The
MONKEY KING'S
Amazing Adventures

Timothy Richard traveled to China in 1868 as a Baptist missionary. When other missionaries were attempting to stamp out the popular local tales of gods and heroes such as *Journey to the West*, Timothy Richard championed them for the universal messages of spiritual challenge and growth they contain. He is also the author of *Forty-five Years in China*.

Daniel Kane was the Head of Chinese Studies at Macquarie University until his retirement in 2011. He has a BA in Chinese from the University of Melbourne and a PhD from the Australian National University. He was visiting scholar at the Department of Chinese at Peking University in 1988 and 1993 and Cultural Counselor at the Australian Embassy in Beijing in 1996.

The
MONKEY KING'S
Amazing Adventures

A Journey to the West in Search of Enlightenment

WU CHENG'EN

Translated by
Timothy Richard

Introduction by
Daniel Kane

TUTTLE Publishing

Tokyo │ Rutland, Vermont │ Singapore

"Books to Span the East and West"

Tuttle Publishing was founded in 1832 in the small New England town of Rutland, Vermont [USA]. Our core values remain as strong today as they were then—to publish best-in-class books which bring people together one page at a time. In 1948, we established a publishing office in Japan—and Tuttle is now a leader in publishing English-language books about the arts, languages and cultures of Asia. The world has become a much smaller place today and Asia's economic and cultural influence has grown. Yet the need for meaningful dialogue and information about this diverse region has never been greater. Over the past seven decades, Tuttle has published thousands of books on subjects ranging from martial arts and paper crafts to language learning and literature—and our talented authors, illustrators, designers and photographers have won many prestigious awards. We welcome you to explore the wealth of information available on Asia at www.tuttlepublishing.com.

Published by Tuttle Publishing, an imprint of Periplus Editions (HK) Ltd.

www.tuttlepublishing.com

Copyright © 2008 Charles E. Tuttle Publishing Co. Inc.
Cover illustration by Chang Huai Yan

Library of Congress Cataloging-in-Publication Data

Wu, Cheng'en, ca. 1500-ca. 1582.
    [Xi you ji. English]
    Journey to the west : the monkey king's amazing adventures / By Wu Cheng'en; translated by Timothy Richard.
        xxix, 226 p. : ill. ; 21 cm.
    ISBN 978-0-8048-3949-5 (pbk.)
    I. Richard, Timothy. II. Title.
    PL2697.H7513 2008
    895.1'34--dc22
2007045249

ISBN 978-0-8048-4272-3

Distributed by

North America, Latin America & Europe
Tuttle Publishing
364 Innovation Drive
North Clarendon, VT 05759-9436
Tel: (802) 773-8930
Fax: (802) 773-6993
info@tuttlepublishing.com
www.tuttlepublishing.com

Japan
Tuttle Publishing
Yaekari Building, 3rd Floor, 5-4-12 Osaki
Shinagawa-ku, Tokyo 141 0032
Tel: (81) 3 5437-0171
Fax: (81) 3 5437-0755
sales@tuttle.co.jp; www.tuttle.co.jp

Asia Pacific
Berkeley Books Pte. Ltd.
3 Kallang Sector #04-01
Singapore 349278
Tel: (65) 6741-2178; Fax: (65) 6741-2179
inquiries@periplus.com.sg
www.tuttlepublishing.com

First edition
25 24 23 22   11 10 9 8   2206TP
Printed in Singapore

Contents

Introduction

(1) The Record of the Western Regions

The Monkey King's Amazing Adventures, also known as *The Journey to the West* is based on a true story of a Buddhist monk, Xuanzang, and his pilgrimage to India to acquire the "true scriptures." Buddhism had entered China from India during the Han dynasty, mainly as the religion of foreign merchants. It spread amongst the Chinese population after the fall of the Han, during the so-called Period of Division, when China was in a constant state of chaos, war, and misery. "I teach suffering," said the Buddha, "and how to escape it." This was very different message from the statecraft of Han Confucianism or the mixture of mysticism, magic, and local religion Taoism had become, and one which found a deep response in the anarchy China had disintegrated into at that time.

Xuanzang's youth coincided with the reunification of China under the short-lived Sui dynasty. He was a precocious child, and received a scholarship (to use the modern idiom) to study in the Pure Land Monastery. When the Sui collapsed in 618, Xuanzang fled to Chang'an, where the new Tang dynasty had been proclaimed. He moved on to Chengdu in remote Sichuan where hundreds of monks had taken refuge. He later travelled throughout the country, learning from the local monks whatever he could about their understanding of Buddhism. He discovered they differed greatly amongst themselves, and came to realise the confusion and limitations on Chinese Buddhism due to a lack of authoritative, canonical texts. The Buddhist scriptures in China had been translated at different times and places, by translators of different levels of ability and understanding of Buddhist doctrines, even translations of translations of translations through the various languages of India and Central Asia. Xuanzang could see that beyond the confusion there was great Truth, but that that Truth could only be found in the original and genuine scriptures of Buddhism. That would entail going to India to get them. He had predecessors: the monk Faxian had visited India between 399 and 414, and had left a record of his travels. Xuanzang was already aware of the various schools of Indian Buddhism, and was particularly interested in acquiring the Sanskrit text of the *yoga sastra*, which taught that "the outside does not exist, but the inside does. All things are mental activities only." That was the basis of the Consciousness Only School of Buddhism, founded in China by Xuanzang. Metaphysical and abstract, it did not become a popular school, but its influence persists. One of the major Chinese philosophers of the twentieth century, Xiong Shili, attempted a fusion of the precepts of this school with Confucianism, and this has influenced several generations of students of Chinese philosophy. On the popular level, anyone who has taken a course in meditation (of any variety) over the past few decades would have heard something along the same lines.

Xuanzang was 28 when he started on his pilgrimage to India. It was a pilgrimage with a purpose, altruistic and not personal: to bring the "true scriptures" to China for the salvation of lost souls. He spent sixteen years away, travelling from what is now Xi'an through Gansu, and from there through the oasis cities around the Taklamakan desert, into Central Asia, then through what is now Afghanistan to India. After his return to China he wrote a detailed geographical description of the lands he had passed through, with notes on the peoples, their languages and beliefs. This book is called *Record of the Western Regions*, in Chinese *Xiyuji*. The Chinese title of *The Monkey King's Amazing Adventures* is *Xiyouji*, a deliberate and direct reference to Xuanzang's records of his travels. In the early twentieth century the *Record of the Western Regions* became a guidebook to many of the "foreign devils on the silk road." Sir Aurel Stein was one of these, who convinced the curator of the secret library of Dunhuang that Xuanzang was his patron saint, thus persuading him to hand over large quantities of thousand year old manuscripts. Much in the way of Heinrich Schliemann with Homer in hand looking for Troy, Aurel Stein and the others relied on

Xuanzang's *Record of the Western Regions* as a guide, located long buried cities under the sands of the Taklamakan desert. Xuanzang, incidentally, visited Dunhuang on his way back to Xi'an—in fact he had been provided with an escort from Khotan, on the emperor's orders. It is not known if the famous portrait in one of the caves is of Xuanzang, or another itinerant monk.

On his way to India, he passed through many kingdoms. In Turfan the king wanted to retain him to such a degree that he would not allow him to proceed, and only agreed after Xuanzang went on a hunger strike. The king was so impressed he provided him with an escort and provisions for the next part of the journey. He also wrote twenty-four letters of introduction to his fellow rulers of the small kingdoms of Central Asia through which Xuanzang would pass. They proceeded to the oasis of Kucha, another stop along the Silk Road, where the red haired, blue-eyed Tokharian ruler, a Buddhist, made him welcome. There he was able to debate with Hinayana Buddhists, who followed the "Lesser Vehicle" road to enlightenment, which was regarded as inferior by adherents of the Mahayana, or "Greater Vehicle," which was the prevalent form of Buddhism in China. Such debates were to continue during Xuanzang's travels, adding to his knowledge of the various schools of Buddhism within India itself.

During the seven days they spent crossing the Tianshan mountains, fourteen men, almost half their party, starved or were frozen to death. They went on to the camp of Yehu, the khan of the eastern Turks, where the letters of introduction from the king of Turfan were helpful. This khan also suggested that Xuanzang go no further, but eventually provided him with a Chinese speaking guide, who accompanied him as far as modern Afghanistan. He passed through Bamiyan, where he described the huge statues carved into the cliff, the same statues which were blown up by the Taliban only a few years ago. He then went to Tashkent and Samarkand, then on to Bactria, near Persia. The local ruler was Tardu, the eldest son of Yehu and the brother in law of the King of Turfan. Tardu's wife had died, and he had married her younger sister, who immediately poisoned him. She and her lover then usurped the throne. It was here Xuanzang met Dharmasimha, who had studied Buddhism in

India, and later Prajnakara, a monk from an area near Kashmir. Xuanzang was coming more and more into the Indian cultural sphere, but he yet had to physically cross the Hindukush into India itself.

When he crossed the Kabul River he was closer to places and events associated with the life of the Buddha. Buddhism was already in decline in India when Xuanzang visited, and many of the famous monasteries, once teeming with monks, were deserted and in ruins. He visited Sravasti, the site of the Great Hall where Buddha preached, Kapalivastu, where he was born and Kusinagara, where he died and was cremated. In one of the most moving passages in the book, when Xuanzang first approaches the *bodhi* tree, under which the Buddha had attained enlightenment, he threw himself face down and wept, wondering what sin he must have committed in a previous life to be born in Tang China and not in India during the lifetime of the Buddha himself.

For eight or nine days he could not bring himself to leave the holy tree, until some monks came from Nalanda monastery, India's most prestigious place of Buddhist learning, to escort him there. The entire community of ten thousand monks came to greet him. He traveled throughout India, to Bengal and Orissa, and almost to Ceylon, but political turmoil there made it imprudent to visit. At one stage he was captured by pirates intending to sacrifice him, but a cyclone swept through the forest and the pirates were so scared they released him. Towards the end of his time in India, Xuanzang met the great Buddhist King Harsha, and explained his mission. Soon after this Harsha sent a delegation to Chang'an, thus establishing what we would now call diplomatic relations with China. Indian monks also urged Xuanzang to stay with them: India was the home of the Buddha, and China was such an unenlightened place it would be unlikely to attain Buddhahood there. Xuanzang explained that was precisely the point of his mission, and he made plans to return to China. During all this time in India, throughout his travels, he had been collecting scriptures and statues. It was now time to pack them up and return to China. He made elaborate preparations, and set off through terrain as difficult and dangerous as the way there. When he was crossing the mile-wide Indus River (on an elephant), his books and statues were thrown into the water by a sudden storm, and several were lost. Xuanzang had to send back to India for replacements before proceeding. His party consisted of seven monks, twenty porters, ten asses, four horses, and an elephant. He eventually arrived in Kashghar, and then Khotan, which he noted was famous for its jade market. At this point his fame had grown to the extent that the Tang emperor instructed the King of Khotan to provide an escort for Xuanzang and his group to Dunhuang, and from there to Chang'an. A vast crowd welcomed him home. Emperor Taizong met him personally, and asked him to write a detailed geographical description of the seventy or more kingdoms through which he traveled. *The Record of the Western Regions* was completed in 646. Until his death the pilgrim retranslated existing works, and translated previously unknown scriptures. He died not long after completing his translation of the long and complex *Diamond Sutra*. His best known translation in the modern world is the *Heart Sutra*, recited daily by millions of believers, and readily available in any modern Chinatown shop selling Buddhist statues and other religious items.

Increased interest in Buddhism, the Silk Road, and growing global awareness has made Xuanzang a significant figure in world history in the twenty-first century. Historically, he can also be considered an extremely influential figure: through him Buddhism, which was to die out in India, was translated to China, and a collection of confused and disconnected ideas which Buddhism was threatening to become was transformed into a profound and complex philosophical and psychological system. From China Buddhism spread to Korea, Japan, and Vietnam. Most of the philosophical schools of Tang Buddhism did not survive the fall of the Tang, one of the great watersheds in Chinese history. What did survive was the Pure Land School, which saw the aim of life as reincarnation in the Pure Land, where one could enjoy the blessings and avoid the sufferings of life on earth. This was to become the basis of popular Buddhism throughout China, and from there into the Chinese communities of Southeast Asia and beyond. The other school to survive was Chan, which did not rely on scriptures, but on meditation to reach enlightenment in a flash of inspiration. This was restricted to a few monasteries in China, particularly the Shaolin monastery, which combined Chan Buddhism with martial arts. Recent interest in Chinese martial arts and innumerable movies about fighting monks have attracted a certain interest in Chan Buddhism itself in recent years. Historically it flourished in Japan under the name of Zen, and it was introduced to western readers through the writings of Daisetsu Suzuki. The other schools are mainly of interest to historians and philosophers.

The most popular and enduring book which has kept the memory of Xuanzang alive for more than a millennium has been one that would have amazed the real Xuanzang. He has become one of the major figures in a novel, translated into the languages of the modern world and modified according to the tastes of the modern world, the other main characters of which were a monkey and a pig. But knowing about transformations and reincarnations, he might well have been quietly pleased that his mission to bring the true scriptures to the world outside India might still be continuing in a new form.

(2) The Journey to the West

The novel is a fictionalized account of the legends that had grown up around Xuanzang's travels. *The Record of the Western Regions* and *The Life of Xuanzang,* a biography of Xuanzang written by a disciple, Huili, were full of stories of strange kingdoms with even stranger customs, attacks from robbers and pirates, mountains, ravines, wild animals, and dangers of all types. Even demons and devils are mentioned. Stories about Xuanzang were told by itinerant storytellers in the market places, mixed with various local folk tales and other traditions. Modified history was the stock in trade of the storytellers, other famous stories deriving from the complex history of China during the Three Kingdoms, after the fall of the Han, or the adventures of a group of outlaws living on a mountain during the Song dynasty. Historical details were not important to the storytellers, but the stories were fleshed out with all sorts of fictional embellishments to attract the interest of the listener, or later the reader. Each "round" would end on a dramatic note, with the words "If you want to know what happened next, you must listen to the next chapter." So the next chapter would start with a brief synopsis of the story so far, before continuing it. This is the origin of the "episodic novel," the usual form of traditional Chinese novels.

The medieval Chinese mind took it for granted that the area to the west, beyond China's borders, was full of demons, monsters, and barbarians of every type. The earliest written version of these stories about Xuanzang himself is *The Tale of the Search for the True Scriptures of Sanzang of the Great Tang Dynasty*, and dates from the Southern Song, but a fragment about the Tang emperor going to hell was discovered in the Dunhuang secret library. In the Southern Song version the Monkey is already Xuanzang's chief disciple, and their encounters involve gods, demons, and bizarre kingdoms. These stories, and others, continued to accrue and develop in various forms, mixed with local folklore and popular religion, and were collected and edited in their present form in the late Ming. The entire book is very long, and the plots and sub-plots, with their myriads of demons and other strange creatures, make very demanding reading. At much the same time abridgements were produced, about a quarter of the length of the original. During the Qing the book was usually read in abridged form, and one such edition formed the basis of the present translation.

On one level *The Monkey King's Amazing Adventures* is an adventure story, and a very funny one. On another level it is an allegory in which the pilgrimage to India is a simile for the individual seeking enlightenment. On the first level, the monkey, the pig, the monk, and the sand spirit, and the innumerable demons and monsters, are characters in an adventure. On the second, they are personifications of our own inner spirits and demons: the pure, idealistic monk trying to achieve spiritual awareness, trying to keep the impetuous monkey, the lazy and lustful pig, and the mournful but reliable sand spirit under control, while all the time being confronted with internal and external demons which must be conquered to continue the way forward. One yet another level for the specialist the book presents an extraordinary range of religious folklore, both Taoist and Buddhist. There is much discussion about how much of the book is Buddhist, how much Taoist: even how much, if any, Confucianism is in it. Xuanzang was a committed Buddhist, of course, but the general theme of the book seems to be *san jiao wei yi* "the three religions are really one." Each deserves to be treated equally: which as far as the Monkey is concerned, is to be treated with equal irreverence. As we shall see, Timothy Richard also saw Christian themes in the novel, an interpretation shared with no one else.

Before the story proper begins, there is a long section which has nothing to do with the monk or his mission, but deals with the exploits of the Stone Monkey, who has learnt an amazing range of skills, including the seventy-two transformations and the secret of immortality, and who claims the title of Great Sage, the Equal of Heaven. His major characteristics are his cheekiness and guts: afraid of no one, irreverent towards everyone, including the Jade Emperor of the Taoists and even Buddha himself, whom he derides as "a perfect fool" until he learns better. He causes havoc in heaven, and eventually the Jade Emperor calls on Buddha's help. He is then trapped under a mountain for five hundred years.

The introduction is followed by the story of how Guanyin, known throughout the Western world as the Goddess of Mercy, is instructed by Buddha himself to bring the scriptures to save lost souls to China, which in the novel is portrayed as being in desperate need of such guidance (reflecting, by the way, the attitude of the Indian monks to China in *The Record of Western Regions*). Guanyin gives this task to the monk Xuanzang, and provides him with three protectors, a monkey, a pig, and a sand spirit. Here we learn that the monk had a past life, in which he was the Golden Cicada, a favorite disciple of Buddha, who failed to pay attention during a sermon and was punished by being reincarnated in China. His disciples are not ordinary monkeys or pigs either: they had all formerly been spirits with official positions in the Celestial Palace of the Jade Emperor, but for various reasons offended their rulers and were sent to earth as punishment. Part-human, part-something-else, they seek to regain their previous status, and agreed to help Xuanzang as an atonement for their sins. The monk undertakes this mission for a variety of reasons. One, of course, is to bring enlightenment to the lost souls of China. Another reason is also to fulfill a vow made by Emperor Taizong, who has seen Hell and ransomed himself out on condition that he would establish a Society for the Salvation of Lost Souls. This provides a secular, as well as spiritual, justification for the trials for the journey.

The last three chapters of the novel describe Xuanzang's entry into Paradise and his return to earth to bring the holy scriptures to China, after which he attains Buddhahood. Between the introductory section and the final conclusion there are 86 chapters. In each of these, the pilgrims are confronted with various demons and monsters, fight with them, defeat them, and continue the journey. Many of the stories extend over several chapters. The geography of *The Record of Western Regions* is real, including modern Xinjiang, Afghanistan, and India; the geography of the novel is a series of kingdoms of barbarians with strange customs, suspicious temples, and monasteries where danger usually lurks, or mountains and ravines inhabited by demons who live on human flesh. These are usually anxious to eat Xuanzang himself, as his holiness would confer immortality. The demons, too, have previous lives: they are usually animal spirits in semi-human form. Apart from the demons, there are formidable physical trials: raging rivers, burning mountains, a kingdom ruled by amazons, the land of spider spirits and so on. After a pilgrimage said to have taken fourteen years, they arrive at the half-real, half-legendary destination of Vulture Peak, where Xuanzang meets Buddha, and explains his mission. Buddha is gracious but a bit condescending; he tells his assistants to provide the Chinese travelers with some sutras, but they cheat them, giving them blank sheets of paper. The last chapter describes the return journey to China (flying with celestial messengers, not on foot as in the real story) and a final trial, where they almost lose the scriptures in the fictionalized version of the crossing of the Indus. Here the elephant becomes a tortoise, and the river separating India from China becomes the demarcation line between the Land of Bliss in Paradise and the land of unenlightened souls on earth. They stay on earth only for long enough to deliver the scriptures to the Tang emperor, after which they are returned to Paradise and their just rewards.

(3) DRAMATIS PERSONAE

The only characters who appear regularly throughout the book are the monk, the monkey and the pig. The horse, a former dragon who has also fallen from grace, is sometimes considered a fourth disciple but rarely appears. His job is less to defend the Master than to carry him to India, and carry the scriptures back to China. The various demons they meet along the way are dealt with and usually not mentioned again, though there are occasionally some references to earlier adventures. There are also a number of supernatural actors of both Buddhist and Taoist persuasion who get involved in both celestial and earthly matters from time to time. These are:

(1) The Jade Emperor: a Taoist deity, he lives in the Celestial Palace. He is served by a bureaucracy rather like an earthly one, but his ministers are various spirits, stars, and planets.

(2) The Queen of Heaven, the queen of the female immortals. Another inhabitant of the Celestial Palace. Her garden contained the peach of immortality, which bloomed only once in three thousand years. She could confer immortality on her guests at her peach banquets.

(3) The Ancient of Days, an unusual and memorable name for the Patriarch, a disciple of Buddha, but in the novel seems to be in the Taoist camp. A sort of adviser and ambassador at large.

(4) The Minister of Venus and the Minister of Jupiter: personifications of the spirits of these planets. Their role is rather like the ministers in a Chinese traditional bureaucracy.

(5) Yama, the King of Hell; Judge Cui, the Chief Judge of Hell, the Ten Judges of Hell; Guardian King Li and his sons Nezha and Mucha, various Messengers and other servants: other officials in the nether world of folk religion where the doctrines and spirits of Buddhism and Taoism become very blurred.

(6) The Buddha. In the novel he was many names: The Incarnate Model, the Ideal, the Buddha to Come, the Cosmic Buddha, Maitreya, Tatagatha, and many others. The historical Buddha was a real person, referred to in the novel as Shakyamuni. Buddha appears early in the novel to help the Taoist Jade Emperor suppress the Monkey, and reminds him of his rather insignificant place in

the grand scheme of things: when the Monkey thinks he can jump as far as the end of the universe, he finds he has not left the palm of the Buddha. This is the theme of one of the most common bronze curios available in the flea markets of modern Beijing. Buddha appears from time to time, but mainly at the end of the novel, where he presents the true scriptures to the monk for the salvation of lost souls in the Middle Kingdom in the East.

(7) Guanyin, the Goddess of Mercy. Her Chinese name means "She who hears the sounds of misery of the world." In some ways the architect of the whole enterprise: Guanyin seeks permission from Buddha to bring enlightenment to the people of the East, which coincides with the vow of the Chinese emperor to found a society for the salvation of lost souls. Whenever in trouble he cannot manage, the Monkey appeals to Guanyin, who comes to the rescue. It is in Guanyin's interests that the mission succeeds, despite finding the tactics of the Monkey and the others a bit distasteful from time to time.

(8) Ananda and Kasyapa: the major disciples of the Buddha, presented in an unflattering light in this novel. They expect to be paid for the scriptures Xuanzang has sacrificed so much to obtain for the benefit of others, and when Monkey threatens to make a fuss, give them scrolls of "wordless sutras"—plain paper. The pilgrims only discover this when they have left, and eventually Buddha's disciples supply them with written scriptures, on the grounds that their level of enlightenment was not enough to enable them to understand the wordless ones.

(9) The Emperor Taizong. Apart from the monk, the only human and historically real character in the book. The second emperor of the Tang, he is widely considered the greatest emperor in Chinese history. When Xuanzang set off on his journey, there was a ban on all travel to the interior because of the general military chaos of the time, but when Xuanzang returned in 645 his fame had come before him, and he was warmly welcomed by Taizong, in both the novel and in historical fact. Incidentally, the Big Wild Goose Pagoda that we can now visit in Xi'an is not the pagoda built for Xuanzang, in which he translated the scriptures into Chinese. This was made of mud and clay, and decayed within fifty years. The

present structure was rebuilt by Empress Wu Zetian (625-705), and has been partially destroyed and repaired several times.

(10) The real Xuanzang is described in his biography written by Huili. The fictional Tang monk is true to the ideals of abstinence, vegetarianism, and refusal to take life, so Guanyin provides him with three powerful disciples who look after the messier side of life for him. In the novel he is typically attacked, either by demons who want to eat him or women who want to seduce him. He cannot defend himself: that is what the disciples are there for. But he is continuously frustrated at the lack of seriousness and dedication of the disciples: the Monkey is violent and rebellious, and quits several times; the Pig is lazy and always in search of food or pretty women. These altercations between the Monk, the Pig, and the Monkey also provide much of the material of the novel that is not dealing with external threats, but internal ones. Xuanzang has a clear and unwavering sense of mission, which provides the novel with a unifying theme.

(11) Sun Wukong. Originally called the Stone Monkey, he becomes the Monkey King, the Seeker of Secrets, the Pilgrim, and Sun Wukong, "Aware of Emptiness." Born of a rock, he established himself as Monkey King by showing his courage in entering the Waterfall Cave at the Flower and Fruit Mountain, where no other monkey dared to go. After some time he became restless and went in search of adventure. He caused so much trouble in Heaven that the Four Heavenly Kings and Nezha, the son of Guardian King Li, leading an army of a hundred thousand celestial soldiers, tried to defeat him, without success. Fearless and irreverent of everybody, he upset many Taoist and Buddhist deities, so the Jade Emperor sought the help of Buddha. He was imprisoned under a mountain for five hundred years, and only rescued when Xuanzang came by him on his pilgrimage and accepted him as a disciple. The meeting was really arranged by Guanyin, of course. He is always depicted with his staff, named "As You Like It," which was originally a pillar supporting the Palace of the Dragon King. This staff, together with his devouring of the peaches of immortality and his ordeal in the eight trigram furnace, which gave him a steel hard body and fiery golden eyes, makes Sun Wukong pretty much invincible. He can only be controlled by a cap of spikes placed around his head

by Guanyin, which he cannot remove by himself. The mantra that can tighten the spikes around his head is about the only thing Monkey is scared of, and is Xuanzang's final resort to try to bring his obstreperous disciple to heel.

(12) Zhu Bajie, also known as Zhu the Pig, or Zhu Wuneng "Aware of Ability." He is usually called Zhu Bajie, the "Eight Prohibitions," a name given him by Guanyin to remind him of his Buddhist vows, so much in contrast with his natural inclinations. Richard translated the term as the Eight Commandments. Once an immortal who was a commander of 100,000 soldiers of the River of Heaven, he drank too much and attempted to flirt with Chang'e, the moon goddess (or "the fairies", as Richard translates), resulting in his banishment into the mortal world. He was supposed to be reborn as a human, but ended up in the womb of a sow, and he was born half-man half-pig. In the original Chinese novel, he is often called *daizi*, meaning "idiot." His weapon is the "nine-tooth iron rake." He and the Monkey seem to be constantly engaged in a sort of game of one-upmanship, and this rivalry provides some of the funniest scenes in the novel.

(13) Sha the Monk, or Sha Wujing "Awakened to Purity." He was exiled to the mortal world and made to look like a monster because he accidentally smashed a crystal goblet at a heavenly banquet. He lives in the River of Quicksand, where he terrorizes travelers trying to cross the river, and occasionally eats them. This is the reason he is often depicted with a necklace of skulls, as in the Japanese television series. He is also persuaded to join the pilgrimage. Like Monkey, who knows 72 transformations, and the Pig, who knows 36, he knows 18. His weapon is the Crescent Moon Shovel, and he is usually depicted with it. Compared with the others he is well behaved, obedient, and reliable, but a bit morose and prone to worrying. At the end of the journey he is made an *arhat* in Paradise, while the Pig is made Official Altar Cleanser, meaning he gets to eat the offerings on every Buddhist altar throughout the country. It is hard to imagine a more perfect image of Paradise for the Pig than that.

(14) The *bodhisattvas* were enlightened souls who chose to forego Extinction in order to remain in the world of mortals to use their

understanding and wisdom to help other people along the road to enlightenment. The most famous were Avalokitesvara, the Indian prototype of the Chinese Guanyin, and Manjusri, in Chinese Wenshu. Samantabhadra, in Chinese Puxian Pusa, also plays a role in the novel. *Pusa* is the Chinese form of *bodhisattva*. The *arhats*, in Chinese *luohan*, are disciples of the Buddha who have already attained enlightenment. They have no role to play, but are often mentioned in the context of the inhabitants of the Buddhist Paradise. There are also a variety of messengers, which Richard calls angels, or occasionally seraphim and cherubim, who have minor roles. Other spirits have delightful names such as The Divine Kinsman and the Barefoot Taoist. Demons are sometimes fallen angels or spirits, or in the allegorical sense, the more evil aspects of human nature.

(4) RICHARD'S TRANSLATION

The first English translations of the *Record of Western Regions* and Huili's *Biography of Xuanzang* were by Samuel Beal, *Records of the Western World*, London, 1906, and *The Life of Hiuen-tsang*, London 1911. Timothy Richard published his translation of *The Monkey King's Amazing Adventures* in 1913. His title and subtitle shows his understanding of the book: "*A Journey to Heaven, being a Chinese Epic and Allegory dealing with the Origin of the Universe, The Evolution of Monkey to Man, The Evolution of Man to the Immortal, and Revealing the Religion, Science, and Magic, which moulded the Life of the Central Ages of Central Asia, and which underlie the Civilization of the Far East to this Day. By Ch'iu Chang-ch'un. A.D. 1208-1288 Born 67 years before Dante.*"

One can scarcely believe this is the same book that Arthur Waley called *Monkey*, or the basis of the TV series *Monkey Magic* and the many other adaptations since. But it is, and it is important to understand why. Confucian China, like Victorian England, was a rather moralistic society. Confucian scholars considered novels frivolous, but like their Victorian counterparts, were not adverse to a bit of nonsense every now and then. Nevertheless, all literature, even the most frivolous, had to contain a moral message. This was the intellectual environment Richard was living in.

To Richard, the moral message of *The Monkey King's Amazing Adventures* was clearly that of the pilgrim struggling against internal and external demons towards enlightenment. Richard was a Baptist missionary, born in 1845 and first assigned to Yantai, in Shandong. He became the editor of the *Wanguo Gongbao,* known in English as *A Review of the Times*, a reformist journal founded by the American Methodist missionary Young J. Allen. Its subject matter ranged from discussions on the politics of Western nation states to the virtues and advantages of Christianity. It attracted a wide and influential Chinese readership throughout its thirty-nine year run from 1868 to 1907. The Qing reformer Kang Youwei said of the publication: "I owe my conversion to reform chiefly on the writings of two missionaries, the Rev. Timothy Richard and the Rev. Dr. Young J. Allen." Kang Youwei and his student Liang Qichao are generally regarded as the most important reformers in late Qing China. Richard was a prolific writer and translator, and one of the most influential missionaries of his day, often ranked with and compared to Hudson Taylor, the founder of the China Inland Mission.

Although a committed Christian missionary, Richard was fundamentally an internationalist, and fervently believed in the cause of modernization. He did not share the general view of the missionaries that Christianity was the only revealed Truth from God; rather, he argued, Christianity and the major Chinese religions, Buddhism, Taoism, and Confucianism, had much in common. Some of these communalities were superficial, like vestments and rituals; others were deeper, including the urge to seek spiritual enlightenment and the belief in a Higher Power, known by different names in different religions, but essentially the same. Richard did not insist that converts burn their tablets to their ancestors: one could be a good Christian and show respect to ones' ancestors, with the appropriate rites, without any conflict. This showed an attitude similar to that of Matteo Ricci in the Ming, but differed from most of the missionaries of his day.

The *Wanguo Gongbao* was extremely influential amongst the Chinese educated classes, and Richard mixed with high officials easily. Clearly he knew Chinese very well, and was well versed in Chinese literature and history, which would have made him even more respected by the Chinese literati. Despite the anti-Christian Boxer Rebellion, during which many thousands of Christians had been murdered, he believed that the Chinese educated classes were not fundamentally opposed to the West, or to scientific progress, or to Christianity itself. So he must have been delighted to discover *The Monkey King's Amazing Adventures*. Many of its themes resonated with his own intuitions: the Three Religions are One, and respect is due to all of them. To this Richard offered his own insight: moreover, many of the characteristics of the Chinese religions, Mahayana Buddhism in particular, are shared with Christianity. Richard thought he had discovered the connection in *The Monkey King's Amazing Adventures*. The other issue Richard was passionate about was that scientific thought was not foreign to the Chinese tradition; was that there was a tradition of scientific knowledge in China, and the evidence was in *The Monkey King's Amazing Adventures*.

Richard's attitudes are reflected in both his translation and in his notes. He often translates the Jade Emperor as God, the Taoist Celestial Palace and the Buddhist Paradise as Heaven and Maitreya, the Buddha-to-Come, as the Messiah. Messengers are angels, Taoist immortals and Buddhist *bodhisattvas* are all saints, and the Buddhist/Taoist paradise is populated with such Old Testament figures as cherubim and seraphim. That the Jade Emperor in his Celestial Palace could see what was going on below proved to Richard that "the telescope was invented by Galileo only in 1609 AD, therefore the Chinese must have had some kind of telescope before we in Europe had it." When the Monkey is showing off his knowledge of Buddhist metaphysics and getting it all garbled, he says "the fundamental laws are like the aiding forces of God passing between heaven and earth without interruption, traversing 18,000 *li* in one flash." To which Richard added a note: "The speed of electricity anticipated."

The last chapter of Richard's translation even has the Buddha berating Xuanzang for not believing in the "true religion," which Richard claims was Nestorianism, a variety of Christianity that flourished during the Tang. And among the many Buddhas and *bodhisattvas* in the final litany, Richard managed to insert a reference to Mahomet of the Great Sea, to the Messiah and to Brahma the Creator. The reference to the Messiah is Richard's translation of Maitreya, the Buddha-to-Come; the reference to Brahma is his translation of the Narayana Buddha. How Richard got "Moham-med of the Great Sea" out of *Chingjing dahai zhong pusa*, "The *Bodhisattvas* of the Ocean of Purity" is a bit of a mystery. He may have misunderstood *chingjing* "pure and clean" as *qingzhen* "pure and true," the Chinese term for Islam. People see things the way they want to see them, and Richard's fundamental approach was that he wanted to see references to God, Jesus, the Messiah, and even Mahomet and Brahma, whether they were there or not.

This was not entirely fantasy. The Nestorian Stele was a Tang Chinese stele discovered in 1625, which proved the existence of Christian communities in Chang'an during the Tang dynasty, and revealed that the church had initially received recognition by the Tang Emperor Taizong in 635. Taizong, of course, was the emperor who welcomed Xuanzang back to China and had the Big Wild Goose Pagoda built to house his scriptures. But any connection between Nestorian teachings and *The Monkey King's Amazing Adventures* has never been made by anyone else.

All of this strikes the modern reader as bizarre. Richard's claims that he had discovered that Mahayana Buddhism was somehow much the same as Nestorian Christianity and that the author of *The Monkey King's Amazing Adventures* was a closet Christian, attracted a good deal of criticism from less eccentric missionaries, in particular Bishop Moule. Richard later translated Ashvagosha's *Dacheng Qixinlun* (The Mahayana Tradition on the Awakening of the Faith), further exploring his theories that Mahayana Bud-dhism was consonant with Christian teaching, and that recognition of this would lead to more rapid evangelization of the millions of Buddhists in China. Despite much public criticism, he persisted in this line of thought till the end of his life. His open approach to religious matters led to unexpected results. Kang Youwei, who ac-knowledged Richard's influence on his thinking, dedicated himself in the later years of his life to the writing of *The Book of Grand Unity*, which curiously reflected many of Richard's ideas: a world ruled by one central government, and the improvement of human-ity through the spread of modern technology.

These comments are by no means meant to belittle Timothy Richard. Along with Hudson Taylor, he is regarded as one of the most influential and prolific missionaries of the non-conformist Christian tradition in China. Richard was closely involved with famine relief in North China as early as the 1870s. During the Boxer Rebellion (1900) some two hundred missionaries and their families were massacred in Shanxi. When the question of reparations was raised, the Prime Minister, Li Hongzhang, asked Richard for his advice. Richard suggested an indemnity of $500,000 be spent on establishing the Taiyuan University College (later Taiyuan University, now Taiyuan University of Technology). Richard was its Chancellor and Moir Duncan its first Principal. The Chinese government also instructed the Ministry of Foreign Affairs to consult with Richard and the Catholic Bishop of Peking on the improvement of relations between the government and the missionaries. Both men were awarded the title of First Grade Officials of the Qing Empire.

Though essentially forgotten because the things he found important and the intricacies of the political situation in China in which he was involved are now history, and rather obscure history at that, that does not diminish his status in the eyes of specialists in the history of the Christian missions in China. His heart was in the right place. It may well be that his translation of *The Monkey King's Amazing Adventures* might well be the work for which he is most remembered so many decades after his death.

(5) LATER TRANSLATIONS AND ADAPTATIONS

Times change, and the missionary zeal of the nineteenth century missionaries is very foreign to the modern reader, just as the preoccupations of late Qing China are foreign to modern Chinese. When the book was written, or compiled, novels were not taken particularly seriously. The question of authorship was not important. It was regularly ascribed to Qiu Changchun, a Taoist in the entourage of Chenghis Khan, who had also written a book with a similar title about his travels in Central Asia. Qing commentators stressed that the book had a "deeper meaning" than an adventure

story about a monkey and a pig, a view reflected in Richard's introduction: "Those who read the adventures in the book without seeing the moral purpose of each miss the chief purpose of the book.
Those who may be disposed to criticize the imperfect character of
the converted pilgrims, must remember that their character is in the
process of being perfected by the varied discipline of life."

The twentieth century saw the fall of imperial China and the
disintegration of traditional culture. The New Thought Movement,
following the May Fourth Movement of 1919, had a number of is-
sues on its agenda, one of which was the creation of a new literary
language based on the spoken language, rather than the language
of the classics two thousand years earlier. Another important issue,
in the words of its main spokesman, Hu Shi, was "the re-evaluation
of all values." And so *The Monkey King's Amazing Adventures* becomes one of the central texts of the vernacular language movement,
because it was indeed written in vernacular Chinese, and was indeed
popular. Literary scholars came to the conclusion that its compiler
was one Wu Cheng'en, and Wu's name is routinely given as its author. Modern specialists feel the evidence for this attribution is too
weak: in Anthony Yu's full and scholarly translation of the novel,
the name of the author is simply omitted. As part of the rationalism
of the New Culture Movement, the "hidden message" of the book
was re-examined and found to be irrelevant, or non-existent. So
Hu Shi, in his *Preface* to Arthur Waley's translation, wrote, "Freed
from all kinds of allegorical interpretations by Buddhist, Taoist,
and Confucianist commentators...*Monkey* is simply a book of good
humor, profound nonsense, good-natured satire, and delightful
entertainment." That is an early twentieth century assessment, and
has influenced the way succeeding generations have read the story.

The original book is very long. William Jenner's complete translation runs to 1410 pages; Arthur Waley's translation has 314 pages.
The first seven chapters of the novel deal with the Monkey's adventures in heaven, before he becomes a disciple of Xuanzang. These
contain many of the most famous stories in the book, and both
Richard and Waley include them. The next chapters, with the exception of a sort of interlude in which the disciples are recruited by
Guanyin to escort Xuanzang to India, are mainly concerned with

their travels, encounters with various demons and other strange inhabitants of the western regions. In the last chapter Xuanzang reaches Vulture Peak, brings the sacred scriptures to China, and returns to Paradise, where he too attains Buddhahood.

The central part of the book covers the adventures of the pilgrims; each translator makes his own choice of adventures to include. Richard chose to translate the first seven chapters, the last three chapters and the chapter on hell in some detail. Waley translated about one third of the book, mainly about the Monkey, but not neglecting the Buddhist aspect of the novel. He translated most of the dialogue, but not the poetry, which, as he said "does not go well into English." Richard included all the chapters, as did the Chinese abridgements from which he was working. He translated the poetry but the dialogue and much of the descriptive passages were shortened and simplified. Some were summarised so drastically they become incoherent: they are little more than "monkey meets demon, monkey fights demon, monkey defeats demon." In his translations of the poetry, Richard conveys a sort of profundity within abstruseness which contributes to the particular charm of this translation. The last two chapters, the *Shedding of the Mortal Body* and *The Mission Achieved*, are the summary and real meaning of the whole book to Richard, which are very moving. The novel ends with a litany of the Names of the Buddha and in homage of all the other *bodhisattvas* and *arhats* of heaven.

The earlier stage versions of various stories in the book in local opera form were incorporated into the much more elaborate and elite Peking Opera repertoire in the late nineteenth and early twentieth century. These also made the Monkey the central character. The role of Monkey was played by many famous actors, included the father and son Yang Yuelou (1844-1889) and Yang Xiaolou (1878-1938); and later by Li Shaochun, Li Wanchun, and Ye Shenzhang. During the late 1930s and early 1940s *The Monkey King* was so popular in Beijing that it was performed in several theatres simultaneously. The image of the Monkey they created is now very famous: standing on one leg, the other crossed over his knee, his hand covering his eyes as he peers into the darkness looking for demons, his eyes twitching nervously, holding his staff, and of course his chatter and his acrobatics.

In 1964 the Monkey King story was transformed into two animated cartoons produced in China, both about the Monkey with no reference to the Monk. These cartoons, *Monkey Causes Havoc in Heaven* and *Monkey Upsets the Peach Banquet*, featured Monkey as a sort of Mickey Mouse figure modelled on the Peking Opera version. There have been many other cartoon versions of the Monkey King, but the popular consensus is that none have surpassed the 1964 animations. After the Cultural Revolution the most widespread depiction of the Monkey on the stage was *Monkey Beats the White Bone Demon*, a modern allegory on Deng Xiaoping outwitting Jiang Qing, the widow of Chairman Mao and one of the so-called Gang of Four.

Outside China, the most significant development in the Monkey myth came during the 1960s with the Japanese series *Monkey Magic*. This was truly weird, with a middle aged woman playing Buddha, and a beautiful young actress, Matsuko Natsume, playing the young monk. Thirty odd episodes were produced, with little reference to the original book. It was based on the original characters, of course, and brought out their characteristics very well: the monk with a mission, the restless, rebellious monkey, the easy going, gluttonous, lustful pig, and the mournful, pessimistic sand spirit. One of the many interpretations of the book is that the many arguments and disputes between these four are in fact an inner dialogue, as we all wrestle with the rebellious, restless, gluttonous, lustful, mournful, and pessimistic personal demons, all of which are somehow kept in check by the higher aspirations of the soul. Freud would have said something about *id, ego*, and *super-ego*. This can easily be read into the pseudo-mystical comments threaded through *Monkey Magic*. The dialogue was dubbed by the BBC in a faux Japanese accent. It became somewhat of a cult, and still has many adherents. A sad postscript is that Matsuko Natsume, who was twenty-one when the series was made, and whose character is constantly reflecting on the transitory nature of life, died of leukaemia at the age of twenty-seven.

Since then there have been musicals, children's theatre versions, a full and serious version produced in China (which stays close to the original book), innumerable *manga* adaptations, video games, and a number of movies and TV series, mainly from Hong Kong. Each of these reflected the tastes of the day. If Richard's translation reflects the general cultural milieu of the late nineteenth century, both in China and Victorian England, and if Waley's translation reflects the taste of the urbane British reader of the thirties, we can say that the Japanese series reflects the good humored innocence of the 1960s and the various *manga,* TV, and film versions of the late twentieth century reflect the technology, and in many cases the taste for violence, of that time.

The latest adaptation is *The Forbidden Kingdom,* which comes at a time when Chinese *gongfu* movies have now become part of Western popular culture, thanks to the pioneering work of Bruce Lee; when Chinese movies of a mystical turn are well known because of *A Touch of Zen* and the like, and when traditional *wuxia* (knight errant) and *gongfu* (martial arts, with a touch of magic) stories like *Crouching Tiger Hidden Dragon* have made this aspect of Chinese culture well known in the West. Outside the Chinese cultural sphere, *The Lord of the Rings* was one of the most popular works of literature of the late twentieth century, and the movie version of the early twenty-first century made it part of the consciousness of the general movie fan, whether they had read the book or not. The idea of the quest through dangerous lands full of demons and ogres, of friendly and unfriendly kingdoms, of determination, fear, courage, and the rest has become a resonant theme in Western culture. It is almost as if the traditional interpretation of *The Journey to the West* is reflected in the mood of the early twentieth-first century, in a new idiom.

Timothy Richard was famous in his day, but has been more or less forgotten by the currents of history. His translation, made with such hopes, may never have had much of a circulation, and was superseded by that of Arthur Waley and more recently by the full translations of Jenner and Yu. In this re-edition of Richard's translation, some of the shorter chapters have been omitted, and many of them have been linked together in what is more or less a coherent sequence of events. Some of the more far fetched translations and comments have been excised, but the general flavor of Richard's translation remains more or less intact. We do not know the process by which Richard made his translation, but I strongly suspect a Chinese colleague read it to him, explaining and commenting along the way, and Richard took it down quickly in English, which he later revised. It cannot really be considered a translation in the modern sense of the word. Anthony Yu, in his preface to his full and scholarly translation of *The Monkey King's Amazing Adventures*, comments, "Two early versions in English (Timothy Richard, *A Mission to Heaven*, 1913, and Helen M. Hayes, *The Buddhist's Pilgrim's Progress*, 1930) were no more than brief paraphrases and adaptations." But few people have the time or energy to wade through 1340 pages, unless they are students of Chinese literature and use the translations as a crib to read the original.

Richard's translation is much more than a brief paraphrase: it is a very readable version and is quite close to the original, though often in an abbreviated and summarised form. It has its quaint and quirky side, but that adds to its charm. It is an auspicious time to rescue it from oblivion and re-issue it for another lease of life. The passage of Xuanzang's story has indeed gone through seventy-two transformations. It has acquired monkeys and pigs, has been reinterpreted in Peking Opera, in musicals, in movies, in *manga*, and most recently as a martial arts epic. Somewhere in this series lies the translation by Timothy Richard. Both Xuanzang and Richard would be amazed, but pleased, to see that the transformations continue while the essence remains.

Daniel Kane
Professor of Chinese at Macquarie
University, Sydney

1

Monkey Gets Restless and Seeks Immortality

Chaos reigned ere order came,
Darkness wrapped the world around,
When at last Pangu appeared.
Light and bright he placed above,
Heavy things he ranged below.
Living creatures he called forth,
All things needed he supplied.
Creation's wonders if you'd see,
Read this journey to the sky.

WE HAVE HEARD THAT THE AGE OF THE WORLD is 129,600 years for one *kalpa*, that these *kalpas* are divided into 12 periods, just as the day and night are divided into 12 Chinese hours, and each period is 10,800 years, or two half periods of 5,400 each. Speaking of the divisions in a day, there are twelve of 2 hours each, from midnight to midnight. But if we speak of the division of the *kalpas*, at the end of each there is a return to chaos and darkness. After the first period of 5,400 years, everything should be dark like night without any living thing. This state is called chaos. After the second period of 5,400 years comes the era which gradually begins to open up with light. Hence the saying, "The winter solstice is the re-beginning." But Nature never changes. Everything is dead. Soon after, life again begins. After a third period of 5,400 years, the lighter parts of matter rise up, forming the sun and moon and stars. Towards the end of a fourth period of 5,400 years, the solid parts combine. The *Book of Changes* says, "How great is Heaven, how perfect is the Earth producing all things. The Earth henceforth becomes solid." After a fifth period of 5,400 years more, all the solids resolve into water and fire, into mountains, rocks, and earth. After a sixth period of 5,400 years, at the end of another *kalpa,* all things are reproduced again. Heavenly influences descend and earthly influences rise, and by the union of the two, all living things are produced. After the seventh period of 5,400 years, men and birds and beasts are produced. Thus we have the three great powers, Heaven, Earth, and Man. The Three Emperors came forth to rule the earth and the Five Sovereigns fixed the social relations.

Then the world was divided into four great continents, and far beyond the ocean there was a country called Aolai. Near this country was a sea, and in the sea there was a famous mountain called the Flower and Fruit Mountain. This was the greatest of all the mountains of the world, the home of the mighty dragon gods. On the top of that mountain there was a living stone, 36 feet 5 inches high, and divided into 365 degrees like the heavens, and it was 24 feet in circumference, from which went forth 24 different influences. Above it there were 9 openings and 8 holes, according to the 9 mansions and 8 diagrams of the *Book of Changes.* Since the beginning of time it had been animated by the finest forces of heaven and earth. Sun and moon had long influenced it, so that it had an internal force, as a child in its mother's womb. On a certain day it split open and produced a stone egg, round like a big ball. After exposure to the air, this was transformed into a stone monkey with the five senses of the body complete, and able to creep and run. It turned and bowed to the four points of the compass, and its eyes glowed like burning light, the rays of which reached the stars, astonishing the dwellers in heaven, even reaching the Jade Emperor in his golden palace in the clouds, and the inner palace where the heavenly ministers were gathered.

They saw the light burning brightly and ordered a telescope to be brought. Two great heavenly messengers returned and reported that the light came from the Aolai country where the Flower and Fruit Garden was on a mountain; on the mountain there was a stone pillar, which had laid a stone egg; when the egg was exposed to the air, it was transformed into a stone monkey that bowed to the four quarters of heaven; its eyes shone with burning light reaching to the stars; it ate and drank, but the light of its eyes was becoming dim. The Jade Emperor took pity on it and said, "That far object below is not strange at all; it is the living principle of life in the universe." The Monkey on the mountain could walk and jump, eat vegetables and drink of the brook, pluck wild flowers and seek for fruit and berries, and make companions of monkeys and birds and join a herd of deer. At night he lay down on a rock. In the day he wandered about on mountain peaks and penetrated into caves. Truly he was the most incomparable of all living creatures. In the greatest cold he did not suffer. In the summer heat he joined a herd of monkeys seeking a cool place in the deep shade of fir trees. After play he would go to the mountain stream to bathe and watch the water rushing down the rocks.

Then one day all the monkeys cried out, "Where does the stream come from? Let us follow it to its source. Call the monkeys all together." All came and shouted out, "Let us go." So they started up the stream and climbed the rocks till they came to its source, which was a great waterfall. Then all clapped their hands for joy and cried, "Beautiful, beautiful!" But the waterfall came from a cave. Then they said, "Whoever dares enter the cave and find the source and comes out without injury, we shall make our king." Three times this cry was raised and agreed to.

In face of these difficulties, suddenly a monkey came forward and cried out, "I will venture in." A fine one he was. He shut his eyes, bent his body and rushed into the midst of the waterfall. Then he opened his eyes and raised his head to see. There was no water, but there was an iron bridge. The water under the bridge filled a hole in a stone and then flowed out and covered the entrance to the bridge. Again on looking at the top of the bridge, he saw a house, most beautiful. After looking at everything for a long time, he jumped over the bridge, and he saw in the middle a stone pillar. On the pillar were cut the words, "The Happy Land of the Flower and Fruit Garden, the Waterfall of Heaven's Cave." The stone monkey was delighted beyond measure. He shut his eyes again and doubled up his body and jumped through the waterfall to the outside.

He sneezed twice and then said, "A grand find, a grand find!" Then all the monkeys gathered round and said, "What is it? Is the water deep?" He said, "There is no water at all, only an iron bridge. On the other side of the bridge is a palace full of treasures." "How do you know that?" they asked. The stone monkey smiled and said, "This water comes from a stone hole under the bridge and flows out as a screen to the entrance. On both sides of the bridge there are flowers and trees and a stone palace. In the palace there are stone pots, stone stoves, stone basins, stone cups, stone beds and stone seats. In the midst there is a stone pillar on which is carved: "The Happy Land of the Flower and Fruit Garden, the Waterfall of Heaven's Cave." There is our true resting place. Let us go and live there, lest we suffer from the weather." All were delighted with the news. "You lead us in and show us the way."

Then the stone monkey shut his eyes, doubled himself up and jumped in, and all the rest followed in the same way, and jumped over the bridge, all of them struggling for the stone pots and pans and beds and seats with all the selfishness of monkeys, till all were quite tired. The stone monkey sat with dignity and at last said, "Sirs, what will become of persons if they are faithless? You said whoever should be first in here and go unhurt, should be made king. I have now found out this Cave of Heaven where you rest in peace and enjoy the happiness of a palace. Why is it that you do not respect me as a king?" They all cried out, "May you live, Oh King, for a thousand years." After this he changed his name and did not call himself the stone monkey, but the Monkey King.

> Living beings all descend
> From three Powers: Heaven, Earth, and Man.
> From the womb of immortal stone,
> Comes the egg from whence the ape.
>
> Shapeless first all life begins,
> Then at last is perfect form.
> Age to age thus reproduced,
> Whether beast or man or sage.

Then the Monkey King led all kinds of monkeys who were princes, statesmen, and their assistants, to the mountain garden in the day, and at night they slept inside the water curtain. They did

孫行者

Sun the Monkey.

not join with the birds of the air, nor with the beasts of the fields, but lived as a kingdom in the enjoyment of the wealth of Nature for many centuries.

One day, when feasting with his monkeys, suddenly the king began to weep. Then all the monkeys gathered round him and reverently asked what troubled him. He replied, "Although I am happy now, I am not without fear of future shadow." They laughed and said, "Oh King, we live daily in this Happy Land and the Cave of Heaven, perfectly free without restraint and with infinite joy: what need is there to fear?" The king replied, "Although today we break no human laws, nor have fear of being conquered by wild beasts, still in time we shall get old and decrepit, and be in fear of the judge of the dead, who will not let us stay amongst the living." Hearing this, all the monkeys covered their faces and cried because they all feared death. At this there jumped from among them a strong one, and cried out with a loud voice, "Oh King, this sorrow of yours is an opportunity to gain Life Eternal. Of all the wonders of the world, three are greatest: the Buddhas, the Taoist Immortals, and the Confucian Sages. These have reached beyond transmigration and will never be reborn to die again, but will endure as long as Heaven and Earth. The king asked, "Where do they live?" The Monkey said, "In the world after death, in the ancient depths of the Eternal Mountain."

On hearing this the king was much pleased and said, "Tomorrow I leave you and go down the mountain and take a flight to a corner of the sea far on the horizon, and find out these three wonders, so that I may never get old, but live for ever and escape the hand of death. This is a happy thought. It is the sudden conversion spoken of in the Buddhist religion, whereby a man can escape the net of reincarnation by transmigration, and become a great saint as lasting as Heaven itself."

At this all the monkeys rejoiced and clapped their hands, saying, "Good, very good! Tomorrow we also go across the mountain in search of fresh fruit to provide a big banquet for our great king."

The next day all the monkeys went in search of fairy peaches and found a strange fruit and some mountain herbs. They laid out a fine table with fairy wine and fairy dishes. Then they placed ten of the stone forms for the banquet, and invited the king to be seated and the monkeys in turn served the guests with wine and feasted themselves the whole day.

The next day the Monkey King got up early, cut up some dried fir trees, and made them into a raft and took a bamboo for a punting pole. He went on the raft alone and punted with all his might and was carried out by the tide to the open sea. There day after day he was carried by the Southeast wind to the borders of the Southern Continent. Then he abandoned his raft and went ashore.

There on the beach he saw some men fishing, others gathering cockles, others evaporating salt. He went up to them and took the form and motions of a tiger, and so frightened the people that they ran away in all directions, leaving behind their baskets and their nets. Finding one who was unable to run away, he stripped him of his clothes, and put them on as men did, and walked with dignity across the country. When he got to the town, he learnt men's manners and their language, took his meals by day and slept at night. He searched with all his powers for the place where the Immortals lived. He found all men were in search of fame or riches, and none sought for everlasting life.

> Ever seeking fame and wealth,
> Late and early men are led.
> Riding horses and their mules,
> Dukes and princes seek high thrones,
> Food and raiment without work,
> Heedless of the doom of death.
> Sons and grandsons all want ease,
> None desiring to repent.

The Monkey King, having no luck in his search for the way of the Immortals, and having spent eight or nine years in vain, suddenly came to the great Western Ocean, where he thought beyond the sea must be the home of the Immortals. Then he got on a raft as before, and sailed as far as the borders of the Western continent, where he landed and searched for a long time.

Suddenly he saw a high mountain most beautiful, covered with forest and jungle. Fearing no wolves, snakes, tigers, or leopards, he went straight to the mountaintop. While looking about, he heard a sound far in the forest like the voice of man. He at once plunged into the forest and listened. It was a man singing, and the song he sang was this:

> When chess I play the haft is burnt,
> The trees are felled all one by one.
> I pass the clouds and slowly mount
> I sell the wood and buy my wine
> I laugh with joy and cry self saved
> The way to heaven in harvest moon.
> I sleep at foot of Tree of Life.
> When I awake 'tis heavenly day.
> Old trees I know, steep hills I climb,
> Beyond the pass make for the plain.
> With hatchet cut the withering vines,
> A bundle make of all my lot,
> Then sing away on road to mart.
> I buy my pints of daily rice,
> And then, why grudge I have no more?
> My price is fair, my price is fair.
> Why should I worry to increase.
> My fame or shame? Quite calm I live,
> Whoe'er I meet Immortal is,
> We sit and talk of heavenly themes.

The Monkey King, on hearing this, was full of joy and said, "An Immortal hides himself here." He rushed forward, and behold, it was only a woodman lifting his axe and cutting wood. The king went up to him and said, "Venerable Immortal, I kneel down before you as your disciple." The woodman hastily threw aside his hatchet and knelt likewise. "I am ignorant, and with insufficient food and clothing, undeserving to be a man, how much less am I an Immortal." The king said, "If you are not an Immortal, how can you speak the language of Immortals?" "What language of the Immortals did I use?" asked the man. The king said, "I heard you say that your companions are Immortals, and when you meet you sit and talk of heavenly themes. Heavenly themes are true words of wisdom and religion. If you are not one of the Immortals, what are you?" The woodman laughed and said, "The truth is, this song is called "The Fragrance that Fills the Hall" and one of the Immortals taught it me. He lives next door to me and he told me to sing it whenever I was in trouble and the trouble would vanish. It is because I was in need that I sang this song and did not expect anyone to hear me." The Monkey King said, "Since you live next door to an Immortal, why do you not follow him and learn how not to become old?" The man answered, "All my life my lot has been bitter. My father died when I was young, my mother is a widow and depends on me alone. I must cut my two bundles of wood and carry them to the market for sale, and then buy rice for my mother's food. I therefore cannot leave my mother." The Monkey King said, "From what you say you are one of the superior men, full of filial piety, and surely you shall have a share of immortality. Please show me where the Immortal lives, so that I may pay my respects to him and learn from him." "It is near, quite near. This place is called the Heart of the Living Mountain. In the mountain there is the Slanting Moon and Three Star Cave. In that cave there is an Immortal called the Fountain of Wisdom, and innumerable disciples taught by him have gone forth. He has some thirty or forty students now. You follow that small path and go southward for seven or eight *li,* and there is the place." The Monkey King laid hold of the woodman and said, "Venerable Brother, you come with me. I shall not forget your kindness." The woodman said, "What a stupid man you are! I have already told you where to find him. I must cut wood and look after my mother. If I go with you I shall be neglecting my business, and who will look after my mother? You go by yourself!"

The Monkey King had to leave him, and went his way out of the forest for seven or eight *li,* and there surely was the cave. There he stopped and looked round—it was so beautiful. The door of the cave was closed and all was quiet with no one about. Raising his head he suddenly saw a stone on which was engraved the words "The Heart of the Living Mountain, the Cave of the Slanting Moon and Three Stars." The Monkey King was full of delight, and looked at the cave for some time, not daring to knock. He climbed to the top of a fir tree that was close by, and began chewing the fir tops. Shortly after he heard the noise of a door opening. It was the door of the cave. Out of it came an Immortal Student who cried out, "Who is making a noise here?" The Monkey King dropped down from the tree, went up to him respectfully and said, "I am in search of Truth and Immortality, and therefore of all places I would not make a noise here." The Immortal Student smiled "and said, "Are you a Seeker after Truth?" The king replied, "I am." The Immortal Student said, "My teacher has just gone up and mounted the platform to preach, and without giving me the reason why, he told me to come and open the door as a Truth Seeker had come, and I was to welcome him. I suppose it is you." The Monkey King smiled and said, "Yes, I am the one, I am the one." The Immortal Student said, "Follow me inside."

The Monkey King adjusted his clothes and moved on respectfully after the student far into the Cave of The Slanting Moon and Three Stars through corridor after corridor, between high places of carnation marble, vermillion mansions, and precious gates of indescribable beauty, right up to the inner sanctum and there saw Wisdom sitting above. On either side of him were ranged his thirty disciples, standing on a platform below.

> Greatest learning of Immortals,
>   Unstained Purity,
> Western Heaven's greatest wonder,
>   Wisdom's Fountain.
> Nor birth nor death experienced he,
>   Perfect Model.
> Forces complete, godlike are all
>   His myriad mercies.
> Silent, unseen, work all the forces
>   As need requires.
> Instincts grow from roots of True Model
>   Without forcing.
> His years like Heaven's endless are,
>   Glorious his form.
> Lasting Wisdom throughout all *kalpas,*
>   Teacher of the Law.

Seeing him the Monkey King fell on his knees and knocked his head upon the ground innumerable times, and said, "Master, I want you to accept me as your disciple." The Master said, "Tell me where you are from and what your name is, and then you can perform the disciple ceremony." The Monkey King said, "I am from the Continent of the East, the Country of Aolai, the Mountain Garden and the Cave with the Water Screen." The Master cried,

悟徹菩提真妙理

Meditation, Seeking Wisdom.

"Turn him out. He is a sower of discord, a false disciple. How can he bring forth any good fruit?" The Monkey King grew alarmed, went on knocking his head without stopping, saying, "What your disciple says is strictly true. I am an honest man." The Master said, "If you are honest, how can you say that you come from the East Continent? Between us and that place there are two great oceans and the Southern Continent. How could you come here?" The Monkey King knocked his head and said, "I sailed across the seas, came ashore and traveled overland in search of Immortals for over ten years before I arrived here." "Since you have traveled so long and so far let it be. What is your surname?" The Monkey King replied, "I have none." The Master said, "What surnames had your parents?" The Monkey King replied, "I never had parents." "Since you had no parents, did you grow like fruit on a tree?" The Monkey King replied, "Although not grown on a tree, I grew from a stone. I only remember that in the mountain orchard there was a fairy stone. One year the stone split open and I was born."

The Master was glad to hear this and said, "This speech shows that you are a child of the Divine Power above Nature. Rise up and let me see you walk." The Monkey King jumped up and walked round twice. The Master smiled and said, "Though your body is not beautiful, you seem like a monkey who lives on evergreen pine and cones. I will give you a surname according to your nature and call you Sun, which means macaque." The Monkey King was delighted, knelt on the ground again and said, "Good! Good! Good! Now that I have a surname, I beg that the Master will be kind and give me another name, to which I can answer when called." The Master said, "We have twelve names, such as Breadth, Greatness, Wisdom, Model, Ocean, Nature, Versatile, and Seeker after Complete Learning, and so forth, from which to choose. The most suitable for you would be Seeker of Secrets. Will that do?" The Monkey King laughed and said, "Good! Good! Henceforth call me Sun, Seeker of Secrets."

2
Monkey Studies Magic

AFTER THE MONKEY HAD RECEIVED A NAME, he settled down to study and remained there over six years. Once the Master lectured and taught:

> Mysterious are the three Religions
> In essence and fruitage all complete
> Now preaching, now praying
> All unite in one essential
> Repentance and sincerity
> As the path of life for all.

The Seeker of Secrets, on hearing this, felt like dancing for very joy, and moved his hands in great excitement. The Master asked him what was the matter. He replied, "Please pardon me, it is nothing but inexpressible delight at hearing such joyful tidings from you." The Master said, "You have now been here seven years. What more do you wish to study? There are hundreds of interesting subjects; which do you want to take up? Do you wish to study the inactive subject, such as the art of calling up genii and obtaining oracles from the gods to avert evil and secure happiness, or do you wish to learn the six Schools of Thought: Confucianism, Taoism, Buddhism, Dualism, the Universal Love of Mozi or the Principles of Medicine? Or do you wish to study Quietism, which means stillness, prayer, and meditation, silence and fasting, sleeping merit, standing merit, and trances? Or do you wish to study various objective activities, such as men and women, inward massage with the breath, the compounding of male and female essences, the use of human milk and such like?" The Monkey asked, "Will any of these show me how not to grow old?" The Master said, "No, not one."

The Monkey King replied, "Not one of them will I study then." The Master jumped down from his platform and said, "You monkey, what will you learn since you will study none of these?" and he hit the king three times on his head and went inside. The Monkey King thought this was only the Master's private hint for him to come and see him at the third watch that night, and he would tell him the secret. At the third watch the Monkey King went in and found his Master's door half open. He went in and waked him. On waking the Master chanted:

> Hard it is, hard it is,
> Mystery of mysteries to solve.
> The Golden Pill give out to man with care.
> The faithless ne'er can prize the gift divine.
> Your breath is spent, you preach in vain.

At this the Monkey King said, "Since you signaled to me to come and get the secret of religion at this time, I have come here and have been kneeling to receive it for some time." The Master thought, "What a rare creature I have in this monkey!" He said, "I will tell you this great secret."

> To discover secret doctrine, perfect and profound,
> One must train the spirit's nature, only this the art,
> This involves three primal forces, sex, mind, and spirit.
> Secret keep this no divulging, fatal to reveal,
> Preserve with care your body's strength,
> Your secret strength conserve, increase.
> Obey my words, and Truth you'll find.
> Forget them not, the gain is great.
> Put off all thoughts of evil lust.
> Seek purity, shine bright.
> Your secret chambers flood with light.
> The moon protects the timid hare,
> The sun grows trees for birds to roost.
> Birds and rabbits join in revels,
> So do dragons have their mates
> Have their mates and new life follows.
> E'en in fire grows a lily
> Differing natures, all converted,
> End their work as true Immortals.

The Seeker of Secrets, having learnt the three secrets of Immortality: mind and spirit and abstinence from sex, memorized these carefully, and went on studying alone for three years more. Then the Master again mounted the platform and preached on the Parable of the Great Judgment. Suddenly he asked, "Where is the Seeker of Secrets?" The Monkey King came forward, knelt and said, "I am here." The Master asked, "What have you been learning all this time?" "Your disciple has mastered the study of the spiritual nature." The Master said, "Then you know the origin of things. But you must be careful of three great dangers." The Seeker of Secrets, after pondering over this for a long time said, "I have constantly heard it said that when one has found Truth and Virtue, then one becomes an Immortal and no sickness can befall him; how then do you speak of dangers to be avoided?" The Master said, "What I teach you is not an ordinary doctrine, for it controls the forces of Heaven and Earth and the secrets of the sun, moon, and stars. When one has arrived at this stage, then one is superior to the evil spirits and the ordinary gods. Still after a time there will come a thunderclap to try your soul and spirit. If unmoved and unshaken in the deluge, you will be like Heaven itself. If you doubt, then you perish. After a long practice of religion again, one is tried a second time. This danger does not come from Heaven, nor from man, but from one's own passions. It burns one's whole body to ashes, and all one's long years of practice are in vain like a dream. After another long term of practice, one is tried a third time by the danger of environment, which blows on one like a typhoon and affects one's whole being. This must be overcome." When the Seeker of Secrets heard this his body shook and his hair stood on end. "Oh Master, have pity on me, and tell me how to overcome these three dangers, and I shall never forget your kindness." The Master said, "That is not difficult. There are two ways to avoid them. One has 36 wonders, the other 72; which do you wish to know?" The Seeker of Secrets said, "I wish to know the 72 wonders." "Come here then, and I will teach you the incantation." Then he whispered it in his ear. The Monkey King felt influences going through every pore of his body, and began to practice the arts and to learn the whole 72 wonders. Afterwards when they were outside the door of the Three Star Cave, the Master said, "Seeker of Secrets, have you learnt all the arts?" He replied, "Thanks to your great kindness I have, and I can fly among the clouds." The Master said, "Let me see what you can do." At this, the Seeker of Secrets bent himself and jumped some 50 or 60 feet in the air and walked on the clouds for about the time it takes one to have a meal, walked for a mile and then descended amongst them. The Master said, "That is not much. It is only creeping on the clouds. The ancient Immortals are said to have mounted in the morning as far as the Northern Ocean, gone round the East, South, and West Ocean, and been back at night." The Seeker of Secrets said, "This is not easy." The Master said, "Easy enough if you have a mind to do it." At this the Seeker of Secrets threw himself on his knees and, declaring he was in earnest, begged his master to be so kind as to show him how to do it again. The Master said, "You jumped when rising, you should only bow and rise. But if you wish I can teach you how to do it by somer-saults." The Seeker of Secrets knelt before him again and begged him to do so. The Master then taught him the incantation. Then with a clenched fist and a spring, the Monkey King was off 107,000 *li*. As it was late the Master and students retired, while the Seeker of Secrets went on mastering how to travel on the clouds, and for many days afterwards would do nothing else.

One day the students had a long talk together, and said, "Seeker of Secrets, you have studied the mysteries of Nature so deeply, that our Master has taught you how to perform many wonders; can we all do this?" The Seeker of Secrets laughed and said, "Truly if the Master teaches and you diligently learn, there is no reason why you should not learn all." They replied, "Show us some of your won-derful arts." The Seeker of Secrets said, "Tell me what you want and I will try." They said, "Change yourself into a pine tree." The Seeker of Secrets recited an incantation, shook his body and was transformed instantly into a pine tree.

> Clouds come kissing virgin pine,
> Wooded through the growth of years,
> Showing monkey traces none,
> Only hoarfrost on each branch.

At the sight the students clapped their hands and cried in great admiration. The Master hearing the commotion, came out and asked what the matter was. When he heard he said, "You pledged yourself not to divulge the secret, and now you play with great things before the unworthy. If you do not divulge the secret to the others, they will kill you." The Seeker of Secrets wept and begged his pardon. But the Master said, "I cannot keep you any longer, you must go, for your life is in danger." The Seeker of Secrets said, "What shall I do?" "Go back whence you came," was the stern reply, "and never tell anyone that you are my disciple, or I will flay you alive." With this, the Seeker of Secrets took leave of the Master and fellow students, recited an incantation, jumped over the clouds and was back in an instant in the East Continent of the Mighty Gods, the Mountain Garden and the Water Screen Cave, and was glad, saying,

> Leaving home I lonely was,
> Mortal frame and mortal seed.
> When born again in spirit land,
> The body light became as air.
> In all the earth none have a mind
> To seek the truth and gather light.

Finally the Seeker of Secrets descended safely from the clouds, arrived at the Mountain Garden and there heard the monkeys crying bitterly. He said, "My children, I have returned, what is the matter?" Ten thousand monkeys, great and small, ran towards him from all the rocks and trees about, knelt before him and cried, "Why did you leave us so long here without protection? We have been longing for your return like men who are hungry and thirsty. Of late we have been troubled by the Chief Disturber of the World's Peace, who wanted to take possession of our cave by force. We fought him at the risk of our lives and many were killed. If you, Oh King, had not returned, there would soon have been no cave left us at all." The Seeker of Secrets became very angry and asked what evil spirit it was that had dared do that. "We will soon have our revenge on him. Where does he live and how far away?" "We do not know. He came with the wind and went away in a fog." At this the Seeker of Secrets said, "I will find him." And with this the Monkey King made a spring and disappeared to the North. There he saw a high and steep mountain.

> Mountain peaks like pencils pierced the sky,
> Mountain streams like gouges carved the rocks.
> There the fount of three worlds bubbled forth
> Giving strength by watering the earth.

The Monkey King hearing voices in this mountain, descended from the clouds and found a cave from which flowed a river. About the entrance some small demons were at play. At the sight of the Seeker of Secrets they ran away. He cried out, "Do not run away. I am the Master of the Mountain Garden and Cave with the Water Curtain in the South. Your chief, the Disturber of the World's Peace, has been frequently assaulting my children, and I have come to get an apology." The little demons ran in and said, "Trouble has come, oh King," and repeated the message of the Monkey King. The Demon King laughed and said, "I have often heard the monkeys say that they had a great chief, and that he had gone away to lead a religious life. I suppose it is he who has come. How is he dressed and how is he armed?" They replied, "He is not armed, but is hatless and dressed in a red gown and yellow girdle and black boots. He is not like an ordinary man, nor like a Buddhist monk or a Taoist priest, and he is waiting outside with no weapons in his hands." On hearing this the Demon King put on his armor, took a sword in his hand and went out, followed by a crowd of little demons, and cried out, "Where is the Master of the Water Screen Cave?" The Seeker of Secrets opened his eyes and saw the Demon King.

> Black helmet crowned his head,
> Red coated was his back.
> Black armor over all,
> Black leather boots he wore.
> His girdle ten times others round
> His height was thirty feet.
> His hand bore a huge sword,
> All polished for the fight.

The Seeker of Secrets cried out, "You incorrigible demon! You have such big eyes but you cannot even see me." The Demon King looked down and seeing him, said, "You are not five feet tall and not more than thirty years old, and have no weapons, how dare you be so mad as to talk to me about an apology?" The Seeker of

Secrets cursed him and said, "You insolent demon, it is plain you cannot see. You think I am small, but if I wish to be big, I can easily become big. You think I have no weapons, but I can stretch my arms to reach the moon. Wait till you get a taste of my fists. Let us have a bout of boxing." The Demon King took off his armor saying, "You are short and I am tall. If you use your fists and I use a sword and kill you, it will be ridiculous. Let me put down my sword and fight with my fists." Having put down his armor, he then began fighting. The Seeker of Secrets got close to him and they fought each other hard, but the long fist beat the air while the short one hit the mark. After the Monkey King had given him several hard knocks, he began to swell. Suddenly the Demon King seized his great steel sword and made a rush to strike him down. The Monkey quickly evaded him, so that he struck the empty air. The Seeker of Secrets then used one of his wonderful arts. He pulled out one of his hairs, put it in his mouth and chewed it into minute bits, then blew them out of his mouth and said, "Transform!" and these bits were instantly changed into hundreds of small monkeys who gathered round him. The Monkey King, since he had discovered this supernatural gift, had 84,000 hairs on his body, and each of these could be transformed in like manner, as he pleased. The small monkeys were so lively that the demon could not hit them on the right or left. They went at him from behind and before, they seized him and pulled him and tripped him, played with his hair and eyes, as if he were a pincushion. The Seeker of Secrets then laid hold of his sword, went up amongst the monkeys, struck the top of the Demon King's head till it split open, and went into the cave, killing as he went, leaving not one of the demons alive. Then he put back the hair in its place on his body again. Those who did not suffer in the cave were a few dozen monkeys, which the Demon King had carried captive before. He ordered them out to light a fire to burn all the demons. Then he told these monkeys to follow him home. "Shut your eyes tight." He then uttered an incantation, and a strong wind carried them over the clouds. When he descended from the clouds he called on them to open their eyes. They then found they were at home again, and were very glad, and ran into the cave as of old. Then all the monkeys assembled in the cave to welcome the king and get ready a banquet. They asked him how he had vanquished the Demon King. The Seeker of Secrets told them the whole story. The monkeys' praises were interminable, and they asked, "Where, Oh King, did you learn all these wonders?" He answered, "That year when I left you, I sailed across the China Sea till I reached the Southern Continent and there I learnt how to become human, and put on clothes and wear boots for some 8 or 9 years, but had not found the secret forces of nature. I then crossed over the great Western Ocean till I reached the Unicorn Continent in the West, and searched for this secret for a long time. Finally I met an old patriarch who taught me the true way of living eternal as the heavens, so as never to become old." All the monkeys congratulated him on having discovered how to avoid all calamities. The Seeker of Secrets smiled on his followers and said, "You may congratulate me on one other thing. You all have a family name now." They all cried, "Oh King, what is thy name?" The king said, "My surname is Sun, which means macaque, and my name is the Seeker of Secrets." When they heard this, they clapped their hands with great joy and said, "The great King is the venerable Sun, we are his sons and grandsons, one family and one nation—all of the same name. Let us all honor our ancestor Sun with cups of coconut wine, grape wine, and fairest fruits, for this is a great joy to the whole family."

3

Monkey Visits the Dragon King

THE MONKEY KING RETURNED HOME with honors. Having killed the Disturber of the World's Peace, he took away his great sword and daily practiced with it. He taught the monkeys how to use it, how to make wooden swords to cut bananas and thistles, and how to build a camp. They played at this for a long time. One day when sitting quietly he suddenly thought, "Perhaps this sham fight may become a real one. We may excite the fear of a human king, or of a king of the birds, or of the king of beasts, and they may say that we are practicing military affairs in order to rebel and lead forth an army to kill. How can we get something better than these wooden weapons?" On hearing this, all the monkeys were filled with fear. Then four great monkeys, two red tailed and two long armed, went up and said, "Great King, if you wish sharp instruments, that is easy. Two hundred *li* to the south of us, across the water, on the borders of Aolai, there is a city full of soldiers. They have workers in copper and iron. If you go there you can buy or have made weapons with which we can practice for the defense of our mountain, and then we shall have nothing to fear."

On hearing this, the Seeker of Secrets was full of joy. He leaped to the clouds and was there in a minute. The city had streets and markets and business, both small and great, a very busy place. The Seeker of Secrets thought, "Here there must be plenty of ready made weapons. I will go down and buy them. But perhaps I had better use my magic power." He pronounced an incantation and drew in his breath, and then blew it out. Then there arose a tremendous cyclone blowing sand and stones, and the people of Aolai were so terrified that they shut their doors, as none dare stay outside. The Seeker of Secrets then descended from the clouds, went to the armory and burst open the doors. Inside were eighteen kinds of weapons, all complete. He rejoiced greatly at the sight. "But I cannot take many alone. I had better call my monkeys by magic." Then he plucked a hair, chewed it into bits, and blew them out with an incantation, and many thousands of monkeys appeared. They cleared the armory of all the weapons, took them through the air, and returned home with them.

Then the Monkey King shook his body, put back the hair and set up the weapons in a heap and called the monkeys together to choose their arms. They came and struggled to get knives and swords, hatchets and spears, bows and arrows, and with these they played all day. Next day they were called to drill as usual, and their king numbered them and found them to be over 47,000. This frightened all the beasts of the mountain. The elf chiefs of the 72 caves on the mountain came to do homage to the Monkey King, and brought their yearly tribute. They were drilled every season, and all paid their taxes regularly, till the Mountain Garden became an iron city, where they drilled daily for military purposes.

In the midst of this splendid success, however, the Monkey King said, "I am not satisfied. My sword is very blunt, what shall we do?" The four elder monkeys came forward and said, "Oh Great King, you are an Immortal Sage, and all human weapons are of no use to you. But we do not know if you can live under water." The Seeker of Secrets said, "Since I discovered the secret of life I know seventy-two magic transformations. I can ride through the air like lightning; I can make myself invisible; I can ascend to high Heaven or descend into the depths of the earth; I can walk in sunlight or moonlight without throwing a shadow; I can go through metals or stones; water cannot drown me, fire cannot burn me. I am in possession of all these powers." The four elder monkeys said, "Since the Great King has all these magic powers, and the water under our iron bridge flows to the Dragon Palace of the Eastern Sea, if you are willing to go down that water in search of the Venerable Dragon King, and ask him for a weapon, you may get what you want." The Seeker of Secrets rejoiced on hearing this and said, "I will go."

He jumped on the bridge, recited an incantation, dived and traveled to the Eastern Ocean under the water. As he went he met some water elves, who wished to stop him and asked him, "Tell us what Holy Sage you are, so that we may announce your arrival." The Monkey King said, "I am Sun, the Seeker of Secrets, a natural Sage from the Mountain Garden, a neighbor of your Venerable Dragon King. How is it that you do not know me?" The water elves, on hearing this, quickly turned and announced him at the Crystal Palace saying, "Outside there is a natural Sage from the Mountain Garden, named Sun the Seeker of Secrets. He says he is your Majesty's neighbor and comes to see you." The Dragon King of the Eastern Sea hurried out to meet him and said, "Honored Sage, please enter." They entered in and saluted each other. After being seated and served with tea, the Dragon King said, "Honored Sage, when did you find the Secret of Life? And what Magic Arts do you possess?" The Seeker of Secrets replied, "After I was born I left home to study religion and discovered secrets without beginning or end, and now I have returned to train my children to defend the Mountain Cave. But alas, I have no weapons. I have long heard that in your jeweled palace there must be abundance of splendid weapons; I have come to beg one of you."

On hearing this, the Dragon King, unwilling to refuse, ordered one of his officers to bring one of the biggest swords and present it to him. The Seeker of Secrets said, "I am not used to swords, please let me have something else." The Dragon King ordered another officer to carry out the nine-pronged fork for him. The Monkey King received it and tried its weight. He then put it down and said, "Too light, too light, I beg of you again to get me another." The Dragon King laughed and said, "Do you not know that this is 3,600 catties in weight?" The Seeker of Secrets said, "It is no use for my arm, no use at all." The Dragon King began to fear and ordered his general to carry out the spear that was 7,200 catties in weight. The Seeker of Secrets took it into his hand and made a few thrusts with it and said, "This is far too light." The Dragon King now feared greatly and said, "This is the heaviest spear I have. I have no other weapons." The Seeker of Secrets laughed and said, "The ancients had a saying that no one need trouble the Dragon Kings unless they bring precious things. Please search once more, and see if there be a suitable weapon, and I will buy it." The Dragon King said, "Really there are no more."

Just as he was speaking, two beautiful women came in at the back door saying, "Great King, this is a great Sage and not an ordinary being. In the sea storehouse there is that miraculous iron from the River of Heaven. Today it sparkles with light as if it desired to come forth to meet this Sage. It is the rod of the great Yu, who regulated the waters of the deluge and judged of the depth of the water." "It is just a divining rod, of what use is that?" The women replied, "No matter whether it be of use or not, let him have it and do what he likes with it." The Dragon King told the Seeker of Secrets, who said, "Let me see it." The Dragon King shook his head and said, "It cannot be carried, it cannot even be moved, it is so heavy. Honored Sage, you must go and see it yourself." The Seeker of Secrets said, "Lead me to it."

The Dragon King took him to the ocean storehouse, and there were innumerable rays of light radiating from it in all directions. The Dragon King said, "That is it, lying there!'" The Seeker of Secrets went up close and touched it. It was an iron pillar as stout as a bushel measure and over 20 feet long. He stretched both his arms around it, then said, "It is a little too stout and too long. If shorter, it would do." At the sound of these words the precious pillar became a few feet shorter and thinner. The Monkey King tried its weight again and said, "Still a little smaller, it would be better." Then it became a fraction smaller. The Seeker of Secrets was greatly delighted at this. Then he took it out of the storehouse to look at it, and behold at each end were golden prongs, but in the middle between the prongs it was black iron, on which was engraved its name "As You Like It." It weighed 13,500 catties. He rejoiced greatly in his heart and thought, "This is a precious thing, such as I wish!" As he walked away, he wished the pillar shorter and thinner, so as to be more convenient. He carried it away. When he arrived outside, it was only 12 feet long and about the diameter of a rice bowl. At the sight of him walking about the Crystal Palace with this magic power, the old Dragon King trembled with fear and the young dragons were frightened out of their wits, and all the reptiles and dwellers of the deep ran away to hide themselves.

The Seeker of Secrets sat in the Crystal Palace of the Dragon King, holding the precious weapon in his hand, and said to the Dragon King smiling, "Many thanks, neighbor, for your great kindness. I have one thing more to say. If there had been no such iron staff, I would have had nothing to ask. But since I have it, I have no armor to match it. Please let me have a suit of armor, and I shall be much obliged." The Dragon King said, "I am sorry, I have nothing of the kind." The Seeker of Secrets said, "A visitor does not trouble more than one host. If you cannot find one, I will never leave this place." The Dragon King said, "Please look through another sea, perhaps you can find some armor there." The Seeker of Secrets said, "It is better to remain in one quarter than to search in two quarters. I beg of you a million times to give me a suit." The Dragon King said, "Truly I have none. If I had, I would give it you." The Seeker of Secrets said, "Since you will not give it, let me try this weapon on you." The Dragon King became much alarmed and said, "Worthy Sage, please do not. Wait till I find if my brother has any, then I will give you a suit." The Seeker of Secrets said, "Where is your brother?" The King replied, "One brother, Aojin, is King of the Southern Ocean. Another, Aosun is King of the Northern Ocean, while the third, Aoyun is King of the Western Ocean." The Seeker of Secrets said, "I will not go to them. A bird in the hand is worth two in the bush. I hope you will find me one somewhere nearby." "You, Worthy Sage, need not go so far," said the Dragon King. "I have here an iron drum and a golden bell. When there is anything very urgent we beat the drum and strike the bell. Then my brothers come here at once." The Monkey King then said, "Beat the drum and strike the bell immediately."

True enough, as soon as the drum and bell sounded, the three Dragon brothers were alarmed and immediately appeared. Aojin asked, "Elder Brother, what is the matter? Why do you beat the drum and strike the bell?" The Old Dragon said, "I am afraid to tell you. There is a Sage from the Mountain Garden come to call on me as a neighbor, and he desires some weapons. I gave him the steel prong, but he said it was too small. When I gave him the carved lance, he said it was too light. Then I took from the bottom of our cave the wonderful iron staff. He was pleased with that, and he now sits in the palace and demands some armor. I have none here; therefore I beat the drum and the bell. My dear brothers, let him have a suit of armor, so that he may go." The brother Aojin hearing this, got very angry and cried, "Let us get soldiers and arrest him." The elder Dragon said, "Do not do that, do not do that! If he touches you with that iron beam, or if it falls upon you, you are dead." The third brother, Aoyun said, "We must not fight with him. The best thing we can do is, to give him a suit of armor so that he may go. We will memorialize High Heaven about him and Heaven will punish him." Then Aosun said, "That is right. I have here a pair of silk sandals for traveling in the air." Aoyun said, "I have with me a chain coat with gold buckles." Aojin said, "And I have a red gold helmet." At this the elder Dragon King was greatly pleased, and led them to the crystal palace to be presented to his visitor.

The Seeker of Secrets took the gold helmet, and the gold buckled coat, and the silk sandals and put them all carefully on. Then he took up the magic beam and walked straight out. The four Sea Kings were greatly displeased at this and discussed how they might memorialize about the matter. But the Monkey King looked for his waterway in order to get back to the top of the iron bridge in his cave.

All the monkeys were there gathered, waiting for him. Suddenly their king jumped out of the water, with not a drop of water left on him, and landed on the iron bridge. At the sight all the monkeys were greatly frightened, and fell on their knees saying, "Great King, how beautifully you are dressed." The Monkey King was mightily pleased and ascended a high throne. He took the iron beam and made it stand on end in their midst. The monkeys were all full of wonder and came round to feel that precious beam, but their strength was like that of flies, and they could not move it the least bit. They all put out their tongues and cried, "Aiyah! Aiyah! It is terribly heavy. How did you manage to bring it? Such a tremendous weight!"

The Seeker of Secrets came up, took it in his hand, and smiled at them. "Everything has a master, so has this precious beam. It has been lying in the storehouse of the sea, who knows for how many thousands of years. But just when I was there, it emitted light in all directions, and the Dragon King thought it only a bit of black iron. But it was called the Pearl of the River of Heaven. None of the people there could move it, so they asked me to go and take it. At that time this precious beam was more than twenty feet long, and stouter than a bushel measure. When I looked at it, I thought it was too big, then suddenly it became less. I thought it still too big, and again it became much less. On it are engraved a few words, "As You Like It." All of you stand back and I will command it to change, so that you can see what it will do in my hand. When I say 'Small, Small, Small,' instantly it becomes the size of an embroidery needle, so that I can hide it in my ear." And so it was.

All the monkeys were greatly astonished and said, "Oh Great King, show us how you handle it." The Monkey King took it from his ear, put it on the palm of his hand and cried, "Big, Big, Big." Instantly it became as a bushel measure in thickness and twenty feet long. He took it in his hand with great joy, jumped outside the cave with it, and then exercised his own magic on it. He doubled up his back and cried out, "High, High, High." In an instant he was 100,000 feet tall, and his head was as high as the peak of Mount Tai. His loins were as great as mountain ridges, his eyes like lightning, his mouth like a bucket of blood, his teeth like sharp spears. He then took the magic lance in his hand, which reached up to the 33rd heaven and down to the 18 hells, frightening the 72 demon kings in hell, so that they all kowtowed to him in fear and trembling. In the twinkling of an eye, he took the precious lance, changed it by magic to the size of an embroidery needle, and hid it in his ear, and then returned to his cave.

After this, all the demon kings came to pay homage to him. Then according to previous arrangement they hoisted the flag and beat the drum. The Monkey King appointed the four elder monkeys to be strong guardian generals. The two red tailed ones, who were called the Horse-like Generals, and two long armed ones, who were called Palm Leaf Generals, regulated all the rewards and punishments in the camp. Since these matters were in the hands of the four generals, the Monkey King was at leisure to mount the clouds, and visit the seas in the four quarters of the world, and see the heroes of all lands.

During this time he met six brothers: the King of the Ox demons, the King of the Crocodile demons, the King of the Roc demons, the

King of the Lion demons, the King of the Gorilla demons and the King of the Baboon demons, and daily discussed with them civil and military affairs, feasting and drinking from morning till eve, and enjoying unlimited pleasure.

One day, he invited the six kings to dine at his cave, and they drank until they were all incapable. After seeing his guests off, while leaning on the iron bridge in the shade of the pine trees, he suddenly fell asleep. The four generals at once surrounded him to protect him, but dared not speak in case they might wake him. The Monkey King dreamt he saw two men carrying a warrant, with the name of Sun the Seeker of Secrets on it, approach him, and without any words bind him with ropes, take his soul away, and carry him off to the gates of a city. The Monkey King saw above the gates of the city an iron tablet on which was written, "The World of Hell." The King said, "Hell is the place where Yama the Judge of the Dead lives; how is it that I am here?" The two men replied, "Your days on earth are numbered, and we two have been ordered to fetch you here." The Monkey King on hearing this said, "I have crossed over beyond the gates of death and am no longer to be counted among mortals and cannot be under the rule of the Judge of Hell. How have you so blundered and dared to bring me here?" The two who had so far dragged him along, were determined to drag him in. The King, getting angry, drew out from his ear his precious weapon. It shone forth as he caused it to grow large, and with it he beat the two men to a pulp. He then tore off the rope that bound him, cast off the handcuffs and making of them a weapon went into the city. He frightened the bull-headed and horse-headed demons, so that they flew in all directions towards the office of Yama. They reported the matter to the great chief crying, "A great calamity, a great calamity. Outside a bearded thunderer has come." Thus they terrified the Ten Officers of the Lower Regions, so that they hurriedly donned their official robes and went to see. Finding the Monkey King so terrible, they cried out loudly, "Excellency, write down your name, write down your name!" The Monkey King said, "If you do not know me, how is it you sent to fetch me? I am from the Mountain Garden, from the Waterfall Cave, a natural Sage whose name is Sun the Seeker of Secrets. Tell me what offices you hold. Tell me quickly or I will thrash you." The officers bowed and said, "We are:

Judge Yama, King of Hell
Judge Qinguang, Prince of Hell
Judge Chujiang
Judge Wuguan
Judge Songdi
Judge Pingdeng
Judge Taishan
Judge Dushi
Judge Biancheng
Judge Zhuanlun,
The Ten Judges of Hell."

The Seeker of Secrets said, "Since you all have attained to the position of Judges in Hell, you should clearly understand the grounds of rewards and punishments. How is it that you do not know the difference between right and wrong? I, Sun, have become one of the genii and shall live forever, for I have transcended the three realms and am beyond the control of ordinary life and death; how is it that you sent men to arrest me?" The Ten Judges said, "Your Excellency, do not be angry. The number of people of the same name in the world are many. It must be that those who arrested you made a mistake" Sun, the Seeker of Secrets said "Nonsense, nonsense. We constantly hear that the officials know how to use their subordinates. The two men who came were quite right. Let me see your *Register of Life and Death* at once." On hearing this, they asked him to go to the office and see it. The Seeker of Secrets, taking his magic club, commanded the judge to bring him the *Register of Life and Death*, which listed those who were due to die. He searched among the stinging animals, hairy animals, feathery animals, reptiles, and creatures in shells, but among them all there was no one with his name. Then he searched among the names of all kinds of monkeys. But monkeys, although somewhat like men, had no names like men, and therefore were like beasts, but not under the control of the *kirin*, like birds, but not under the control of the phoenix. There must be another register. The Seeker of Secrets looked for it himself. Under the name Soul No. 1350, he found his own name, Sun, the Seeker of Secrets, a naturally born stone monkey, who should live 342 years, and then die a natural death.

閻羅王

Judge Yama, the Chief Judge of Hell.

The Seeker of Secrets said, "I do not know my own age myself. Let me strike out the name." He took up the pen, dipped it deep into the ink and went through the list of monkeys. Everyone that had the name of Sun he struck out, and then threw the register down and said, "That is the end of your registration. That is an end of your registration. I am no longer under your control." Then with his magic club, he cleared his way out of hell. The Ten Judges did not dare to go near him, but all went to the Feathery Cloud Office to worship the Chaplain Prince, and consult him as to how to memorialize High Heaven. The Monkey King, having got out of the City of the Dead, stumbled against a bundle of straw and fell. This woke him up and he realized that it was only a dream.

He stretched himself out and heard the four generals and all the monkeys saying, "The Great King must have drunk an immense amount of wine to sleep as late as this." The Seeker of Secrets said, "After I had slept a little, I dreamt that two men had come to take me to the City of the Dead, and I have only just waked up. In my dream I had a quarrel with the Ten Judges of Hell, saw the *Register of Life and Death*, and struck out everyone that had our name, so that they might never be under the control of these fellows." All the monkeys fell on their faces and kowtowed. From that time there were many of these mountain monkeys who did not get old at all, because their names were not to be found on the fatal Register. We will not further describe how the Monkey King daily enjoyed himself.

But we will relate how one day the Jade Emperor, sitting in his Golden Palace of the Clouds in the Divine Court of the Sky, called together all the civil and military ministers of Heaven. During the morning audience, an official unexpectedly announced, "The Dragon King Aoguang of the Eastern Ocean has arrived to memorialize and is waiting to be called in his turn." The Jade Emperor commanded that he should be admitted. Aoguang was called to approach the throne. After bowing, he presented his memorial as follows: "Your humble Dragon Master Aoguang of the Eastern Ocean of the Continent of the Mighty Gods, on earth for ages, memorializes the Sacred Sovereign of High Heaven, the Great Ruler of the Universe, that: Sun, the Seeker of Secrets, a monster from the

Mountain Garden of the Waterfall Cave, has insulted your humble petitioner, forced himself into our Ocean Palace, demanding weapons and armor. I and my brothers gave him the precious magic iron club, a red gold helmet, chain armor and sky boots, and saw him off most civilly. But he played his tricks, used magic to frighten us with his threats and power, so that he was most difficult to manage. We humbly appeal to your sacred judgment, and beg that you send legions from Heaven to arrest this monster, so that the ocean and rocks may not be troubled, and our ancient home will be at rest."

When the Jade Emperor had read the memorial through, he ordered the Dragon King to return to his ocean home saying, "I will send generals for the monster's arrest." The old Dragon King kowtowed, thanked him and went away.

Next there was another ancient worthy who memorialized thus: saying, "There is one of the Judges of Hell, named Prince Qinguang, who brings a complaint from the Chaplain of Hell. The complaint reads: 'Hell is the earthly prison of the dead. In heaven there are gods, in Hell there are demons. Birds and beasts are begotten into male and female, according to the order of Nature. Now in the Mountain Garden and the Waterfall Cave, Heaven has produced a monstrous monkey, named Sun, the Seeker of Secrets, who is cruel and does evil without control. He misuses his magic, and has killed nine of the demons of Hell. Relying on his strength he frightened and wounded the Ten Judges of Hell, and had a struggle with Yama the King of Hell himself. By force he obtained the *Registers of Life and Death*, and struck out the names of many monkeys, and added to the age of others. Thus there is no record remaining of transmigration, as we cannot know the time of their birth and death. We beg that you send legions from heaven to subdue this monster, so as to restore the natural order of things, and give permanent peace in the nether regions.'"

When the Jade Emperor heard the memorial, he commanded the Judge from Hell to return, saying, "I will send generals to arrest him." Then Prince Qinguang also kowtowed, returned thanks, and retired. The Jade Emperor then asked all the civil and military ministers of heaven when this monkey monster was born and in what age he appeared, for there must have been some reason for his appearance. One of the ministers in the company replied, "This monkey was born 300 years ago. Nature gave birth to a stone monkey. At that time there was no special notice taken of him. But we do not know how he discovered during these years the way to become an Immortal, able to subdue dragons and demons and to take the *Register of Life and Death* by force." The Jade Emperor said, "Let the gods of that region go down and subdue him."

Before he had finished his commands, the Minister of Venus appeared, bowed down, and said, "Your Majesty, all who have complete mental powers in the three realms may become Immortals if they practice the art. This monkey is a product of Nature, begotten by the sun and moon. Since he has now become indestructible and can subdue dragons and demons, perhaps he can be reasoned with like a human. Your minister suggests that you be merciful, and issue an edict to call him to a peaceful audience. Let him come to the upper world, and confer on him some official position to look after something. If he is loyal, then let him have a rise. If he is disloyal, then arrest him. In this way you will not need to trouble many legions to go after him."

The Jade Emperor was very pleased with this idea, and according to his minister's suggestion ordered the God of Literature to prepare an edict, and the Minister of Venus to carry it to the Monkey King. The Minister of Venus took it and went outside the South Gate and proceeded down on an auspicious cloud, till he got to the Mountain Garden of the Waterfall Cave. There he said to the crowd of small monkeys, "I am an ambassador sent from the Jade Emperor himself with an imperial edict to invite your Great King to go to heaven. Go and tell him at once!" The little monkeys outside the cave rushed in at once to the depths of the cave and said, "Great King, outside there is an old man who says he is an ambassador sent from the Jade Emperor with an edict to invite you to heaven." The Monkey King was very delighted to hear it, and said, "These last few days I have just been thinking of going to heaven to look for myself. Quickly invite the messenger in." The Monkey King hurriedly put on his clothes and went out to meet the Minister of Venus who came inside and standing with his face to the South said, "I am the Minister of Venus from the Palace of the Jade Emperor. I have been sent down to earth with a dispatch to invite you to heaven for an audience, and to become one of the officials in heaven." The Seeker of Secrets smiled and said, "I am much obliged to you, Minister of Venus, for coming down to see me. We must arrange for a worthy banquet." The Minister of Venus, replied, "I have the dispatch with me and I must not tarry long. I beg of you to return with me." The Seeker of Secrets called his four strong generals and commanded them saying, "Be careful to drill my monkeys while I go to heaven to find out how to get there, so that I may later take you with me there." Having given his commands, the Monkey King with the Minister of Venus rose amongst the clouds and passed beyond them.

4

Monkey Declines Being a Stud Master

THE MINISTER OF VENUS AND the Monkey King traveled together above the clouds, but the Monkey King traveled so quickly that the minister was left behind, for the Seeker of Secrets was perfectly skilled in the art. He arrived at the South Gate, and when about to enter, was led by one of the Heavenly Princes into a trap. On all sides were strong legions guarding the gate and they would not let him in. The Monkey King said to himself, "This ancient minister of the planet Venus is treacherous. Since he invited me to heaven, why is he setting guards with swords and spears to bar the gate of heaven, and so prevent me from entering?" In the midst of the confusion, the ancient minister arrived. The Seeker of Secrets with a face full of anger said, "You old fool, why did you deceive me? You said you came by the order of the Jade Emperor to invite me. How is it then that you have these men barring the gate of heaven and not allowing me to enter?" The minister smiled and said, "Great King, do not be angry. You have never been in heaven before, and none of the guards know you, how could they dare to let you in? Wait until we have an audience with His Majesty and you are given an official position up here, then you can go in and out as you please." The Seeker of Secrets said, "Very well then, we shall see. I refuse to go in." The minister laid hold of him and said, "You must go in with me." He called out in a loud voice for the guards to make way, "This is one of the genii of earth. I have been commanded by His Majesty in a sacred edict to invite him to heaven."

玉
帝

The Jade Emperor.

> Glorious light in myriad rays,
> Thousand forms of radiant cloud;
> Gold and silver were the courts,
> Decked with flowers fit for gods.

The minister led the Monkey King towards the Palace of the Jade Emperor. The minister fell on his knees. The Seeker of Secrets, however, stood upright and looked on without any signs of reverence. The minister said: "Your minister, having received your august command, presents the Seeker of Secrets." "And who is that?"

It was only then that the Seeker of Secrets bowed and replied, "It is I, Old Sun!" All the heavenly ministers were greatly alarmed at his manner and said, "Why does this wild monkey not do obeisance at an audience, and not only rudely reply, 'It is I, Old Sun?' He should be killed, he should be killed!" His Majesty said, "Sun, the Seeker of Secrets, is a monster spirit from the lower world, having only been transformed into man for the first time, and has not yet learnt court etiquette. We therefore forgive him." All the heavenly ministers cried out, "Thank Your Majesty for his mercy." But the Monkey King faced the Jade Emperor and cried out with a loud voice, "And so you should!" The Emperor then ordered the civil and military ministers of state to find where there was an empty official post, and let Sun the Seeker of Secrets fill it. At the side there was a military official who said, "In the heavenly court there is no empty post, but in the imperial stud they need a Horse Master." All the ministers called out, "Thank you, Your Majesty, for your kindness!" But the Monkey King only faced the Jade Emperor and with a loud voice cried "And so you should!" So the Jade Emperor then ordered the Minister of Jupiter to go with him to his office as Horse Master. The Monkey King was delighted, and went with the Minister of Jupiter to his new post.

The Monkey King called together his subordinates, the heads and their assistants, the clerks and servants, so as to have a clear knowledge of his duties as Horse Master, and found there were only one thousand horses. He examined the registers and verified the number of the horses, the superintendents of accounts and of fodder, and the servants who fed and cleaned the horses. The superintendents and subordinates worked night and day looking after

太白金星

The Minister of Venus.

the stud of horses, so that they became frisky and fat. The Monkey King's subordinates were much pleased and in about a fortnight decided to give him a banquet, partly of welcome, and partly of congratulation on his promotion.

In the midst of the banquet, the Monkey King asked, "By the way, what is the official rank of the Horse Master?" They answered, "He has no official rank." The Monkey King said, "Since he has no rank, the position must be very high and unequalled." They replied, "No, not at all, it is not great at all. It is just above not having any rank at all. It is the lowest. The ministers think you are only good enough to look after the horses. After having taken so much care of the horses as you have done, all you can expect is that they are pleased with you, but if there is anything wrong you will be censured, and if very wrong, you will be punished." When the Monkey King heard this, he became very angry, ground his teeth and said, "This is an insult! In my Mountain Garden they call me King. How dare they invite me here merely to look after horses? Is this the way they should behave towards me? I will not stand it! I will not stand it! I am going!" In an instant he pushed over, with a great noise, the table at which public justice was administered, pulled out his precious weapon from his ear, and having got it to its proper size, rushed out through the gate of the Imperial Horse Yamen, and proceeded straight towards the South Gate. All the guard knew he had been given an official position in heaven as Horse Master, so did not dare to stop him as he passed outside.

In a moment he mounted a cloud and reached his Mountain Garden in no time. There he found the four great generals drilling the monkeys.

The Monkey King cried out, "My children, your old father Sun has come back." All came out to welcome him, and then entering the cave invited the king to sit on a high throne. In a side room they prepared a banquet in honor of his return. "The Great King has been away in heaven over ten years. What high honors he must have secured!" The Monkey King replied, "I have not been away a month, what do you mean by saying it is over ten years?" The monkeys replied, "Great King, when in heaven, you were not aware of the flight of time. One day in heaven is one year in the reckoning of mortal men. May we know, Great King, what official position you occupied there?" The Monkey King waved his hand and said, "I am ashamed to tell you. It nearly killed me. The Jade Emperor does not know how to choose men. He only appointed me to be Horse Master, simply to look after the feeding of his horses, the lowest official position of all. When I arrived at my post, I did not know it. But today when I learnt it from my colleagues, I was filled with wrath and came away." The monkeys said, "The Great King is happy in his home, and is acknowledged king with much reverence and joy. Why should he go and become a stable boy? Let us get some wine, so that he may forget his humiliation."

Whilst they were drinking wine together, there came in a man, who said, "Great King, at our gate there are two one horned kings, who wish to see you." The Monkey King said, "Let them come in." The two kings outside straightened their clothes, entered the cave, kowtowed and said, "We have long heard of the Great King who is in search of worthy officials, but we had no opportunity of meeting him before. Now we have heard that the Great King has been given a post in heaven. He must be pleased, and have come back with honors. So we have come to present him with a yellow robe as a token of congratulation. If he will kindly accept it, please let him use it as he does his horses and dogs." The Monkey King was very pleased, put on the yellow robe and appointed the demon kings as viceroys under him.

Having thanked him for his favor, the demon kings said, "You were in heaven a long time, what rank did you occupy there?" The Monkey King replied, "The Jade Emperor did not respect me, and simply appointed me to look after some horses." The demon kings said, "Since you, Great King, have marvelous magic powers, how did you submit to merely looking after horses? If you had called yourself the Great Sage, the Equal of Heaven, there would have been nothing you could not have done." The Monkey King was delighted beyond measure on hearing this, and could not refrain from repeating, "Good, Good, Good!" several times. He ordered his four generals to make him a banner on which was to be written in large letters, "The Great Sage, the Equal of Heaven." He put up a tall flagstaff and hoisted the banner, and cried, "Henceforth never again call me the Great King, but the Great Sage, the Equal of Heaven. Report this to all the demon chiefs, so that they may know."

The day after the Monkey King had left his post in heaven, when the court was about to assemble, the Master of Ceremonies brought in the two assistant grooms instead of the Horse Master. They knelt before the throne and said, "We beg to say that the new Horse Master, not satisfied with the low position assigned to him, has left Heaven altogether." The Keeper of the South Gate then entered and reported that the Horse Master had passed out at the South Gate without giving any reason. When the Jade Emperor heard this, he commanded that the two officers should return to their respective posts, and said, "We shall send heavenly legions to arrest this truant." From among the courtiers, there stepped forward a heavenly king, named Guardian King Li, and his third son Prince Nezha, and said, "We beg to suggest that, although we have no ability, Your Majesty issue an order for us to subdue this monster." The Ruler was glad and appointed Li the Guardian King and his third son, to the command of the expedition. The expedition was ordered to start for earth forthwith.

After this the two commanders returned to their respective palaces, and divided the forces into three armies, and the Great Victorious Spirit led the vanguard. All the forces at once left the South Gate of Heaven and arrived at the Mountain Garden, where they encamped, ready for battle. When they reached the Waterfall Cave, they saw innumerable demons drilling with spears and swords as if in battle. The Great Victorious Spirit cried out, "You wild animals, go and announce to the Horse Master that I am a great commander sent to subdue this place. Tell him to come out at once and surrender, lest you all be destroyed." The demons flew into the cave and cried, "Woe to us! Woe to us! Outside our entrance is one of the commanders from Heaven, who styles himself a holy official, and says he has come by the order of the Jade Emperor to subdue this place, and calls on you to come out at once and surrender, lest we all be destroyed."

The Monkey King on hearing this, merely said, "Bring me my coat of mail." He put it on and took his magic beam in his hand, and ordered all to go outside and put themselves in battle array.

The Great Victorious Spirit screamed out, "You wretched monkey, do you not know me? Guardian King Li has been sent down to earth by the order of the Jade Emperor to receive your submission. You had better yield at once, and submit to his mercy, lest you perish. If you hesitate a moment, you will be at once beaten to powder." When the Monkey King heard this, he became very angry and said, "You rotten hairy demon! You had better cease from your tall talk. I can easily kill you all with one blow, but as there would be none left to report the matter in Heaven, I will spare your life. But you must go back at once and say to the Jade Emperor there, that he does not know how to engage worthy officers." The Great Victorious Spirit said, "You impudent monkey!" Sun quickly replied, "What hairy spirit are you? Old Sun has never met you before, tell me your name at once! I have infinite resources; how then did your boss send me merely to look after horses? Look at my banner. If he promotes me in accordance with my title, then I will not fight, and there will be peace in heaven and on earth. If not then I will fight and besiege heaven itself and the throne of the Jade Emperor, and it will not be long before I sit on the throne myself." When the Great Commander from Heaven heard this and saw clearly on the banner outside the cave in great letters, "The Great Sage, the Equal of Heaven" he smiled and said; "You wretched monkey, do you consider yourself equal to the Jade Emperor, and call yourself the Great Sage, the Equal of Heaven? Very well then, just have a taste of my battle axe." With this he aimed to split his head, but the Monkey King parried his blow with his magic beam. The Great Victorious Spirit was no match for him, and his head was badly hurt. He then took the handle of his axe and broke it in two, and ran away for his life. The Monkey King laughed and said; "You coward! Hasten back to heaven and report."

The Great Victorious Spirit returned to the camp, went to see Guardian King Li, knelt before him, and said, "The Horse Master certainly has immense magic power. I was no match for him and was beaten. Punish me as you like." Guardian King Li became angry and said, "For this inability, you must be beheaded." Then his son, Prince Nezha stepped forward and begged his father the King not to be angry, but to forgive the Great Victorious Spirit. "Let me go forth and lead the forces once, then we shall know the truth about the matter." Guardian King Li ordered the Great Victorious Spirit to return to the camp to await punishment. Prince Nezha, clad in full armor, then jumped out of the camp, and on arriving at the Waterfall Cave, found the Seeker of Secrets drilling his soldiers.

Seeing Prince Nezha coming up with a rush, the Monkey King went up to him and said, "Whose little boy are you, daring to come to my cave, and what is your business?" Nezha replied, "You wretched monkey, I am the third son of the great Guardian King Li, who has now been ordered by the Jade Emperor to come and arrest you." The Seeker of Secrets smiled and said, "Young Prince, you have not yet shed your milk teeth, nor the down in which you were born, how dare you engage in this tall talk? But I will spare your life. Look at what is inscribed on my banner on the flagstaff. When I go to see the Jade Emperor it will be with that rank. Then there will be no need to trouble our armies to fight. If not, I shall certainly take my armies and besiege Heaven itself." Nezha lifted his head and saw in great big letters, "The Great Sage, the Equal of Heaven." "What great magic power this monkey must have, to dare to use this banner" he thought. "Are you not afraid to have a taste of my sword?" The Seeker of Secrets said, "I will stand still and let you strike with your sword as you wish." Nezha got very angry, made a great shout, "Transform!" and he was changed, having three heads and six arms. With a fierce look he held a different kind of weapon in each of the six hands, one instrument to behead the monster, a second to cut him down, a third to bind him, a fourth to beat him, a fifth a silken ball and the sixth a large fork with which to rush on him. When the Seeker of Secrets saw this, he was afraid and said, "This little boy after all has some skill. It would not be out of place to show him my skill." The Seeker of Secrets then cried out, "Transform!" and in an instant he also had three heads and six arms, had multiplied his magic spear into three, and with his six hands grasped them.

And so they fell to and fought. It was truly like an earthquake when these mighty spirits battled for thirty rounds. The six instruments of the prince were multiplied into ten thousand. Sun the Monkey King therefore multiplied his magic spears into ten thousand. It seemed as if a shower of shooting stars were falling, and it was difficult to know which would be victor. But the Seeker of Secrets was quick of eye and skilful of hand. In the thick of the battle, he pulled out a hair and called out, "Transform!" and in an instant he was changed into his original form, and held the magic spear in his hand as he made for Nezha. The prince tried to parry the thrust, but he was struck by the spear on the back of his head and on his left arm. With great pain he fled, having been completely beaten, and returned to camp.

At this Guardian King Li was greatly alarmed, changed color and said, "How can we withstand this kind of magic?" The young prince replied, "Outside his cave there is a flagstaff with a banner on which is written in large letters 'The Great Sage, the Equal of Heaven.' This name he boasts, and says that the Jade Emperor must recognize him as an equal, and then there will be no trouble at all. If the Jade Emperor refuses, then he will certainly fight, even up to the Court of Heaven." Guardian King Li said, "Since matters are so bad, on no account have anything to do with him just now, but let us return to Heaven and report and ask for more legions to subdue him."

So they departed for Heaven. The Monkey King, after his victory, returned to the Mountain Garden, and the seventy-two demon kings and the six brothers all came to congratulate him. Then they drank and rejoiced in the cave. The Monkey King, sitting opposite the six brothers said, "Since my title is now The Great Sage, the Equal of Heaven, you also shall be known as great sages." The Ox Demon King cried out, "What you say is most reasonable. I myself shall be The Great Sage, Victorious over Heaven." The Crocodile Demon King said, "I shall be The Great Sage of the Sea." The Roc Demon King said, "I shall be known as "The Great Sage Rebellious in Heaven." The Lion Demon King said, "And I shall be the Great Sage who Removed the Mountains." The Gorilla Demon King said, "And I shall be The Great Sage who Permeates All Things." Another Demon King said, "I shall be The Great Sage who Repelled the Deities." Thus the seven Great Sages took names to themselves and titles just as they pleased, and played together all day.

Meanwhile Guardian King Li, had returned with his third son to Heaven, and memorialized thus: "We, your ministers, by your command, led forth an army to subdue the monster the Seeker of Secrets, but as we did not know that his magic power was so great, we did not overcome him. We therefore hope Your Majesty will add more heavenly hosts to destroy him." The Jade Emperor said, "How can one monkey demon have such ability that you need an additional force?" Then the third son said, "I hope Your Majesty will forgive your minister, and not put him to death. That Monkey Demon had an iron spear with which he first put to flight the Great Victorious Commander. Then he wounded me in my arm. At the entrance of his cave he has hoisted a flag on which is written in large letters "The Great Sage, the Equal of Heaven." He says if you give him this position and title, he will cease fighting; but if not, he will lay siege to Heaven itself." The Jade Emperor, hearing this, was much astonished and said, "How dare he be so mad as that?" and ordered all the generals to go and destroy him at once. Just as he spoke, the Minister of Venus stepped out of the ranks and said, "That monkey demon knows how to make big demands, but does not know how far he can go. If you send more heavenly legions to fight him, they will not subdue him easily, so it will cause great trouble to the army. Would it not be better that you should pardon him, and send an edict, granting him the title that he asks? But let it be only an empty title, without any emolument." The Jade Emperor said, "What do you mean by that?" "Let him come and take up his abode in Heaven," said the minister, "so that his ambition might be satisfied, and he will no longer create any disturbance, and Heaven and Earth may be at peace again." The Jade Emperor, having heard this, granted the request. He ordered that an edict be written, and that the Minister of Venus should take it to the Monkey King. The Minister, therefore, left the South Gate of Heaven and came to the Mountain Garden and the Waterfall Cave.

When he came near, things looked very different from what they had done on his previous visit. There were great displays and an appearance of deadly earnestness. Every one of the demons had a spear and sword, and all were shouting and running about. As soon as they saw the Minister of Venus, they approached as if in fright. But he said, "Wait a little. Go tell your Great Sage that I am an ambassador from the Jade Emperor himself, and have an invitation from him to your chief."

The monkeys ran and told their king what had happened. The Seeker of Secrets said, "I am glad he has come, I am glad he has come. He is probably the Minister of Venus, who came here before, and through whom I was invited to go above and occupy a position that was far too low. Since he comes again, it must be for the good." Then he ordered all his chiefs to unfurl their banners, beat their drums, and put themselves in battle array to receive him. The Great Sage, with helmet on his head and clothed in armor, came out of the cave and made obeisance, crying out, "Ancient Minister, please come in." He came in and stood with his face turned towards the South and said, "Now I must announce to the Great Sage that since you despised the position of Horse Master which was assigned to you, and left your office, the Jade Emperor has considered the situation. He says that as all officials begin with inferior positions and rise step by step, you should not have rejected the position because it was low. Guardian King Li and his son were sent down to arrest you. They have returned saying that you, Great Sage, have put up a standard, claiming to be the Equal of Heaven. All the generals of Heaven wanted to come down and fight, but I excused you and exerted my influence on your behalf, so as to avoid the mobilization of the troops. I begged the Jade Emperor to give you a more fitting appointment. This he granted. Hence I am come to invite you to go back with the title you claim." The Seeker of Secrets smiled and said, "Once before you troubled yourself on my behalf. Now you do so again. Very many thanks to you. But I did not know that there was such a position in Heaven as "Great Sage, the Equal of Heaven." The Minister of Venus replied, "My request was that you should be appointed to that post, and it has been granted. That is why I come to invite you. Put away all your doubts." The Seeker of Secrets was greatly delighted, and invited him to a banquet, but he said he could not delay.

Therefore together they mounted the clouds and reached the South Gate of Heaven. All the generals of the heavenly legions presented arms to receive them. Then they went straight to the Throne Room and the Minister of Venus fell on his knees and said, "Your Minister, in obedience to your command, has fetched Horse Master Sun, the Seeker of Secrets, into Your presence." The Jade Emperor said, "Sun, Seeker of Secrets, I have decided to appoint you the Great Sage, the Equal of Heaven. Here I expect you to act worthily." The Monkey King only faced the Jade Emperor and said, "Thanks a lot!" The Jade Emperor then commanded two officials to erect a mansion for him on the right side of the Peach Orchard and to put up a tablet inscribed, "The Mansion of the Great Sage, the Equal of Heaven." Two officials were appointed to wait upon the Monkey King in the mansion, with a number of servants to wait upon each. The Jade Emperor also sent the Minister of the Five Pole Stars to accompany him to his new palace, presenting him with two big jars of wine and ten golden flowers. He told the Monkey King to have his mind at rest, to live at peace, and not to leave his post again. The Monkey King received this envoy, and that very day went with the Minister of the Five Pole Stars to his mansion, where he opened the wine jars so that all might drink and rejoice together. The Minister of the Five Pole Stars then returned to his own palace, and the Monkey King was full of happiness, rejoicing in his heavenly mansion, without care of any sort.

5

Monkey Upsets
the Peach Banquet

THE GREAT SAGE, having been given the title of the Equal of Heaven, was not certain of the degree of his official rank. But he had two servants waiting on him in his palace all day long. They had nothing to do but to eat their three meals a day, and to sleep all night. The Equal of Heaven had perfect freedom to visit his friends in the palaces and to make new friends. When meeting the Three Pure Ones, he styled himself Old Sun, and when visiting the Four Rulers he called himself, "Your Minister." When meeting the Forces of the Nine Bright Stars, the Generals of the Five Regions, the Forces of the Twenty-eight Constellations, the Four Guardians of Heaven, the Twelve Morning Stars, the Elders of the Five Regions, all the Stars of Heaven, and the Spirits of the River of Heaven, he addressed them all as equals.

One day he went to the East, another day to the West, mounting on the clouds without any fixed purpose. Then one day at the morning audience of the Jade Emperor, an official said, "That so called Equal of Heaven is daily wandering about without anything to do. It is to be feared that some day trouble will arise. It will be better to give him some work to do."

The Jade Emperor then summoned the Monkey King, who gladly came forward, saying, "Your Majesty has called Old Sun. What honor are you about to confer on him?" The Jade Emperor replied, "I see you have nothing to do, I therefore appoint you to a special service, to guard the Peach Orchard." The Great Sage joyfully thanked him and retired.

He then went to look at the Peach Orchard. Servants were there who refused to admit him asking, "Where does the Great Sage wish to go?" He replied, "I have been appointed by the Jade Emperor to take charge of the Peach Orchard, and have come to see it."

Then the servants called the others, and all kowtowed to him, leading him in to the orchard. It was full of magnificent trees with fine branches. They were not common trees, but had been planted by the Queen of Heaven. The Great Sage, after admiring them for a long time asked the servants the number of the trees. They replied, "The first row has three thousand six hundred trees, their blossoms and fruit are small. They take three thousand years to ripen. If men eat the fruit they become immortal and can understand the laws of nature. Their constitutions will become strong. The middle row has twelve hundred trees, bearing more blossom and sweeter fruit. They take six thousand years to ripen. If a man eats one of those he can ascend to the heavens floating like a cloud, and can live forever without getting old. The third row has also twelve hundred trees with red fruit and small stones. It takes nine thousand years for them to ripen. When a man has eaten of them, he will live as long as the heaven and earth, and attain the same age as the sun and moon."

When the Great Sage heard this, he rejoiced exceedingly. After examining the trees with great care he returned to his palace, and every few days he went to the orchard, without visiting his friends or wandering on the clouds. One day, seeing the peaches ripe on the trees of the third row, he was anxious to taste them, but the laborers in the orchard and his own servants were all in attendance on him. So he thought how he could get rid of them, and said, "You can all leave me. I am going to rest awhile here." So they all went out. Then Monkey King took off his official robes and climbed up the great tree. He picked the ripest peaches, sat on the branches, and ate his fill. After this, he donned his clothes, and called for his servants to accompany him to his own palace.

After a few days, he went again to the orchard to get fruit to his heart's content. Now it happened that the Queen of Heaven had a birthday that day, and had provided a great banquet in one of her palaces on the lake. This was called the Peach Banquet, and for this she sent seven companies of fairies in various uniforms of red, blue,

西王母

The Queen of Heaven.

grey, black, purple, yellow, and green ornamented with flowers on their heads, to gather peaches from the orchard. The seven companies of fairies arrived at the orchard and found the servants watching at the gate. They said, "We have come by order of the Queen of Heaven to fetch peaches for the Peach Banquet." The servants replied, "Just wait a little. This year is not the same as before. The Jade Emperor has appointed the Great Sage, the Equal of Heaven, to guard the orchard. We must go in and announce you to him."

The fairies asked, "Where is he?" The servants replied, "He is inside the orchard sleeping in the pavilion."

"Go and fetch him and be quick about it," ordered the fairies. The servants went on to the pavilion, but could not find him. His clothes were there, but he was gone.

It happened that the Great Sage, after eating some peaches, had suddenly transformed himself into a man only two inches in height, and was sleeping amongst the leaves on one of the branches of a tree. The servants returned to say they could not find him. The seven companies of fairies replied, "We came in obedience to the Queen's command. How can we go back empty handed?"

Some of the servants standing by said, "Since you fairies have come in obedience to the Queen, and there is no doubt of her command, you had better go in and pluck the peaches yourselves. The Great Sage must have wandered out of the orchard to visit his friends."

They went in and found very few peaches, and those that were there were hairy and green. The Monkey had eaten all the ripe ones. The fairies looked East and West and only on the South found a few partly eaten remnants, some red and some white. The blue fairies pulled a branch down. It was on this branch that the Great Sage was sleeping. The red fairies picked the fruit and then let go of the branch. This sudden jerk woke the Great Sage and he resumed his original natural size. He pulled out of his ear the steel needle, which grew as large as a beam, and cried out fiercely, "What fiends you are to dare to come and steal my peaches!"

At this sight the seven bands of fairies fell down on their knees and begged him not to be angry, saying, "We are not fiends, but are fairies sent by the Queen of Heaven to get peaches for her banquet. When we arrived, you could not be found anywhere. Fearing to be late, we came in to pick some fruit. Pray forgive us."

On hearing this, the Great Sage ceased his anger and smiled, saying, "Rise! Whom has the Queen of Heaven invited to the Banquet?"

The fairies replied, "Those invited are, according to ancient custom, the Buddha of the Western Heaven, *the bodhisattvas*, the *arhats*, Guanyin of the Southern Ocean, The Merciful Emperor of the East, the Venerable Immortals of the Ten Provinces and Three Islands, the Mystic Divinity of the North Pole, the Great Immortal of the Center, The Five Elders of the Five Regions. Besides these, are the Prince of the Five Northern Stars, Spirits of the Upper Eight Caves, the Three Pure Ones, the Four Rulers and the Heavenly Immortal called the Great Beginning. There are also the Jade Emperor and the Gods of the Nine Mountains and Seas of the Middle Eight Caves, the King of Hell, the Dark Teacher of the Lower Eight Caves, the Spirits of the Earth. All the Major and Minor Deities of all the Halls and Palaces will meet at the banquet to congratulate the Queen."

The Great Sage laughed and asked, "Am I invited?" The fairies replied that they did not know.

The Great Sage said, "I am the Great Sage, Equal of Heaven. Why should I not have been invited among the honored guests?"

"These are those who have been invited in the past. We do not know who are invited now," replied the fairies.

"I do not blame you," he said. "Wait a little and let me go and enquire." The Great Sage then pronounced a spell towards the fairies and said, "Stop, Stop, Stop," and in this way fixed the body of each of the beautifully robed fairies. They turned the whites of their eyes and stood transfixed in the peach orchard. The Great Sage then mounted a cloud and came out of the orchard and directed his course towards the celestial lake. As he was going, he saw before him a bare footed Taoist. The Great Sage bent his head and decided to play a trick. He asked the Taoist where he was going. He replied, "I have been invited by the Queen of Heaven to the Peach Banquet." The Great Sage said, "You do not know, Sir, that the Jade Emperor has ordered me to mount on the clouds and instruct the guests, who come from all directions, to go first to the Dongming Hall to learn their proper places at the banquet." The spirit was an honest soul and did not doubt his words, so he turned and directed his course towards the Dongming Hall.

The Great Sage mounted a cloud and repeated an incantation to change his body. He was at once changed into the likeness of the bare footed Taoist, and directing his course to the celestial lake, soon got to the Banquet Hall, and finally entered inside. There he saw carnation incense coiled round princely red batons with embroidered silks. In front were arranged the nine pink phoenix feathers and eight precious purple seats; on the table were dishes of dragons' liver, phoenix marrow, bears paws, a hundred different things, strange fruit and fine dishes, everything new and fresh. All were arranged in perfect order, but as yet no guests had arrived. The Great Sage noted everything. Suddenly he smelt some wine, turned round quickly and saw several jars of carnation sauce and sweet fermented spirits under cover of the right partition, so that his mouth watered and he wanted to taste it. But those that served the wine were all in attendance. He therefore used his magic, plucked a few hairs, put them in his mouth and chewed them small and pronounced an incantation saying, "Change!," and the bits of hair were all changed into sleeping insects which flew on the men's faces and soon their hands were limp and their heads heavy and all fell into a deep sleep.

The Great Sage then tasted those fine dishes, went to the right partition where the wine jars were, opened them and drank till he became tipsy. Then he said to himself, "This will never do, for the guests will soon arrive and I shall not be surprised if they arrest me. What shall I do? It is better that I should return to my home and have a sleep." So he strolled away, but lost his way, and instead of getting to his own palace he got into the Polar Star Mansion, from whence spirits start from heaven to become incarnate on earth. At the sight of this he suddenly became sober and thought, "The Polar Star Mansion is above the Thirty Three Heavens, and is the home of the Ancient of Days. How have I made this mistake? Never mind, I wanted to come and see this place and have never succeeded, now that I am here I may as well take the opportunity and see it."

So he straightened his clothes and went in, but there was not a soul present, for the Ancient of Days and the Creator of Light were preaching in the three-storied vermillion palace above and all the ministering spirits were in attendance. The Great Sage went in to

亂蟠桃大聖偷丹

The Monkey Upsets the Peach Banquet.

the Immortal Pill Chamber in search of someone, but could not find anyone. He saw beside the crucible, where the pills were prepared, five gourds. These five gourds were filled with Immortal Pills already made. The Great Sage was very glad and said, "These are the most precious things of the Immortals. I would like to prepare some pills to help men, but I have no time at home. Today providentially I have hit upon these pills. As the Ancient of Days is not at home, let me eat a few of these." So he turned the pills out of the gourds and swallowed them all as he would have swallowed some peas. With the pills and the wine working in him he did not feel comfortable, and said, "If the Jade Emperor is disturbed I shall fear for my life. It is better for me to go down and be a king upon earth." So he ran out of the Polar Star Mansion. He had not gone far from the Western Gate of Heaven before he made himself invisible, got on the clouds, and returned to his old home in the mountain.

Then he shouted out, "My little ones, I have returned." They all knelt and cried out, "You, Great Sage, have been very thoughtless of us; you have left us for so long a time without coming back." He replied, "Not long, not long at all," and as he spoke he walked on and went far into the cave. When the four generals had kowtowed before him, they said, "Oh Great Sage, you have been in Heaven for a hundred years, what honors have you received?" The Great Sage laughed and said, "It seems to me only six months since I left you. Why do you speak of a hundred years?" The generals said, "One day in heaven is equal to one year on earth." The Great Sage said, "I am glad to tell you that the Jade Emperor was kind to me this time, and gave me the title of being Equal to Heaven, and let me live in the Palace of the Equal of Heaven, and I had servants to wait on me. Seeing that I had nothing to do, he appointed me to look after the Peach Orchard. Then followed the great Banquet of the Queen of Heaven. Because I was not invited to it, I went to the Celestial Lake Palace where the banquet was to be held, and finding none of the guests had arrived and that everything had been prepared and all the dishes laid out, I stealthily tasted them and drank the wine. On leaving I lost my way and got into the Mansion of the Ancient of Days, where I found five gourds full of the Pills of Immortality. These I also stealthily swallowed. Fearing that the Jade Emperor might find fault with me, I left Heaven altogether and returned here."

On hearing this, all the little monkey demons greatly rejoiced and prepared refreshments in honor of his return, and gave him a bowl of coconut wine. He tasted it; then made a wry face and said, "It is not good, not good at all. This morning I enjoyed myself in the Celestial Lake Palace, where on the side of the dining hall was abundance of a delicious carnation sauce, which you have never seen. When I go there again I will take a few jars and bring them home to you so that you may taste it and each become immortal." All the monkeys rejoiced beyond measure. The Great Sage then went out of the cave, jumped and made himself invisible and made straight for the Peach Banquet Hall. When he got there he found all the wine servers still asleep, so he took up two jars, one under the right arm and the other under the left, and two others, one in each hand, and, mounting a cloud, he returned to the cave and served the monkeys with the wine of the Immortals, which greatly delighted all.

Now the seven companies of fairies, since they had been turned into immovable statues, were not able to move for twenty-four hours. When they awoke again they took up their baskets and returned to the Queen of Heaven, who asked them, "How many peaches have you brought?" They replied, "We have only two baskets full of small peaches, and three baskets full of middle size ones. When we got to the best peach trees there were no peaches left, for the Great Sage had eaten them all. When we were looking for him, he suddenly appeared before us. He was very angry and was about to beat us. Then he asked for whom you were providing this banquet. After that, by some magic, he made us all immovable so that we could not stir until now." The Queen of Heaven, on hearing this, went to the Jade Emperor and told him everything. Just as she had finished, the wine servers and the officials came and reported that some one, whom they did not know, had secretly drunk all the fine wine, and eaten all the dishes.

Then the four great generals announced that the Ancient of Days had arrived. The Jade Emperor and the Queen of Heaven went out to meet him. After having saluted them, he said, "I had prepared five gourds of Immortal Pills to present to you at your great banquet. Unfortunately a thief came and stole them, so I have come to explain." The Jade Emperor, on hearing this, was alarmed. Shortly after, there came a messenger from the Palace of the Equal of Heaven, who kowtowed and said, "Sun, the Great Sage, is neglecting his duties. He went out yesterday and has not come back, and we do not know where he has gone." The Jade Emperor was still more alarmed. Then the bare footed Taoist said, "Having received the Queen of Heaven's invitation to the banquet, I met the Great Sage, the Equal of Heaven, who told me that the Jade Emperor had ordered us to go to the Dongming Hall, to learn our proper places before proceeding to the Banquet Hall. So I turned round and went to the Dongming Hall, but I did not see Your Majesty there, so I hastened and came here." The Jade Emperor was greatly alarmed and said, "This was a false order, deceiving my guests. Make haste and call the police superintendent, and make enquiries about where he has gone."

The superintendent went out and made enquiries everywhere. Then he reported and said, "The disturber of the celestial guests is none other than the Great Sage, the Equal of Heaven," and he then told the story of his doings. His Majesty was very angry, and ordered the four Princes of Heaven together with Guardian King Li and his son Nezha to call on the Forces of the Twenty-eight Constellations and the Nine Bright Stars, the Five Morning Stars, the Examiners of the Five Legions, the Great Rulers, the Four Eminent Officials, the Spirits of the East and West and the North and the South, the Guardians of the Five Mountains and all the Stars of Heaven, altogether a hundred thousand heavenly hosts, to go down to earth and surround the Fruit Garden in the Mountain and seize the Great Sage.

All the hosts of heaven arranged themselves in order to leave heaven. Guardian King Li gave orders that all should encamp around the Mountain Fruit Garden, and let no water go into it. In all there were eighteen regiments. The Officers of the Nine Bright Stars were sent first. They surrounded the cave outside, yelling "Where is the Great Sage? We have been sent from Heaven. We are heavenly hosts sent down to take you. Submit yourself at once! If you hesitate in the least, we shall annihilate you all." The little monkey demons were frightened and ran in saying, "Outside there are nine fierce spirits, who say that they have been sent as messengers from Heaven to capture the Great Sage. They are cursing and swearing outside the gate." At that time the Great Sage was drinking wine with his four great generals. Though he heard these words, he paid no attention to them and said, "This morning we have wine and we will take our fill, and never mind what is outside." Before they had finished speaking, a whole crowd of little monkeys rushed in and cried, "Great King, the nine fierce gods have broken through the gate and are rushing in and killing all before them."

The Great Sage was very angry, ordered his commander-in-chief, "Lead out twenty-two generals of the monkey demons to fight. I and my four bodyguards will follow." Then the commander-in-chief led them out to meet the enemy and the nine fierce officers annihilated them all before they came to the iron bridge. In the midst of the strife there, the Great Sage arrived with his iron spear and, throwing aside his armor, came out to fight, crying, "Make way for me!" At the sight all the nine officers fell back, arranged themselves in battle array and said, "You foolhardy monkey, are you not afraid of death? You have committed ten crimes. First you stole the peaches, then you stole wine, then you upset the banquet, afterwards you stole the Pills of Immortality, then you stole the imperial wine, and here you are enjoying yourself with these things. Are you not aware that you have committed crime upon crime?" The Great Sage laughed and said, "It is true that I have committed these things. What are you going to do about it?" The Nine Stars replied, "We have come by order of the Jade Emperor; you must submit yourself at once, lest the lives of all these should be imperiled." The Great Sage was very angry and said, "What strength have your gods of straw, that you dare to talk like this?" Then the Monkey King brandished his steel club and the Nine Stars fought with him with all their might until they were tired, and one by one they turned round and dragged their weapons after them, until they were all vanquished.

They hurried back to the central tent in the camp, and said to Guardian King Li, "That Monkey King is certainly wonderfully strong, we are no match for him, and have had to retreat before him." Guardian King Li called for the Four Celestial Princes and the Forces of the Twenty-eight Constellations all to come forth and fight. Still the Great Sage seemed to have no fear, but sent forth his commander-in-chief and seventy-two of his demon generals from the cave, and his four generals, and arranged them in order of battle outside the cave mouth. The battle lasted from morning until sunset. The commander-in-chief and seventy-two generals of the cave demons were all seized. But the four generals and the hosts of monkeys hid themselves in the cave inside the waterfall. The Great Sage with his iron club stopped the four heavenly generals and fought most fiercely with Guardian King Li and Prince Nezha in the air for a long time. Then, seeing that it was getting dark, he plucked a bunch of hair, chewed it small, and blew it forth, crying out, "Change!" and it was changed into a hundred thousand Great Sages, each with an iron club, and so they beat back Prince Nezha and the Four Guardian Generals of Heaven.

When the Great Sage had gained the victory, he called back the scattered hair and returned to his cave. Then were seen on the iron bridge the four generals leading their followers to welcome the Great Sage. They groaned three times in sorrow and tears, then three times they broke forth into cheers and laughter. The Great Sage said, "Why do you come and greet me both weeping and laughing?" The generals said, "Thinking of the battle this morning, when our seventy-two generals and commander-in-chief were all taken by the celestial hosts and we only escaped alive, we could not but weep, but now seeing our Great Sage return after his victory without a scratch on him, we are filled with laughter." The Sage replied, "Victory and failure are common things among soldiers, why should you be in distress? Only let us be on our guard, let us have something to eat, then we can sleep and be refreshed. In the morning I will show you a great miracle. I will take these celestial hosts and have my revenge on them." Then all the monkeys retired to sleep.

The Four Guardians of Heaven called back their soldiers after the battle and rewarded them according to their respective merits. They had seized tigers and leopards and wolves without number, but had not got a single monkey amongst them. Those who toiled hard were rewarded, and all the companies of soldiers were thick like bees, and were called together to surround the Mountain Garden, only waiting for the daylight to begin the great battle. All were on the watch to hear the command of the prince.

6

The Great Sage Captured

WE WILL NOT NOW DISCUSS HOW the heavenly host besieged the cave nor how the Great Sage resisted, but will tell of Guanyin, who arrived from the Southern Sea through the mouth of the Indus.

After Guanyin had been invited by the Queen of Heaven to the banquet, she and her chief disciple, whose religious name was Hui Yan and lay name Mucha, another son of Guardian King Li, went together to the Celestial Lake Palace, where they saw the Banqueting Hall in the greatest disorder. Although some guests had arrived, none of them were sitting down, but all were discussing matters very seriously. After Guanyin and the rest had greeted each other, a Taoist immortal told them everything that had taken place. Guanyin said, "Since there is no banquet, pray come with me to see the Jade Emperor." So all followed her to the Dongming Hall. There the four great barefooted Taoist immortals received them. Guanyin said, "I wish to see the Jade Emperor, may I trouble you to announce us?" A messenger went into the palace to know if they might enter. At the same time the Ancient of Days accompanied by the Queen of Heaven went there also. Guanyin then led her followers in. After having paid their respects, and having greeted the Ancient of Days and the Queen of Heaven, they all sat down and asked about the Peach Banquet. The Jade Emperor said, "Once a year we meet together for a happy banquet, but this year that monkey demon has upset everything. On this account I am greatly troubled, and have therefore sent a hundred thousand of the hosts of heaven down to earth to capture him. Today I have not received any report and do not know whether there has been a victory or not." When Guanyin heard this, she ordered Hui Yan to leave

Heaven at once and go down to the Mountain Garden and enquire about the battle, and added, "If the two parties should be about equal in strength, you must give a helping hand to the celestial hosts and return quickly with the tidings."

Hui Yan straightened his clothes and, taking an iron staff in his hand, mounted a cloud and went straight to the mountain, which he saw covered with soldiers, regiment upon regiment. Then he called upon the gatekeeper of the camp to announce his arrival, saying, "I am Guanyin's chief disciple, Hui Yan, the son of Guardian King Li, sent to enquire how the battle goes on." Guardian King Li invited him to enter. When Hui Yan saw the Four Guardians of Heaven and Guardian King Li, he fell on his knees and paid his respects. The king asked, "My son, where do you come from?" He replied, "I came with Guanyin to attend the Peach Banquet, but when we arrived and saw everything in disorder, Guanyin led all the guests to see the Jade Emperor. He told us how he had sent a host to subjugate the monkey demons, but had not received any tidings as to the progress of the war, consequently Guanyin sent me down here to make enquiries and report." Guardian King Li then told him all about the previous day's battle. Before he had finished speaking, there appeared a man outside the gate, saying that the Great Sage had led out a whole army of monkeys ready for battle. The Four Great Guardians of Heaven and Guardian King Li then discussed how to send soldiers to meet them. Mucha said, "Father, since Guanyin has ordered me to come down to make enquiries and render help in case of need, I am ready to go and see what kind of being this Great Sage is." Guardian King Li said, "My son, you must be very careful."

The son seized his iron staff, jumped outside the gate and shouted out, "Which is the Great Sage, the Equal of Heaven?" The Great Sage replied, "Who are you that dares to ask me?" Mucha said, "I am the second son of Guardian King Li, my Buddhist name is Hui Yan and I am a disciple of Guanyin." The Great Sage said, "Why do you come here instead of practicing religion at your home in the Southern Ocean?" Mucha replied, "I have been sent by my teacher to enquire about the war, and to see that these ferocious monkeys are captured." The Great Sage said, "How dare you talk like this

to me? Wait till you have a taste of my club." Mucha took his iron
staff to meet him, and there on the side of the mountain, outside
the camp, the two fought several bouts with each other. Hui Yan,
being no match for his enemy, was beaten and fled. The Great Sage
gathered his monkey soldiers and put them in battle array outside
the cave. Meanwhile, Mucha had already gone inside the camp,
and said breathlessly to his father, "This Great Sage is most wonderful, his powers are really marvelous. I could not vanquish him
and had to retreat before him." The prince was alarmed at this and
ordered a memorial to be written and sent to Heaven requesting
help. He then sent one of the Great Guardians to accompany his
son Mucha, bearing this memorial to Heaven.

When Hui Yan met Guanyin, he told her the evil tidings that
they had been beaten. The Jade Emperor opened the memorial and,
seeing that it was a request for help, smiled and said, "What shall
we do with this wild monkey? He seems to have wonderful powers,
for he is more than a match for a hundred thousand heavenly hosts,
and the Guardian King Li begs for more help; let the celestial soldiers help him." Before he finished speaking, Guanyin begged him
to wait. "Let me recommend someone that is able to capture this
monkey." The Jade Emperor said, "Whom do you recommend?"
Guanyin said, "Your worthy relative the Divine Kinsman. Formerly
he drove away six legions. He has younger brothers also on Plum
Mountain, with one thousand two hundred spirits, and their magic
powers are very great. But they only obey the command of the Jade
Emperor. Will you therefore issue an edict commanding them to go
and help? In this way you will succeed in capturing the monkeys."

When the Jade Emperor heard this, he ordered an edict for this
end and sent one of the chiefs forth to carry it out. When this chief
came to the mouth of the Guanzhou River he did not tarry a moment, but went straight to the Divine Kinsman. The doorkeepers at
once announced his arrival. Guardian King Li and all his younger
brethren came to receive him, burnt incense, and opened the edict.
It said, "In the Mountain Garden there is a monkey demon who
calls himself the Great Sage, the Equal of Heaven, and he has created a great disturbance. He has thrown the great Peach Banquet
into disorder. Although a hundred thousand heavenly hosts have

been sent down to the Mountain Garden, they have not been able to put him down. Therefore I call upon my worthy relative and all his faithful followers to go to the Mountain Garden and help in stamping out the rebellion. After the work is done he will be highly promoted and greatly rewarded." The Divine Kinsman replied, "I shall with pleasure go at once to help."

The Divine Kinsman called his six brethren of the Plum Mountain, namely, the Four Governors and the two Commanders-in-chief, to go with him. The brethren joyfully went together and called the roll of their hosts, with their hunting hawks and hounds, and their bows and arrows. They went before the wild winds and in no time crossed the Eastern Ocean and arrived at the Mountain Garden. But it was so thickly surrounded by rows upon rows of soldiers that they could not get near. The Divine Kinsman cried out, "I am the Divine Kinsman, commanded by the Jade Emperor to come and take the monkey demons. Quickly open the gate." At once the gatekeeper announced his arrival, and the Four Great Guardians and Guardian King Li came out to meet him. Having been asked how the battle was getting on, Guardian King Li told the whole story. Then the Divine Kinsman laughed and said, "Now that I have come here, I will make a change. You, sirs, do not scatter yourselves on the mountain, but keep close by, and wait until I fight the Great Sage. Please allow Guardian King Li to use his telescopic vision to watch the Monkey from afar, for I am afraid that when he is defeated, he will try to escape to some other place. We must all keep a sharp look out lest he should get away."

The Jade Emperor ordered things to be carried out as directed. The Divine Kinsman led the four governors and the two commanders-in-chief, including himself seven in all, out to the camp to fight, and the generals carefully watched round the camp, and had all their hunting beasts ready. Then all the lower ranks of soldiers received their orders. The Divine Kinsman went straight to the waterfall outside the cave, and saw the hosts of monkeys encamped around in perfect order. In the center of the camp there was a flagstaff with a flag on which was written, "The Great Sage, the Equal of Heaven." The Divine Kinsman said, "How is it that this demon dares to call himself the Equal of Heaven?" When the little monkeys saw the Divine Kinsman, they ran in and announced his arrival. The Monkey King seized his steel club and, putting on his armor, jumped outside the camp gate, and looked at the Divine Kinsman. He was really beautiful and was dressed superbly. When the Great Sage saw him, he smiled inwardly and lifted his steel club and shouted out, "What minor general are you who dares to come and fight with me?"

The Divine Kinsman shouted back, "You foolish fellow, you seem to have eyes, but cannot see. Do you not know me? I am the Divine Kinsman of the Jade Emperor, come here by order to take you. But you, foolish one, defy us and do not know what is good for you." The Great Sage said, "Now I remember the Jade Emperor's sister had an idea of coming down to earth to marry a certain Mr. Yang. They had a son who used to go to Peach Mountain with a hatchet in his hand. Can you be this one? Well, sir, I will not fight you. Go back quickly and tell your Four Great Guardians of Heaven to come forth." The Divine Kinsman, hearing this, was very angry, and said, "You wretched monkey, do not be so foolish. Take a cut from my sword." The Great Sage raised his steel club and the two fought with all their might. They fought three hundred bouts, and it is difficult to say who had the better of it. Then the Divine Kinsman roused himself terribly, shook himself and cried out, "Change!" and he was so changed that he was a hundred thousand feet high and he held in his hand a trident with sharpest points, each as strong as the peak of a mountain. His face and teeth were black, and his hair vermillion red. Looking at the Great Sage, he aimed a blow at his head. The Great Sage also used his magic art and changed himself so that he looked exactly like the Divine Kinsman. He raised his magic club, which was as huge as a peak of the Himalayas, and opposed the Divine Kinsman and so terrified the standard bearer that he could not hold the flag, and the two generals Peng and Pa that they could not hold their swords.

The four governors, together with the two commanders-in-chief gave orders the troops to go to the waterfall outside the cave, and carry with them the falcons and hounds and the bows and arrows to kill everybody outright. The poor monkeys were throwing away their spears and armor, their swords and lances, and were running and screaming, some fleeing to the mountains, others to the caves.

The Great Sage, suddenly seeing all the monkeys of his camp fleeing in terror, was himself alarmed, and, thinking of hiding himself by magic, retreated with his club. The Divine Kinsman followed and said, "Where are you going? Submit yourself at once and we will forgive you!" The Great Sage had no desire to fight, so he fled away, but when he came near the mouth of the cave, he met the Four Governors and the Two Commanders-in-Chief, who stopped his way and said, "Where are you going, you wretched monkey?" The Great Sage, trembling hand and foot, took his club and made it as small as a needle and hid it in his ear, shook his body and was transformed into a magpie and flew to a branch on the top of a tree.

The six brothers were confounded, and searched for him in all directions but could not find him. So they called out, "We have lost him!" Whilst they were talking of this, the Divine Kinsman arrived and asked, "How did you lose him?" They replied, "Here, where we had surrounded him, he suddenly disappeared!" The Divine Kinsman looked around with his phoenix eyes and saw the Monkey King in the form of a magpie on the top of a tree. He threw aside his spear and bow and used his magic to change himself into a starving falcon, and flew towards the magpie. The Great Sage, seeing this, flew away and changed himself into an eagle and made for the sky. The Divine Kinsman, then, quickly fluttered his feathers and changed himself into an ocean roc, and flew up to the cloud to pounce upon him. The Great Sage, seeing this, transformed himself into a fish in a stream and disappeared. The Divine Kinsman followed him to the brook side but could see no trace of him. In his heart he thought, "This monkey must have gone into the water! I must transform myself into a cormorant, and I shall surely get him!" So he changed again into a cormorant and floated down on the waves of the water and rested awhile. The Great Sage, having changed himself into a fish, was also carried down by the stream. Then he suddenly saw something flying like a bird, somewhat like a mandarin duck or a heron, but without red legs, and divined that the Divine Kinsman had changed himself into a cormorant and was waiting for him. He then turned round and made a sudden whirl in the water and disappeared. The Divine Kinsman, seeing this whirling fish, first like a carp but without a red tail, then like a perch but without scales, then like a black fish but without a star on its head, then like a bream but without a needle on its head, thought, "How is it that at the sight of me this fish disappears? It must be that it is no other than the Monkey changed into a fish!" So with his beak he tried to snatch the fish. The Great Sage then escaped out of the water and changing himself into a water snake on the edge of the river, rustled into the grass where he hid himself. Then the Divine Kinsman, hearing some noise in the water, and seeing a water snake coming out, recognised it as the Great Sage, and changed himself into a grey heron. With his long pincers like a beak he tried to pounce on the snake and swallow it. The water snake wriggled out and changed itself into a fetid tree, on the top of an acrid sandy beach.

After some more changes the Divine Kinsman shot at him when he was like a cuckoo. The Great Sage took advantage of that and rolled down to the bottom of the hill like a dead thing, and then changed himself into a local temple, transforming the various parts of his body into the parts of the temple. There was a difficulty about the tail, but he finally turned it into a flagstaff. The Divine Kinsman, looking about for the shot cuckoo, saw a tiny shrine with a flagstaff behind, and smiled and thought, "And so the Monkey has changed into this now. I have seen many temples and shrines, but I have never seen a flag staff put up behind one before! He thinks he can deceive me and get me to enter, and then he will swallow me with one gulp. But I am not going to be tempted into entering it. I will first break through the door and windows with my fists." The Great Sage, on feeling this pounding said, "What smart eyes he has! If he destroys the door and windows, he will destroy my eyes and teeth and I shall be hopelessly wounded." So he jumped like a tiger and suddenly disappeared in the air.

The Divine Kinsman looked for him all round, but only saw the Four Governors and the Two Commanders-in-chief rushing towards him and eagerly saying, "Have you caught the Great Sage?" The Divine Kinsman laughed and said, "The Monkey had just changed himself into a temple and thought he would tempt me to go in, but when I was about to break through his door and windows, he got away and disappeared altogether, leaving no trace behind him. Most mysterious! Most mysterious!" They were all alarmed and looked round in all directions and still they found no trace of him. The Divine Kinsman then said, "Stay here, brethren, and watch, and I will go up to the sky and look for him." When he got there, he saw Guardian King Li with Nezha on the clouds, high up in the air, scanning all round with his telescopic vision. The Divine Kinsman called out to Guardian King Li and asked, "Have you seen the Monkey King?" "No, I have not, we are here looking for him." The Divine Kinsman then told the story of all the magic changes of the Monkey, until he changed himself into a temple and then disappeared completely.

When Guardian King Li heard this, he peered around with his telescopic eyes and then he smiled and said, "Go at once, go at once, the Monkey has used the magic of making himself invisible. After leaving the camp, he went to your Guanzhou River." When the Divine Kinsman heard that, he also spirited himself away to the mouth of the river. But after the Great Sage had got there, he changed himself into the form of the Divine Kinsman himself, came down from the clouds and entered a temple. As no one could distinguish the fraud, all came and kowtowed, and he in their midst surveyed the burning of incense, and then read the written prayers and heard Li Hu paying his vows of three animals for sacrifice, Zhang Long offering thanksgiving for blessings received, Zhao Jia begging for a son, and Jian Bing begging to be relieved of his duties on account of ill health. As this performance was going on, there came a man to announce that an old man had come. All quickly turned round to see and were greatly frightened at his demeanor. The Divine Kinsman, for he was the old man, said, "Has the Great Sage, the Equal of Heaven come here?" They replied, "No, we have not seen the Great Sage, but there is an old man inside burning incense." The Divine Kinsman rushed inside. The Great Sage at sight of him appeared in his true form and said, "Do not make any disturbance, Prince, the temple belongs to the Sun family." The Divine Kinsman raised his trident, with its double edged blades, rushed on him to cut him down, but the Monkey King evaded his thrust, took out his embroidery needle from his ear and when it grew as large in circumference as an arm or a leg, rushed to meet him and there was a fierce struggle between them. They got out of the temple and fought in the air as they went, until they reached the Mountain Garden, where they terrified the Four Great Guardians of Heaven and their followers, who were surrounding the place. The Four Governors and the Two Commanders-in-chief came to meet the Divine Kinsman and with all their might tried to surround the Great Sage. Then the Chief, having called the six brethren and their soldiers together to take the Monkey King, returned to Heaven to report.

The Jade Emperor, Guanyin, and the Queen of Heaven, together with all the Taoist spirit officials in the Lingshao Hall were talking and saying, "Since the Second Prince has gone to the battle, we have not heard any tidings today." Guanyin said, "Your humble servant begs you and Buddha to go outside the South Gate of Heaven, and see for yourselves how the battle goes on." The Jade Emperor replied, "That is a good suggestion, let us go outside the South Gate."

So the gate was opened and they looked far and wide, but only saw the heavenly hosts thick all over the place defending the four gates. Guardian King Li and Nezha were still peering around, with their telescopic visions, and the Divine Kinsman was still fighting the Great Sage. Guanyin said to the Ancient of Days, "The Second Prince whom I recommended has great magic power and who is engaged in battle with the Great Sage, has not yet laid hold of him. May I go and help? We shall soon have him seized." The Ancient of Days said, "How can you help?" Guanyin replied, "I will take my bottle of clear water and willow branch and throw them on the head of the Monkey. He will not be killed, but he will fall. Then let the Divine Kinsman seize him." The Ancient of Days said, "This bottle is porcelain, and if you hit him, all is well: but if you do not hit his head but simply hit his steel club, then your bottle will be broken. Wait a moment, do not move, let me have a try." Guanyin said, "And what weapon do you use?" He replied, "I'll show it to you."

Then from his left arm he drew forth a ring and said, "This is my weapon, which was forged by me when preparing the Pill of Immortality. It is full of spiritual efficacy and transforming power. Neither fire can burn it, nor water destroy it. It can be changed into a noose to capture all things and is called the Diamond Coil.

李老君

The Ancient of Days.

It was formerly used to civilize the barbarians and transform them into Buddhas. It has very great merit. In the end it is sure to give protection. Wait until I throw this down." Having said that, he dropped it from the Gate of Heaven, and it rolled down over the top of the camp of the Mountain Garden, and straight on the head of the Monkey King. He was so busy fighting, he did not know that a new weapon with wonderful effect had fallen from Heaven. He could not stand steady on his legs, and fell over. He turned on his side and was about to get up again, when the hounds fell upon him, and the heroes bound him with ropes, and hooked swords that prevented him from transforming himself any more. He cursed and said, "You death hounds, why do you not go and look after your own homes? Why do you come to bite Old Sun?"

Then the Ancient of Days withdrew the Diamond Coil and invited the Jade Emperor, Guanyin, the Queen of Heaven, and all the rest to return to the Lingshao Hall. The Four Great Guardians of Heaven, together with Guardian King Li and the rest called their hosts together and went up to the Divine Kinsman and congratulated him, saying, "It is all your wonderful prowess." But he said, "No, this is owing to the great blessing of the Ancient of Days. The merit does not belong to me." The Four Governors said, "Take this slave to the Jade Emperor." The Divine Kinsman said, "As some of you have not been registered in Heaven, you cannot see the Jade Emperor. Let the six first ranks of the heavenly spirits ascend to Heaven and report. Let the generals of the army remain here to search the mountain. When you have searched it all then return to the Guanzhou River and wait until I get you a reward so that we may rejoice together."

So the governors and the two commanders-in-chief remained behind and the Divine Kinsman with his company mounted the cloud and sang a song of victory, as they wended their way to Heaven. Soon they arrived at the Dongming Hall. The heavenly generals said, "The Four Great Heavenly Princes and their followers have now caught the Monkey Demon, and have arrived here to await your commands." The Jade Emperor then ordered that the chief and all the heavenly hosts should be quartered in the new demon terrace, and that the captive should be flayed alive.

7
Imprisoned for 500 Years

WHEN THE GREAT SAGE WAS ESCORTED by the heavenly host to the new demon terrace, he was slung to a beam, but neither knife nor hatchet nor sword had touched his body. The Southern Star with all the stars of heaven burnt as usual, but none could burn him, and the gods of thunder rolled forth their thunder, but did not injure him in the least.

The Chief Executioner then said, "We do not know what kind of armor this Great Sage has, for nothing can hurt him. We have tried swords to cut him and hatchets to flay him, thunder to terrify him and lightning to burn him, but all is of no avail. What shall we do?" The Jade Emperor, having heard this, asked, "What shall we do to this demon?" The Ancient of Days said, "The Monkey has eaten of the immortal peaches and drunk the immortal wine, and taken the Immortal Pills and swallowed them all. Tried by heavenly fire, he has become a piece of diamond that you cannot smelt. He cannot be harmed. Let him go with me, and I will put him in the eight diagram crucible, and let all the fire of civil and military arts burn him, so that I may get the true Immortal Pill, and his body return to ashes."

The Jade Emperor, hearing this, said, "Let the six guards take him away, and give him to the Ancient of Days." Then he called for the Divine Kinsman and ordered him to be presented with a hundred gold flowers, one hundred jars of heavenly wine, strange and precious pearls with silks and embroideries, to be divided with his brethren. The Divine Kinsman, having thanked his Majesty's grace, returned to the mouth of the river Guanzhou.

The Ancient of Days went to the Polar Star Mansion, unbound the ropes on the Great Sage, opened the handcuffs and pushed him inside the eight diagram crucible, and ordered the servants to kindle the fire so as to burn his dross. This crucible consisted of the eight diagrams: Qian, Kun, Zhen, Xuan, Kan, Li, Gen, Dui.

Now he took his body and put it under the Xuan diagram. Xuan is wind; and if there is wind, then there is no fire, but the wind makes the smoke arise until both eyes become red to the great injury of the sight. Hence it is called the golden essence of the fiery eyes, truly a fleeting reflected light. In forty-nine days the conversion was complete.

On the day the crucible was opened to get the pure metal, the Great Sage took both his hands and hid his eyes, which were weak and full of tears. Hearing some noise above the crucible, he opened his eyes and saw a light that he could not endure. So he bent himself and jumped out of the crucible, upsetting it with great noise, and went forth and terrified those tending the fire, who came to lay hold of him. He took them one by one and threw them on the ground. He was like a mad white-faced tiger or a one-horned dragon. The Ancient of Days came up and laid hold of him, but the Great Sage flung him also on the ground, and escaped, carrying his magic needle in his ear, where it was being shaken by the wind. When it grew larger he took it in his hand, and rushed madly on everyone he met, beating the ministers of the nine bright stars so that everybody shut the doors and disappeared out of sight.

> In chaos time the soul immortal is,
> Through thousand changes, changeless nature is,
> In darkness, dark; unmoved the first cause lies
> The Ideal, the First Mystery,
> The lead and silver furnace is not life,
> But life eternal lies outside matter,
> Ever changing and transforming.
> Of three creeds and five laws we need not speak,
> A spark of light divine shines in vast space,
> Lasts long or short as man wills to spend it,
> Peaceful or warlike as he pleases.
> The monkey heart is like the heart of man,
> This monkey tale is deepest allegory;

八卦爐中逃大聖

Sun Escapes from the Crucible.

> The Great Sage and Equal of Heaven,
> Official rank as stud master has man,
> The horse and monkey, heart and mind,
> Within the man subdued must be.
> To find true life there is but one true law
> Man and Ideal must be a true pair.

At this time the Monkey King, having no regard for high or low, whirled his steel club in all directions, so that no one dared to approach him, and made straight for the Dongming Hall, outside the Lingshao Hall. Fortunately, on the right there were Taoist official spirits, and on the left the officials of the Lingshao Hall. Seeing the Great Sage coming and brandishing his steel club, the Taoist spirit officials wanted to stop him and said, "You impudent Monkey, where do you want to go? Do not behave like a fool." The Great Sage did not trouble to answer them, but raised his spear to strike them. A spirit official quickly met his attack, and the two fought fiercely in front of the Lingshao Hall. Before it was clear which was victorious, the spirit on the right sent his assistant general to the Thunder Palace and requested thirty-six thunder generals to come and help.

They came together and surrounded the Great Sage on the terrace. They all looked most warlike, but although they came very near him with their knives and spears and swords and lances, the Great Sage had no fear and merely shook his body. By magic he changed himself into a being with three heads and six arms, and the steel club by a twist became three, and the six arms, wielding three clubs, twirled about like a spinning wheel on the terrace.

> Perfect life, shining bright
> Down all ages without fail,
> How can man understand it?
> Fire cannot quench nor water drown it,
> Like a diamond, swords and spears cannot hurt it.
> It can be good or ill as chance commands.
> Doing good transforms one to a god.
> Doing evil makes a horned and hairy demon,
> Ever defying heaven, unarrested in his course
> By gods of thunder and all the hosts of heaven.

Then all the generals closed up around him but could not get near his person. They fought terribly with such a noise that the Jade Emperor heard it and sent two officials to go to the West, and invite Buddha to come down.

As soon as these two officials received this command, they went to a grand service in the Spiritual Mountain in the West where Buddha's Temple was. There they paid their respects to the four Temple Guardians and the Eight Bodhisattvas and begged them to announce them. These led the officials to the Precious Lotus Terrace, saying, "Lord Buddha invites you two officials to see him. Go three times round in procession and wait. Lord Buddha asks what the Jade Emperor wishes by sending you here." The two officials told the story of the Great Sage from beginning to end and added, "The matter at present is very urgent and the Jade Emperor invites Lord Buddha to come to the rescue." On hearing this, Buddha spoke to all the other Buddhas Past and Future and said, "All of you sit here in this temple hall, while I go and tame the demon and ease the Jade Emperor's mind." Then he called upon the two chief disciples, Ananda and Kasyapa, to go with him.

They left the service and went to the Lingshao Hall where the Jade Emperor resided, and heard a terrible noise of battle, with the thirty-six thunder generals surrounding the Monkey. Lord Buddha gave the order: "Let the thunder generals stop their fight and open the cordon to let the Great Sage come out, so that I may speak to him." The generals obeyed and the Great Sage assumed his natural form and with a loud shout of anger cursed and said, "Who are you, and where do you come from?" The Buddha smiled and said. "I am Shakyamuni, from the Paradise in the West. Praise be to Amitabha. I hear you are wild and mad, frequently troubling the Palace of Heaven. I do not know where you have been brought up, nor why you are so fierce." The Great Sage said:

> Born I am a natural genie,
> As monkey lived in mountain grove,
> My house a cave behind a waterfall,
> Asking all how best to find the life eternal,
> I practiced many arts to be immortal,
> I learnt all magic without limit.

And hating the one span of human life,
I fixed my heart on joining gods divine,
The halls of heaven were not full at first,
From age to age the saints of earth ascend.
If they succeeded, why not also I?
A hero he who wins the race.

When Buddha heard these words, he laughed and said, "Aha! So you are a monkey seeking to become a hero, are you? How dare you have no conscience and usurp the Celestial Palace? The Jade Emperor has continued with great self sacrifice from eternity, and throughout a thousand five hundred and fifty *kalpas*, each *kalpa* being a hundred and twenty nine thousand six hundred years. And how many years do you think that is? It was in this way that he was able to gain that position of infinite power, while you are still only an animal. You are not even human yet. You must speedily repent and not say a word of complaint, otherwise you might meet with an enemy that will at once rob you of your life, and to end your career would be a great pity." The Great Sage replied, "Although the Jade Emperor has made great sacrifices for many *kalpas,* he should not live there for ever. Leaders should rule in turn, next year should be my turn and he should give way and give me the Celestial Palace. If not, I will certainly make trouble again and there cannot be peace." Buddha replied, "Since you have been deprived of the magic of life eternal, how can you by victory get the Celestial Palace?" The Great Sage said, "I know seventy-two magic arts, I can outlive all the *kalpas*. I can ride on the clouds and with one leap can cover eighteen thousand *li*. How can I not sit on the throne of Heaven?" Buddha said to him, "Let me try your skill. Since you have a skill in making great leaps, stand on the palm of my right hand and let me see if you can jump out of it. Then I will acknowledge that you have won, and there will be no further need of weapons to fight, and the Jade Emperor will go away and yield the Celestial Palace to you. If you cannot jump out of the palm of my hand, you will have to go down below and become a demon again, and practice religion for a thousand *kalpas* more before you come and make further disturbance."

The Great Sage secretly rejoiced and said to himself, "This Buddha must be a perfect fool. I can jump eighteen thousand *li* at once, and his palm is not more than a foot in length. How could I not jump out of it?" Then he spoke aloud, "Since you propose this, I agree to it." Buddha said, "Agreed, agreed!" and opened his hand. His palm was only about the size of a small lotus leaf. The Great Sage took his magic steel and made a leap and rested on Buddha's palm, and said, "Here I go!" He thought he was traveling invisibly on the clouds, and that Buddha was watching him going fast like a windmill. The Great Sage, thinking he was rushing on the clouds, suddenly saw five pillars of red flesh in front stopping him, beyond which was darkness. He then said, "This must be the end of the journey. I will go back now, and Buddha is my witness that the Lingshao Hall of the Jade Emperor is mine now!" He was about to call out to show he had stopped, when he thought he would mark where he had arrived and show it as a proof to the Buddha. He therefore plucked a hair, chewed it, blew it out and cried out, "Change!" and it was changed into a pencil covered with ink. On the middle pillar he wrote, "The Great Sage, the Equal of Heaven, has traveled thus far!" and then put back his hair in the original place. Then at the bottom of the first pillar, he urinated, after which he thought he had jumped up to the clouds and returned. He found himself still standing on the palm of the Buddha's hand. He said, "I have been away and have come back! Now call upon the Jade Emperor to yield his throne to me." Buddha said, "Impertinent monkey, you have never left my palm!"

The Great Sage replied. "Do you not know that I went to the very end of Heaven, and saw five pillars of red flesh in front of me, beyond which was darkness, and I left my mark there in proof of my arrival there? Will you dare to go and look at it with me?" Buddha said, "There is no need for me to go! Bend down your head and look." The Great Sage opened his big eyes and looked and Buddha showed him what he had written. "The Great Sage, Equal of Heaven has traveled thus far." At the root of the first finger there was the stinking monkey mark. The Great Sage was greatly afraid at this. "Yes, truly there was such a thing as this. I wrote these characters on these pillars. But how are these on your fingers? Can it he that there is a magic by which one can foretell things? I do not believe it. Wait until I go there once more and see!"

The Great Sage flexed his body to jump out of the palm as before, but Buddha turned his hand upside down, and the Monkey King was thrown outside the West Gate of Heaven. The five pillars became a mountain joined together, and were called the Five Elements Mountain, and Buddha gently covered him up under the mountain. Then all the thunder gods, together with Ananda and Kasyapa, one by one, put their palms together and cried out, "Wonderful, wonderful!"

> Once we vowed to sacrifice self,
> In the thousand sorrows of life how few succeed!
> But a change comes sudden to all resolved.
> When the next change comes, who can tell?

When Lord Buddha had subjugated Monkey, he called on Ananda and Kasyapa to return with him to the West. Then the immortal heavenly leaders came out of the Lingshao Hall and begged the Buddha to wait a little, till the Jade Emperor arrived. When Buddha heard this, he turned his head and looked up, and there were eight brilliant carriages and nine colored umbrellas, full of choristers singing, praising the Infinite Spirit, and scattering precious fragrant flowers. They came in front of Buddha and said, "Thanks to thy great mercy, the Monkey Demon has been subjugated. Will you not stay a day longer with us so that we may invite all the gods to a thanksgiving banquet?" Lord Buddha put his palms together and thanked them and said, "I came here in obedience to the Jade Emperor. Whatever power has been shown has been owing to his great blessing and all the gods. Please thank him for his kind thought."

Then the Jade Emperor ordered the Board of Thunder and all the gods to arrange themselves, and the Three Pure Ones and the Temple Gods, the Five Elders, the Six Officials and Seven Originals, the Eight Points, the Nine Stars, and the Ten Boards, in all ten thousand sages and saints; and all thank Lord Buddha for his favors. He also ordered the Four Celestial Generals and the Fairies of the Nine Heavens to open the Pearl Palace and the Precious Palace of the Great Mystery and the private rooms and invite Lord Buddha to sit on the top of the seven storied throne, and that seats be arranged for each guest and dishes with dragon livers and phoenix marrow, wine and peaches. In a short time appeared the Taoist divinities:

> The Senior of the Heavenly Host,
> The Most Potent of the Heavenly Host
> The Most Virtuous of the Heavenly Host
> The Five Saintly Spirits,
> The Ministers of the Five Great Stars,
> The Three Officers,
> The Four Sages,
> The Ministers of the Nine Lights of Heaven,
> The Heavenly Prince of Dark Space,
> Prince Nezha, Son of Guardian King Li,
> All the Powerful Spirits, seated in pairs,
> With canopies above them,
> Holding lustrous pearls most precious,
> With fruits immortal and rarest flowers.

They lifted their dishes and said, "Thanks to Lord Buddha's infinite power, the Demon Monkey has been captured, and now since the Jade Emperor has invited us to this thanksgiving banquet, we would like to know what name Lord Buddha gives to this banquet." The Buddha replied, "A Banquet for the Peace of Heaven." All the gods and spirits said, "Good, truly it is a Great Peace!" Then each sat down in his seat, scattered flowers and made music. It was a joyous occasion, and all were glad. Then they saw the Queen of Heaven, and several companies of lovely fairies who danced before Buddha. They said, "Formerly the demon monkey disturbed the Queen of Heaven's Peach Banquet. Today, Lord Buddha, by his great power, has locked up the Monkey. We rejoice in this Banquet for the Peace of Heaven. We have nothing to present, we only bring a few peaches as offerings." Buddha put the palms of his hands together and said, "But you have also offered your singing and dancing."

Not long after, a great fragrance tilled the place, and the Spirit of the Star of the Southern Cross arrived. After paying his respects, he was told to go and see Lord Buddha, to whom he said, "When we first heard that the Monkey Demon had been taken by the Ancient of Days to the Polar Star Mansion and had his dross burnt there, we thought all trouble was at an end and little expected it would break forth again. Happily Lord Buddha has come and seized this monster, and to celebrate the conquest this banquet has been arranged. Therefore we have come, but we have nothing to offer but some purple fungus of immortality, some jade grass, and some Immortal Pills."

> The years of the Buddha are as countless as the sand of the Ganges.
> His Golden Body twice eight feet in height,
> On nine lotus tiers he sits enthroned,
> Invisible Lord of the seen and unseen world,
> The chief of the gods of matter and spirit.

Lord Buddha received him graciously. The Minister of Mercury sat down, and then the barefooted Taoist arrived and paid his respects to the Jade Emperor. He went to Buddha and thanked him, saying, "I thank you profoundly for your great power in putting down that monkey monster, but I have nothing to offer you but two pears, and a few baked dates." Buddha thanked him, and called Ananda and Kasyapa to collect together all the offerings, after which he went up to the Jade Emperor and thanked him for the banquet.

After this the police superintendent reported that the Great Sage had put out his head from under the mountain. The Buddha said, "That doesn't matter." Then he pulled out from his sleeve a piece of paper on which was written a few golden characters, *om mani padme hum*, which he gave to Ananda, and told him to place it on the top of the mountain. Ananda then went out through the Gate of Heaven and, reaching the top of the Five Element Mountain, made the paper fast on a square rock. That mountain had a hole with a hinge that moved with beats of breathing. This he took away without moving the body. Then Ananda returned and reported what he had done. Buddha then took leave of the Jade Emperor and all the gods. As he, with his two disciples, passed through the Gate of Heaven, they pronounced a blessing. Guanyin called one of the local gods and some Tartar soldiers of the surrounding regions to guard the mountain. "When the Monkey is hungry, give him an iron pill; when he is thirsty, give him some copper syrup,

and when the days of his punishment are ended, there will come
someone to deliver him."

> I ask what is the use of prayer
> And numberless petitions?
> Are they not all in vain,
> Grinding a brick to make a mirror,
> Heaping up snow for corn,
> Wasting years of precious time.
> Swallowing an ocean of fur for meat,
> Storing a mountain of straw?
> The glory of heaven smiles on you!
> When you awake, you are beyond
> The ten stages, the three religions.

Lord Buddha went back to the West, where he was welcomed
by the Eight Messengers 3,000 *bodhisattvas*, 500 *arhats*, and innumerable other spirits and deities.

Buddha Provides Sacred Scriptures for the Salvation of Men.

8

Guanyin Recruits the Disciples

AFTER DELIVERING A SERMON, Buddha looked on the Four Continents of the world, and said, "I find men both good and bad. Those in the Eastern continent worship Heaven and Earth, and are intelligent and peaceful. Those in the Northern continent live on flesh, and are without intelligence. Those in the Western continent are mild and long-lived, without avarice. Those in the Southern continent are fond of pleasure and fighting. Our sacred scriptures are a guide to virtue for the three realms of saints in heaven, of men on earth, and of demons and the lost below. It is in 25 books and 15,144 volumes. I desire, without fear of the great distance, or of the great difficulties, to send it to the Eastern continent, where men are ignorant. Who will volunteer to go there and get a man of faith to come and fetch them?" Guanyin volunteered, and was given a Cassock of Peace, which would protect the Scripture Messenger from death and re-incarnation; a pastoral staff, which would save him from fatal danger and a cap of spikes, which would pierce the head, cause the eyes to swell, the head to ache, and the skull to crack. It could be controlled by uttering a mystical incantation, and was essential for punishing the obstreperous. Guanyin received them gladly, and called her chief disciple, Hui Yan to go with her as a bodyguard. He had an iron staff weighing 1,000 catties.

Soon they came to a quicksand desert and water of 3,000 *li,* so light that a feather would sink in it, and met a fierce demon there. They demanded to know who he was. He said, "I am the second son of the Guardian King Li. I was punished by the Jade Emperor, and banished here, where every seventh day I am tormented with swords of remorse." Guanyin said, "Why do you not repent and help to fetch the Sacred Scriptures from the West? Then you will no more be tormented with remorse." He agreed, and Guanyin put her hand in blessing on his head, and gave him the name Sha Wujing, the Seeker after Purity, and bade him remain there till the Buddhist pilgrim came from the East.

Soon after, they met another demon, and asked him who he was. He said, "I was a general in the River of Heaven, but, having misbehaved with some fairies when drunk, I was sentenced to be born among men. By some mistake I was born of a sow, hence my head is that of a pig. I live in this place called without any calling, living off other people. Oh Guanyin, pardon me and save me." Guanyin said, "If you wish to be saved, you must not do what will ruin you. Having sinned in Heaven and been sent down here, you must not sin again. If you have a good purpose in life, Heaven will help you to succeed." "I wish to follow the right, but having sinned against Heaven, what can I do?" Guanyin said, "I have been authorized to go to the East in search of a Chinese pilgrim who will go to the West for the Sacred Scriptures. If you follow him on his journey, and learn from him, then your sin will be forgiven for your good services." The demon said, "I agree." Thereupon Guanyin put her hand on his head and gave him the name Zhu, which means pig, because his face was like a pig in appearance. His religious name was Zhu Wuneng, the Seeker after Strength. He too was to wait for the coming of the Buddhist pilgrim.

Soon they met another creature, a dragon. Guanyin asked, "Who are you, and what are you doing here?" He replied, "I have been sent down from Heaven because I let one of the palaces burn, and soon I am to die for the crime. I pray you, Guanyin, save me!" Guanyin then went to see the Jade Emperor and said she was authorized by Buddha to go to the East in search of a Chinese pilgrim. The pilgrim would need to have a carrier for his baggage. She begged the Jade Emperor to modify the sentence, and let this dragon become a horse and carry the pilgrim's baggage, and in this way make up for his past negligence. Her request was granted, and the dragon was instructed to wait in a deep valley till the pilgrim arrived from the East.

Soon after, they came to the Five Elements Mountain where the Monkey King was still imprisoned under the magic words, *om mani padme hum*. Though he could not move his body, he could speak. On seeing Guanyin, he said, "Merciful Guanyin, a day in this place is as long as a year, and no one comes to see me. I have been here 500 years unable to move. I pray you to save me, and I shall henceforth lead a new life." Guanyin said, "If you are really in earnest and desire to be good, I will help you. I am going in search of a Chinese pilgrim who is to fetch the Sacred Scriptures. When he arrives, he will deliver you if you are willing to become his disciple. There are two others who have already pledged themselves to become his disciples. You shall be the third."

Soon after this she arrived at Chang'an, the capital of the great Chinese Empire in the Tang dynasty. Some time earlier Taizong, the emperor, had issued an edict that he would hold an examination to discover the best men for government service. A student in Haizhou, named Chen, told his mother that he would like to go to the capital, and try the examination. He went and succeeded in coming out first among all. The daughter of one of the leading statesmen was given him in marriage, and he was appointed to a post at Jiangzhou. Proceeding to his post, he took his mother along with him. On the way the mother fell ill, and seeing a man selling fish, the son bought a fine one for her. But looking at it, he saw it winking its eyes, and having heard that such fish were not proper for eating, as they might be human beings, he took pity on it, and put it back in the river, so as to save its life. His mother said, "Go on to your post and I will rest here a few days and come on later." The husband and wife soon arrived at the Hong River, which they had to cross. Here a great calamity befell Chen, because of a wrong he had done in a former existence. One of the boatmen, Liu Hong, seeing the beautiful bride, arranged with his comrade to murder the husband, and throw his body into the river. He threatened to kill the wife if she did not obey him. She was watched and prevented from committing suicide. He collected her husband's documents and decided to impersonate Chen.

The night demons announced to the Dragon King that a man had been drowned. He ordered his body to be brought before him.

At sight of it, he recognised the very man who had saved his life when he had been in the form of a fish, and had been bought for the mother. "One good turn deserves another! I must save this man, and restore his life."

In the meantime the villain Liu Hong arrived at Chen's post, and was joyfully welcomed by all. One day when Liu Hong was away, Mme Chen became very sad thinking of her husband and mother-in-law, and suddenly became faint, and gave birth to a son. Guanyin warned her that her false husband would be sure to destroy this son unless she found some way to save him. She wrote his story with her own blood, and put him on a plank in the river, praying that some good man would save him. The plank floated down to the Golden Mountain Temple, where the abbot saved the infant and brought him up till he was eighteen years of age, when he was ordained a monk and given the name Xuanzang. After this he found his mother, his father's mother and his mother's father, who after hearing all about the rascality of the boatman, memorialized the Throne, and was authorized to take 60,000 soldiers to surround the false official.

Finally the scattered Chen family was reunited. The Dragon King restored the soul into the body of the husband, who became first Secretary of State, while Xuanzang became abbot at the Hongfu Temple in Chang'an.

9

The Emperor Goes to Hell

A FISHERMAN AND A WOODSMAN in Chang'an were loud in praises of a certain fortune teller, who always advised the fisherman where to cast his net, with the result that his net was full of fish. One of the water spirits, overhearing their words, carried the news to the Dragon King, crying that all the fish in the waters would soon be caught, because of the fortuneteller. The Dragon King became very angry, and visited the fortuneteller, and asked him about the weather. The fortuneteller predicted a heavy fall of rain the following day. The Dragon King said, "If you are right about your promised rain, and it comes exactly, I will give you fifty taels; but if you are wrong, then I will smash your house and sign board, and you shall leave the city, so that the people shall not be deceived any more."

After the bargain was agreed to, the Dragon King went back to the deep. After relating the matter to his followers, they said, "It is only you, the Dragon King, who knows when rain shall come. How dare this false prophet know?"

Before these words were finished, they heard that a dispatch had been brought for the Dragon King from the Jade Emperor, and they saw a yellow robed official bearing an edict, which said, "I command the Dragon King to ensure that tomorrow there shall be heavy rain all over Chang'an." This was exactly what the fortuneteller had predicted. At this loss of face the Dragon King was much perplexed. One of his assistants proposed to him, "If you, Dragon King, arrange that the rain should not come at the exact time, or in the quantity predicted, then you need not give the fortune teller the fifty taels." After acting on this suggestion, the Dragon King went to the fortuneteller's shop and smashed up everything, saying,

龍
王

The Dragon King.

"You are deceiving men and must be driven away. You deserve to die." The fortune teller replied, "I have done no wrong, and do not fear to die, but I fear you have so sinned as to deserve death, for you have broken the law of the Jade Emperor both as to time of rain and the quantity of it." At this the Dragon King was terribly alarmed and begged the fortuneteller to save him from death. "I cannot save you myself, but I can tell you how you can be saved. Tomorrow, three quarters of an hour after noon, you must go to the Minister of Justice and ask him to help you."

The Dragon King did not sleep a wink that night, but wandered as a spirit in the air near the bedroom of Emperor Taizong. The emperor was dreaming that he had gone for a walk, and met a man begging that his life should be spared. The emperor asked him, "Who are you?" He said, "I am one of the celestials, and have broken one of the laws of Heaven for which I must forfeit my life." The emperor promised him pardon, saying, "I will see that the Minister of Justice does not execute you."

At noon, however, the emperor sent for the Minister of Justice to play chess with him, and forgot to tell the Minister that he had pardoned the Dragon King. At three quarters of an hour after noon, before the game was finished, the Minister put his head on the table and fell fast asleep. The emperor did not disturb him. Shortly after, the Minister woke up and went on his knees, saying he deserved to die for going to sleep in the presence of the emperor.

Then there was a great uproar outside, and a man came in carrying the Dragon King's head dripping with blood, and flung it before the emperor. The emperor ordered him to explain. The man said, "I was at the execution ground at three quarters of an hour after noon, when this head fell from the sky." The emperor asked the Minister of Justice what it meant. He replied that, when he had slept for a few minutes, he had dreamt that he had been to the execution ground and had carried out the emperor's orders, and had beheaded the Dragon King. The emperor both greatly rejoiced and greatly grieved over the matter. He rejoiced that he had such a faithful minister to carry out his orders, and grieved because he had not saved the life of the Dragon King as he had promised.

In the end the emperor fell very ill, and evil spirits gave him no peace, throwing bricks and stones over the walls, and latterly the headless spirit of the Dragon King came and laid hold of the emperor, threatening to drag him to judgment before Yama, the King of Hell. In this dilemma, when none of his Ministers or Doctors could heal or save him, Guanyin, the Goddess of Mercy, came with her jar of water and sprig of willow and made the Dragon King's head grow on his body again, and the emperor was no more haunted. But the emperor's illness grew worse, and when he was on the verge of death, the Minister of Justice sent a letter to a friend of his, Judge Cui, through whose influence the emperor might return and resume his duties on earth again.

> A hundred years run like a stream,
> And all our affairs float on top of it.
> Yesterday we were as beautiful as peach blossoms,
> Today we are snowflakes floating by.
> Like fighting ants our struggles are but dreams.
> Listen to the bird's call to repentance.
> From of old life can be prolonged.
> Those who seek not self are perfected by Heaven.

It is said that the spirit of Taizong mysteriously passed in front of the Five Phoenix Gate, where a host of horsemen invited the emperor to go out for a hunting expedition. Taizong was delighted and went with them. After having gone a long distance, he saw neither men nor horses about him, only a great wilderness. In his astonishment he was at a loss to find his way, but at a distance, he heard a man calling to him, "Emperor of the Great Tang Dynasty, come this way!"

On hearing this, Taizong lifted his head and saw a man in a netted coat with a leather belt, and a black silk hat, holding in his hand an ivory tablet, such as officials carry to court on which to take notes. He knelt on the roadside and said, "I pray your Majesty to forgive me for being late in coming to meet you.'" Taizong said, "Who are you?" The other answered, "Your humble officer when living on earth had a father who was the magistrate of Cizhou, and in time became the Vice President of the Board of Ceremonies. His surname was Cui and his given name Ru. He is now the Chief Judge in Hell. He saw the affair of the ghost of the Dragon King and knew that your Majesty would arrive here today, and has come

唐太宗

The Emperor of China.

specially to meet you." Taizong was greatly pleased at this, and quickly stretched out his arm and lifted him up on his feet, saying, "My former minister Wei gave me a letter of introduction to you, and I am very glad to meet you." He pulled out the letter from his sleeve, and gave it to Judge Cui, who tore it open and read:

"From the Court of Justice of the Great Capital, I beg to present this letter to my Elder Brother Judge Cui. Formerly we were intimate, and your face and voice are still before me. But several years have now passed and I have had no opportunity of receiving from you more instruction, such as you often gave me before. But in my dreams I receive your advice, and thus know you have been highly promoted. But alas, we are now separated by the great gulf of life and death, and cannot see each other face to face. Now, because my emperor is gone from the living, his case will be brought before the Court of Hell, and he is sure to meet you. I beg of you to remember a thousand times our former friendship, and devise some means by which my emperor will be restored to earth again without much difficulty, for which I shall be eternally grateful to you."

Judge Cui was much pleased with the letter and said, "I know all about Judge Wei beheading the Old Dragon in his dream. He has been kind to my descendants. Since I have received this letter about you today, you can set your mind at rest. I, your humble minister, shall not fail to have you restored to the land of the living, and to your throne again." The emperor thanked him. As they were talking, two young men dressed in black approached them. They were carrying official umbrellas and streamers, and called out with a loud voice, "Yama the King of Hell invites you in." The emperor, accompanied by Judge Cui and the two black robed young men, entered the portal. Suddenly there appeared a city, and over the city gate was written in large golden letters:

THE GATE OF GHOSTS

The black robed pages moved on with their umbrellas and streamers into the city and led Taizong through the streets. On the street he saw his father Li Yuan and his two brothers. When these heard it said that the emperor had come, they rushed on him before he could avoid them, and demanded his life. Fortunately Judge Cui called a blue-faced big-toothed demon and ordered him to take them away, and thus the emperor escaped. He had only gone a mile or two when he saw a palace roofed with jade, truly beautiful. The emperor looked at the outside and saw it was built of precious stones. In front was a pair of lamps, behind them were the Ten Judges of Hell, who descended the steps and came near, bowing most respectfully to the emperor. The emperor, out of respect to them, declined to go before them. The Ten Judges said, "Your Majesty is a ruler among men on earth, we are only rulers among ghosts and demons in Hell. It is your proper place to go first, you must not be too modest." The emperor replied, "Pray excuse my rudeness to you, I dare not discuss the relative position of men and demons." Thus the emperor was obliged to go first, and they arrived at the Sunluo Hall.

After paying their respects they sat down as hosts and guest. After a while Judge Qin bowed with his hands, and said, "The spirit of the Dragon King has charged your Majesty with having promised to spare his life, and then executing him. What about that?" The emperor said, "I dreamed that the Old Dragon had come to me and begged to be forgiven. I assured him that he need not fear. I did not then know that he had broken one of the laws of Heaven and should suffer death for it. Judge Wei, who looks after such cases, executed him without my knowledge. I had called Judge Wei to play chess with me. Being tired, he fell asleep, and in his dream, knowing that the dragon had committed a crime deserving of death, had him executed." The Ten Judges of Hell bowed and said, "Even before the dragon was born, the *Records of Life and Death* distinctly stated that he would be executed by an officer on earth. We all know that. But he insisted on having the case tried and that you should appear here before the three tribunals. We have sent him to be reborn again, but now he troubles you to come here. We hope you will forgive our urgency."

After this they ordered the officer in charge of the *Records of Life and Death* to bring it at once. "How many years should His Majesty's life and honors on earth last?" Judge Cui at once searched the records of all the rulers on earth and saw the name of the Emperor Taizong of the Great Tang dynasty in the Southern Continent, and the statement he should reign thirteen years. Judge Cui, alarmed at this, quickly got a thick brush and changed thirteen into thirty-three and then handed back the *Records of Life and Death*. The Ten Judges of Hell looked through the book, and saw that Taizong was to reign for thirty-three years. They asked the emperor, "When did you begin to reign?" He replied, "Thirteen years ago." Yama, the King of Hell, said, "Your Majesty need not be alarmed, you have twenty more years to live on earth. Since you have come, we have carefully enquired into the matter. You can now return to earth." On hearing this, the emperor bowed and thanked them. The Ten Judges of Hell sent Judge Cui and Executioner Zhao to accompany the emperor back. The emperor, before leaving the Sunluo Hall, kowtowed, and asked, "Are all well in my earthly palace?" The Judges replied, "Yes, all are well there, but we fear your younger sister has not long to live." The emperor bowed again and thanked them, saying, "When I return to the world, I have nothing but melons to send you as a present." The Ten Judges rejoiced and said, "We have abundance of Eastern and Western melons, but have no Southern melons." Taizong said, "When I return home, I will send you some." After this they bowed again and separated.

The executioner seized his flag and led the way. Judge Cui followed and protected the emperor. They passed through a dark office, which was not the way they had come. Then the emperor said to the Judge, "We have surely lost the way." The Judge replied, "No. There is only one way to reach Hell and there is no return from it. Now we shall take your Majesty through the starting place for transmigration, in order, on the one hand, to let you see the underworld, and, on the other, to let your Majesty escape the round of transmigration." So the emperor had to follow these two men for some *li*. Then he saw a high mountain with dark clouds covering the bottom with mist. The emperor asked, "What mountain is that?" The Judge said, "It is the Chilly Side of the Shadow of Death." The emperor was afraid, and said, "How can I pass that way?" The Judge said, "Your Majesty need not fear! We will lead the way." The emperor with fear and trembling followed his two guides, and passed by many courts, from all of which were heard fearful cries. The emperor asked, "What is this place?" The Judge answered, "These are the Eighteen Hells Behind the Dark Mountain." "By what names are these known?" The Judge replied, "I will tell you. They are:

1. The Hanging by the Muscles Hall,
2. The Dark Mad Hell,
3. The Deep Furnace Hell,
4. The Urban Living Hell,
5. The Tongue Pulling Hell,
6. The Flaying Hell,
7. The Grinding Hell, for all sorts of disloyalty, disobedience, wickedness, and hypocrisy,
8. The Pounding Hell,
9. The Tearing on the Wheel Hell, for all sorts of unrighteousness and deceitful words,
10. The Icy Hell,
11. The Unmasking Hell,
12. The Pulling of Bowels Hell, for using false weights and measures, and for cheating the ignorant and helpless, and bringing troubles on them,
13. The Boiling Oil Hell,
14. The Mad as Hell Hell,
15. The Sword Mountain Hell, for violently injuring the good, and for secret wrongdoing,
16. The Hell of the Lake of Blood,
17. The Hot as Hell Hell,
18. The Balancing Hell, for murder to get gain, for deep scheming, for cruelty to animals and killing creatures.

From these they cannot escape for a thousand years, or forever for that matter, though they call on both Heaven and Earth to save them."

On hearing this, the emperor was greatly distressed. After proceeding a little further, he met a company of demon soldiers carrying banners, who knelt by the roadside and said, "The Officer of the Bridge has come to meet you." The Judge shouted to them to get up, and lead on. They led them across a golden bridge. The emperor saw beside it a silver bridge. On the bridge were several good and honest people, just and honorable, who also carried banners, to meet them.

Close by there was another bridge with bitter wind freezing the blood, and a continuous wailing. The emperor asked, "What is the name of that bridge?" The Judge replied, "Your Majesty, that is called the Bridge of Despair. When you get among the living, do not forget to tell them of this bridge!"

It was a mile or two long, but only three narrow planks in width. Its height was a hundred feet, and the depth of water below was a thousand feet. It had no balustrades. Below, there were dreadful demons trying to snatch souls away from guardian angels. On the side of the bridge were struggling souls and demons. In the depths were sinful souls in dreadful agonies. On the withered branches of the trees there hung the corpses of concubines, who had quarreled with the wives of their husbands. Down a steep precipice crouched daughters in law, who did not get along with their mothers in law. They were being bitten by serpents, and devoured by dogs as powerful as brass and iron. These were punished forever on this Bridge of Despair.

As they were talking, they found that those who had come to meet them on the bridge had already gone back. The emperor was alarmed, for the Judge and the Executioner, whom he followed, had already crossing the dreadful river, which was the boundary.

Before them was the city where lived the spirits of those who had died unjustly. He heard them shouting from one to the other, "Li Shiming has come! Li Shiming has come!" Li Shiming was Taizong's original name. On hearing all this shouting, the emperor, trembling with fear, saw a company of deformed ghosts with broken backs and arms, with feet but no heads, who stopped him and cried out, "Restore our lives! Restore our lives!" At this the emperor was so terrified that he wished to hide himself. He called out to Judge Cui, "Save me, save me!" The Judge said, "These ghosts are the innocent souls of those who suffered wrongly with the sixty four rebels, and the innocent souls of those who suffered wrongly with the seventy-two robbers; they are without any redress, and cannot be reborn on earth, as they have no money for traveling expenses. They are all orphans, poor starving ghosts! Your Majesty should give them some money and then I can save you."

The emperor replied, "I have come here empty handed, how can I give them money?" The Judge said, "On earth there is a man who has gathered much gold and silver, which he has stored up in Hell. If your Majesty writes an order for one of his stores of money, I will become security for you. You can distribute this money among these starving ghosts, and they will let you pass." The emperor asked, "Who is this wealthy man?" The judge replied, "He is from Kaifeng, and his name is Shang Liang. He has thirteen treasuries of gold and silver here. If you borrow from him here, you can repay him after you return to earth." At this the emperor, greatly relieved, gladly wrote the order, and gave it to Judge Cui, who borrowed a whole treasury and let the Executioner distribute it. The Judge then said to them, "Now take this money and divide it equally amongst you, and let your emperor pass, as he has not yet finished his life on earth. I have been directed by the Ten Judges to guide his soul back to earth again in order that he may establish a great Society for the Salvation of Souls, for all those who have perished on land or sea. So do not make any more disturbance!" When the hungry ghosts heard this and had received the money, they cleared the way for him. The Judge and Executioner then took up their flags and guided the emperor out of the city where the wronged souls lived, and continued on by this great highway with flying banners. After a long time they came to the six roads of transmigration.

The emperor asked, "What is the meaning of this?'" The Judge said, "Your Majesty is clear sighted. Do not forget what you see now, and let it be known when you return among the living. These are called the Six Paths of Transmigration. The good ascend in their progress, the faithful are reborn in the way of the honorable, the filial are reborn to happiness, the righteous are born among men, the virtuous are born rich, but the bad will fall to Hell and into the pathways of demons." The emperor nodded his head and took careful note of this. The Judge then led the emperor to the path of rebirth that led to honor, and, bowing to him, said, "Your Majesty, this is your way out, your humble officer must now return, but I have ordered Executioner Zhao to accompany you one stage more." The emperor thanked him for accompanying him all this long way. The Judge said, "When your Majesty returns to earth, you must on no account forget to found the Society for the Salvation of Souls. If there are no complaints in Hell, then the people on earth shall enjoy happiness. If all evils are redressed, and all men instructed how to be good, then I guarantee that your descendants will be long lived and your Empire permanently safe." The emperor took note of each of these things and bade the Judge farewell.

He then followed the Executioner and with him entered the gate. The Executioner saw a horse inside the gate, already saddled, and urged the emperor to mount it. When the Executioner had helped him up, the horse went off like an arrow and soon arrived at the banks of the Wei River. In the water were a pair of golden carp playing together. At this sight the emperor was delighted, stopped the horse and seemed as if he would never tire of watching them. The Executioner said, "Your Majesty had better let the horse go on, so that we may enter the city early." But the emperor was loath to leave the spot. The Executioner then gave the horse a kick and shouted out, "Why do you not go, what are you waiting for?" With this he gave a push, and the horse plunged into the Wei River, and thus the emperor left the territory of Hell, and returned among living men.

At that time both the civil and military officials were gathered together about the heir, and the Empress Dowager and palace ladies were at the White Tiger Hall, weeping, and discussing how to put forth an edict about the emperor's death, so as to inform the whole empire, and announce the accession of the heir to the throne. But Minister Wei said, "Let us wait one day more before doing this, as the emperor's soul is sure to return to his body." But one of the ministers stepped forward and said, "Do not listen to these strange words of Minister Wei. From of old who does not know that spilt water cannot be gathered up again, and that when life is gone it does not return? Why do you raise these false hopes?" Minister Wei replied, "I have had some experience in these matters from my youth and know well some things. I am sure the emperor is not dead."

At this moment they heard repeated loud cries from the coffin, "You are drowning me, you are drowning me!" This terrified all the civil officers and military generals. The Empress and all the ladies of the court trembled with fear, and none dared approach the coffin. Happily the upright Duke Xu Mao, the fiery Prime Minister Wei Zheng, the brave Qin Jiong and the strong Hu Jingde all went to the coffin and cried, "What is it that troubles Your Majesty? Or is it some demon that is alarming the whole family?" Minister Wei said, "It is not a demon, it is only the emperor's soul returning. Bring implements to open the coffin at once!" They did so and then they saw the emperor sit up, still crying, "You are drowning me! Who will take me out of the water?" Xu Mao and others went forward and said, "Do not be alarmed! Your Majesty is waking up from a dream. Your ministers are all here looking after your safety." The emperor opened his eyes and said, "I have come from great trouble and have just escaped from the hungry demons of Hell and from drowning." The ministers asked, "What dangers were your Majesty in?" The emperor said, "I was riding, and when I got to the Wei River, I saw two fish playing with each other, and watched them until the Executioner Zhao pushed me into the river, and almost drowned me." Minister Wei said, "Your Majesty is still ill and your mind is wandering. You must get the doctor at once to give you medicine to restore you to your natural health of body and mind."

It should be stated that the emperor had been dead for three days and nights when he returned to earth again. It was now evening and the ministers advised the emperor to sleep and they all retired. Next morning they put off their mourning robes and appeared in their court robes, each with his red and black hat, purple silks, and badges, waiting outside the door to be called in. The emperor had a good sleep the whole night and was much refreshed. He rose at daylight, dressed, and went into the throne room to give audience to the civil and military officers.

Then they heard an order, that those who had business should enter in their respective order, and if they had no business, they were to return to their homes. Wei Zheng, Hu Jingde, and the others went forward together, knelt, and said, "Your Majesty had a long troubled dream. What was it about?" The emperor then told them all about his journey to Hell, and his return to earth, and then said, "When I parted from the Ten Judges of Hell, I promised to send them a present of some melons. After leaving the Sunluo Hall and seeing the faithless, the unfilial, the rude and the unrighteous, the destroyers of harvests, those who cheat and insult both in public and in private, the users of different kinds of weights and measures for buying and selling, the thieves, and the licentious fellows suffering the grinding, the burning, the pounding, the cutting in pieces, the flaying alive, and the thousand other punishments in Hell, I was deeply grieved. Passing by the city of wronged souls, countless innocent ones, who suffer there, stopped me on the way and demanded money. Fortunately, thanks to the good offices of Judge Cui, I was able to borrow from Shang Liang of Kaifeng a whole treasury of gold and silver to ransom their souls, and thus was allowed to pass. Judge Cui told me that on my return to earth I was on no account to forget to establish a Society for the Salvation of Souls of all those lost on land and sea, and the rescue of all homeless souls."

When the ministers heard these things, they all congratulated the emperor, and made the news known throughout the empire so that all the officials might give thanks. The emperor issued an edict to pardon all the prisoners of the empire. There were then over 400 great criminals deserving of death, who were all released and set free to go home to see their parents and brothers, and stay with their relatives for one year, after which they were to return to prison, and await their punishments. All the prisoners were grateful for the emperor's favor.

The emperor also issued an order to relieve the helpless ones, and finding that there were 3,600 women, young and old, in the palace, he arranged marriages for them. After this all his subjects became very good.

In addition to this, he issued an edict that was read throughout the empire:

> Heaven and Earth are very great, the Sun and Moon shine everywhere, the Universe is extensive, and there is abundance for all, without need of robbing one another, or scheming. Rewards and punishments are found in this world. The good man does right in gratitude for past benefits, and seeks happiness without talk of the hereafter. Ten thousand kinds of scheming are not equal to the performance of one's duty. If one is tender hearted, there is no need of much exercise in prayer. If one has a mind to rob others, one has studied good books in vain.

After this there was not a man in the whole empire who was not moved to virtue The emperor also issued another edict ordering the treasury to pay gold and silver to Hu Jingde, who was sent to Kaifeng to seek Shang Liang, and to repay the emperor's debt. Another edict called for a volunteer to take the melons to Hell.

Some days after the issue of these edicts, there appeared a good man, who was willing to present the melons. He was from Junzhou, by the name of Liu Chun, and he possessed some ten thousand strings of cash. But because his wife had given her hairpins to a poor monk, he accused her of being unfaithful to him. The wife could not endure the false accusation, so committed suicide, leaving behind her a little boy and girl, who cried night and day for their mother. The father could not endure their cries, and contemplated suicide. He was therefore willing to die and take the melons to Hell. He took the edict, and went with it to the emperor. He was told to go carefully select a couple of Southern melons to carry with him. On the way he chewed some poison and died, and his soul took the melons to Hell.

He soon got there and told the matter to the demon gatekeeper. The demon welcomed Liu most heartily, and led him to the Sunluo Hall where he saw Yama, the King of Hell and presented him with the melons, saying, "I come to present these by order of the distant Tang Emperor of China, in return for the kindness shown to him by the Ten Judges." Yama was much pleased, and said, "What a faithful and good emperor he is." He received the melons, and asked the man his name and whence he came. Liu replied, "I am from Junzhou and my name is Liu Chun. As my wife had committed suicide, I was willing to leave my home and children, and to sacrifice my life for my emperor, and therefore present the melons as my tribute." When the Ten Judges heard this, they sent one of the demons to find the soul of Liu's wife, and bring her to see him. The Judges also looked up the *Records of Life and Death*. Both the husband and wife were destined to become immortals. Yama said to one of his demons, "Go at once and bring her here." The demon replied, "She arrived here long ago and her corpse has decomposed by now. Where can we put her soul?" Yama turned up the *Records of Life and Death* again. "The emperor's sister, Princess Li Ruying, should be dead by now. Take her body and let the soul of Liu's wife occupy it." Having received his orders, the demon took Liu and his wife out of Hell. And so the princess' body was given Mrs. Liu's soul. The emperor, seeing his sister reviving, began to congratulate the royal princess, but she, possessing the soul of Liu's wife, was indignant, saying she was not a princess, but the wife of a common man. It took some time for Liu to get used to the idea of his wife's soul in the body of the princess, but in time they remembered their former earthly experiences together, and were reconciled.

觀世音

Guanyin.

10
Xuanzang Starts Out on His Mission

THE EMPEROR SENT ONE OF his Ministers to Kaifeng in Henan in search of the man Shang Liang, who had laid up great treasure in Hell, and from whom the emperor had borrowed. The emperor sent an immense amount of gold and silver to repay the loan, but the man denied that he had lent money to the emperor, and would not receive it. On hearing of the disinterestedness of the man and his wife in refusing the money, the emperor ordered a temple to be built in honor of the family. The temple was called the Shang temple. On the day of its opening, the people were ordered to select the best man in each of the three religions, Confucianism, Buddhism, and Taoism, to conduct the opening ceremony. The Buddhists chose Xuanzang, the son of the famous scholar Chen Hui. Being deeply versed in all the Buddhist Sacred Scriptures, he was appointed by the emperor to be the head of all Buddhists in the Empire. The emperor then called together 1,200 monks for a religious festival in Chang'an, lasting seven times seven days, during which Xuanzang gave an outline of the Buddhist Sacred Scriptures, and spoke of heaven, of hell, and of the many on earth who had lost their way, and whom he desired to lead back to the truth.

While this great movement was going on in Chang'an, Lord Buddha had sent Guanyin to earth in search of a religious man to go to the West in quest of the Sacred Scriptures. She heard that the monk Xuanzang was none other than the Golden Cicada, who had become incarnate again to save men. Guanyin and her disciple Mucha appeared in the streets in very poor garments, carrying with them a beautifully embroidered cassock and a nine ringed pastoral staff, which they offered for sale. For the one they asked 5,000 taels and for the other 2,000 taels. But the price was too high for anyone to pay. The Prime Minister, returning from the temple, heard of the articles and asked, "What good is there in buying them?" "He that possesses them will neither be reborn, nor fall into hell, nor be poisoned, nor be killed by wild beasts!" was the reply. On hearing this, the Prime Minister dismounted from his horse, and thought these two magic things most suitable for Xuanzang. The emperor wished to buy them, but Guanyin refused all offers of money, wanting to present them as a gift to the right person. So, wearing poor garments, Guanyin joined the throng, and listened for a time to Xuanzang's discourse on the Sacred Scriptures. Then Guanyin called out to him in a loud voice, and said, "You have only explained to us Primitive Buddhism. Now explain to us Higher Buddhism. Early Buddhism cannot save the dead, but Higher Buddhism can take them to Heaven, can save men from trouble, can make them long lived without being reborn again in this world."

The emperor then asked for some one to volunteer to go to fetch the Sacred Scriptures of Higher Buddhism from the West. Xuanzang came forward and offered to go. So he was given a white horse to carry his baggage and started on his pilgrimage.

But one of his chief ministers sent in a memorial, expostulating as follows:

"In Buddhism there is no distinction of Prince, Minister, Father, or Son, but that of the three worlds of Heaven, Earth, and Hell. They preach the six ways of transmigration, by which the multitudes are deceived. Its followers dwell on the sins of the past, and speculate on the happiness of the future. They read Sanskrit prayers in the hope of avoiding deserved punishment for evil. Short or long life depends on natural causes. Is man able to punish past sin or to predict future happiness? The present custom is merely to trust in powerful fate, but they say it is Buddha's will. In the days of the Five Emperors and the Three Kings there was no such thing as Buddhism. The sovereigns were intelligent, the ministers were loyal and they lived long lives. Buddhism only began in the days of Emperor Mingdi of the Han dynasty, as a religion of barbarians.

観音赴會問
原因

Guanyin attends Xuanzang's discourse.

Even according to its own teachers, this religion from the western regions is not fully to be believed."

The emperor handed this memorial to his ministers for discussion. The Prime Minister bowed and said, "Buddhism has existed for several dynasties. It leads men to do good, and stop evil, and thus indirectly helps the Government. It should not therefore be disallowed. Buddha was a Sage. Without Sages there is no law. I advise severe punishment for this opposition."

Another minister countered: "The Prime Minister supports a religion which recognizes no fathers, and therefore there can be no filial piety in the nation." The Prime Minister's only reply was to bow and say that this talk would lead to the strife of hell.

After this the emperor appointed two other ministers to inquire into this matter. They reported: "Buddhism is purity and kindness. Buddha himself is unseen, but the fruit of the religion is good. Throughout the ages, Buddhism has been honored, and the incarnations of the great Patriarchs of Buddhism, and the appearance of Dharma amongst mortals are well known. From of old till now, all speak of the three religions as most worthy. That Buddhism should not be destroyed or done away with, we beg your Majesty to decide." With this the emperor was very pleased, and said, "If any one hereafter objects, let him be punished."

And so Xuanzang started on his journey to the West. He arrived at Fayun Temple, where 500 monks received him. He said to them, "From the heart come all sorts of evil spirits. By the heart you can overcome them." As he went he was not certain of the road, and fell into a pit. Then the chief of the evil spirits ordered that Xuanzang's two servants be killed and served up as food. But Xuanzang himself was saved by the spirit of a bright star, who rode on a crane, and said, "I am the bright star from the West, and have come specially to save you. Further on you will be guarded by a group of disciples. Do not be discouraged on the journey."

Some time later he met the Guardian of the Mountains, who welcomed him as a fellow countryman. He told how he lived in the mountains among tigers, wolves, snakes and poisonous creatures. On the monk protesting that he never ate meat, the women gave

唐三藏

The Master.

him vegetarian food, and he then gave thanks and ate. While there, Xuanzang offered prayers for the dead in his host's family. Finding him gentle and ignorant of the road, the host accompanied him for a day's journey. He could not go further, as they had arrived at the borders of the Tartar country, which he dared not cross. At the end of that journey a voice, with a sound like thunder, was heard at the foot of a mountain, crying, "Oh my Master, you have come, you have come!"

> Buddha is in the heart, and the heart is in Buddha.
> The two are most important and should be inseparable.
> If you know that nothing is without a mind,
> That is the essence of the True Ideal.
> The essence of the True Ideal has no form
> It is a spark of light including everything.
> The bodiless is the real body, the formless is the real form.
> It has no color, but is not nothing.
> It does not come, nor go, nor return.
> It is not different, it is not the same.
> It is neither possession nor loss.
> It is difficult to take or give away.
> It cannot be heard or counted on.
> The vital spark inside and outside is everywhere the same.
> There is a whole kingdom of heaven in one atom.
> There are numberless worlds in one grain.
> There is but one principle in body and soul.
> He who knows this must follow the mystery of nature.
> The pure is that which is untainted and clean.
> All the ways of good and evil are impotent.
> This is the teaching of the glorious Shakyamuni!

When Xuanzang heard the thunder cry, "Oh my Master, you have come!" it frightened him very much. But the people there said, "These must be the cries of the Monkey King." "Who is that?" asked Xuanzang. "He is one that cannot be frozen or starved, and lives on nothing but iron pills and copper syrup. He has been imprisoned here for 500 years."

Xuanzang let him out of the prison under the mountain, and the Monkey King followed the pilgrim as his disciple, and was given a new name. He was no longer Sun the Seeker of Secrets, but Sun the Pilgrim. Their first encounter was with a tiger which

Sun easily killed, and made himself some fur clothes with its skin. But then they were suddenly attacked by six robbers, who were more difficult to deal with. They were Mr. Eye, who loved change, Mr. Ear, who became angry too easily, Mr. Nose, who smelt love, Mr. Tongue the Taster, Mr. Thought the Coveter, and Mr. Sad the Dissatisfied. They fell on Sun and beat him badly. But as his head seemed to be made of iron, the beating had no effect on him. Then he took out his magic needle from his ear, made it into his steel spear, went for them, and killed them all.

The Master was angry with him for killing instead of correcting them, and rebuked him. Sun was not in the habit of being rebuked, and so fled away 18,000 *li,* and returned to the East, leaving his poor Master helpless by his white horse on the road. Greatly distressed, the Master saw an old woman coming; he was afraid of her, but she was none other than Guanyin. After hearing his story of the loss of his disciple, she presented him with a cassock and a cap of spikes, which he was to give to the disciple when he came back. She also taught the Master some incantations which, when the disciple was disobedient again, would make the spikes pierce his head like nails. In the meantime, Guanyin herself warned Sun the Pilgrim that if he did not keep his vow to go with Xuanzang, he would forever remain a demon, and must be prepared for the consequences. So Sun promised to reform, and returned to the Master.

The Master and his disciple traveled several days through the icy mountains, and were wounded by snakes and dragons. One dragon ate the white horse, and this terrified the Master. Sun said he would go and look for another horse. The Master would not let him go, lest in his absence he should be attacked by something worse. Sun was angry with the Master for not letting him go. Then a voice from the sky was heard to say, "We are the Guardians of the Five Regions and the Four Directions, all here to protect you." So Sun left the Master in their charge and went to fight the dragon who had just eaten the Master's horse. He fought bravely, but the wild dragon could not be subdued. They had no choice but to ask Guanyin for help. Guanyin appeared, accused the dragon of disobedience, reminding him of their agreement. He said he had never been told that this particular monk was the Master he was supposed to carry

鷹愁
澗意
馬收
韁

A Dragon Transformed Into a Horse.

to the West. So Guanyin turned him into a white horse to carry the Master, and they started on their journey again.

In the evening they saw what appeared to be a temple and the Master was pleased to see it, hoping to rest there.

The travelers entered, and asked for lodgings, and the abbot, an old man of 270, entertained them well with his best. Having learnt that they had come the whole way from China, he asked what precious things they carried with them. The Master said they had nothing precious, but the Monkey said, "Yes, we do have that precious cassock." The monks laughed at the idea of reckoning a cassock as precious, and said they had scores of them, and brought out some lovely robes to show them. The Monkey said, "Let me show my Master's robe." The Master whispered to the Monkey that it was dangerous to excite their cupidity by showing it. At the sight of the robe, brilliant with all the colors of the rainbow, the abbot was bent on stealing it.

One monk, named Great Knowledge, said, "The travelers are now asleep. They are only two, let us all arm ourselves, and kill them, and the precious cassock will be the abbot's."

Another monk, named the Great Schemer, said, "That is not a good plan, for it will mean some difficulty. As for that pewter faced one, it is easy to kill him, but that hairy-faced one would not be easy to dispose of. Let us set fire to the temple and then say that the cassock was burned." It was so agreed and the monks brought firewood and piled it around. The Master slept, but the Monkey was awake and, hearing the tramp of men, suspected something. He transformed himself into a bee and went out through one of the cracks and discovered what was taking place. At once he mounted the clouds, reached Heaven and asked for a shade to put over the place where his Master slept and over his cassock and that the wind should blow till everything else was burnt. In spite of this, however, the cassock disappeared!

Next morning, the monks denied all knowledge of the cassock. The Monkey asked, "Is there a demon near here?" "Yes, in the Black Wind Mountain, only 20 *li* off." "I am sure to find the cassock," he told the monks, whom he had called together. "You must take good care of my Master, and his white horse. If there is the

slightest carelessness I will show you how I can beat with my staff."
Then he struck a burnt brick wall with his staff and seven or eight
walls at once fell with his blows. At this every monk was paralyzed
with fear, and they fell on their knees and kowtowed, saying, "Have
mercy on us. You can depend on us being faithful during your absence." At this the Monkey was off on the clouds, and the monks,
greatly terrified at all this, knew he was a god.

Monkey found the Demon of the Black Wind Mountain. A
Taoist priest was on his left, and a Buddhist monk on his right.
They were talking of celebrating a birthday with the precious cassock. Hearing them talk of the cassock, Sun jumped down from
the clouds, brandished his steel spear and said, "Return to me the
stolen cassock, or you shall answer with your life." "Who are you
to talk to me thus? What can you do?" said the Demon of the Black
Wind Mountain. Sun then related some of his mighty deeds, and
the two fought some ten bouts, but neither was victorious. The
demon then said, "Wait till I have had my dinner, and we shall go
at it again." Now this meal was a birthday feast. Sun went back
to the temple for his meal. On the way he passed a small demon
carrying a card case. On opening it, he found that it was an invitation to the aged abbot at the temple, who was 270 years old,
to attend the feast. Sun transformed himself into the abbot and
presented himself in order to steal the cassock when it was shown.
But Guanyin did not think this was a good idea. Then they met a
Taoist immortal, who was going to present two Pills of Immortality to the Black Wind Demon. Sun suggested he transform himself
into one of the pills, and Guanyin approved. When the demon
swallowed them, Sun created such pains inside, that the demon,
in agony, returned the cassock at once. Guanyin took the Black
Wind Demon with her to India, where he repented and promised to
behave himself. She ordered the Monkey to take the cassock back
to his Master and not to make a display of it again.

That day the Master and disciple departed with their horse, but
had not gone far before it grew dark. Seeing a village, they asked
for lodgings, and met a man, who was in a hurry, going to look for
an exorcist. His master had a daughter twenty years of age. Three
years earlier she had married a demon, and the demon had lived,

豬八戒

Zhu the Pig.

as son-in-law, with him ever since, treating his wife badly, and not allowing her to come out of her room. Sun said, "Take me to your home, and I will bring with me my Master, who is a great exorcist." On getting to the house, they heard the story from the father, who said that the demon not only abstained from eating meat, but seemed to have control over the air, traveling in a whirlwind of sand and stones. He had been a clever handsome man at first, but had become extremely ugly with a snout like a pig and with long napping ears. Sun said, "Show me where his room is." Armed with his steel club, he went behind to the room that was locked, and burst it open. The daughter was given to her father, who took her out. Then Sun assumed her form, and waited for the demon, who was in the habit of going away by day and returning by night.

On his return there was a fierce quarrel between the two, and the pig-like husband ran out of the house in a thousand flames, followed by Sun, who mounted the clouds, and followed him saying, "Where do you go? If you go to heaven, I will follow you. If you go to hell, you cannot escape me there. Return your so called wife to her father."

The demon changed back into his natural form, ran into a cave and brought out a nine-pronged spear with which to fight. Sun cried out, "Tell me what your skill is, and hand your weapons over to me, or I will kill you, false demon!" The demon was defeated, of course, and told Sun, "Since I was born, I have been stupid and loved ease, night and day. But I met a spirit, who showed me the way of the immortals. He bade me repent and leave the common way of men, and make myself familiar with the way to heaven above, and hell beneath. I received the Pill of Nine Transformations and studied all the arts by which man could be united to the Powers and Forces above and below, till at last I was able to fly with a light but strong body, and was a guest in the Celestial Court, where I freely mixed with all at the peach banquet. But getting drunk, I made love to some of the fairies, and was expelled back to earth, but by some mistake in transmigration, I got into the womb of a sow instead of that of a woman. That is why I am called Zhu the Pig."

"Oh, you are one of the water fairies sent down to live among men?" "Yes, and you are that terrible monkey, who made such disturbance, and got us all into trouble in Heaven!" They fought again and Sun was victorious, cursing him for daring to marry a good girl.

Then the demon asked if the father had sent for him. Sun replied, "No, I and my Master were passing by on our way to fetch the Sacred Scriptures of the West, and he asked us to save his daughter." On hearing they were in search of the Sacred Scriptures, the demon at once fell on his knees. "I have been waiting for this pilgrim for many years. Take me to see him." He was led to the Master, and said he had kept the five major commandment and the three extra ones as well, fasting all this time waiting for him. "Guanyin has already given me a name in religion. I am Zhu Wuneng, the Seeker of Strength." "That is an excellent name," said the Master. "It fits well with the name of your fellow disciple, which is Wukong, Seeker of Emptiness. But I will also give you a new name: Zhu Bajie, the Keeper of the Eight Commandments."

So Zhu Bajie, now the Keeper of the Eight Commandments, bade farewell to his wife. Seeing he had now become a pilgrim, his father-in-law presented him with a cassock, and two pairs of new shoes. He also offered them some two hundred taels for expenses on the journey, but they were refused, as the monks were expected to live entirely on daily alms.

The Master and his two disciples then started on their journey again. After a month and a half they met a Man of Religion, who happened to know Zhu Bajie. He congratulated him on the privilege of going to the West, and said, "The greatest difficulty lies not in the long distance, but will come from evil thoughts, which lead you astray. When beset by them, repeat the following sacred words. They will act as talisman." He then taught the following to the Master:

> *Buddham saranam gacchami*
> *Dhammam saranam gacchami*
> *Sangham saranam gacchami*

> I take refuge in the Buddha
> I take refuge in the Dharma
> I take refuge in the Sangha

Then the Man of Religion was about to rise to the clouds and depart, when the Master seized him and asked him the way to the West. The Man of Religion smiled and said:

> The road is not difficult,
> Listen to me.
> You must cross a thousand mountains and a thousand streams,
> And you must pass through dark places, where fiends abound,
> If you come to what seems the end of all things,
> Have no fear but press on,
> Close your ears and tread on firm ground.
> Beware of the dark pine forest.
> Fiends and foxes infest that road.
> Cunning spirits fill the cities.
> Demons abound in the mountains,
> Tigers usurp official palaces,
> Leopards keep the official records.
> All lions and elephants are called kings.
> A wild pig bears the baggage,
> The water spirit leads the way.
> The old stone monkey is no longer full of passion.
> You ask this disciple:
> He knows the way to Heaven.

The Monkey did not like his remarks, thinking they were sarcastic. But Zhu Bajie said, "Do not be suspicious. This Man of Religion knows a great deal about the past and the future." Then the Monkey said to the Master, "Mount the horse and let us go!"

> Religion springs from the heart, and religion dies at the heart.
> On whom does the rise and fall depend?
> If it only depends on self,
> Why need we help from another?
> Strive to get blood out of iron.
> Put a ring through your nose,
> And fasten yourself to distant space
> And to the tree of nature.
> Recognize no traitor as friend,
> Follow no artificial rules
> Lest you be deceived.
> Strike hard with your fist,
> But without malice.
> The apparent method is not real,

The light of sun and of moon,
Wherein lies their difference?

Having traveled on, they came to a village where they sought lodgings, but the people were greatly frightened at the sight of Zhu Bajie with his long snout and flapping ears. So Sun advised him to hide his snout in his bosom and fasten his ears, to prevent them flapping. Food was served them, and the Master asked a blessing. Zhu Bajie ate ravenously. The host's name was Wang and he said, "Before you there is a great mountain 800 *li* to cross. You should be well armed, as the mountain is full of robbers and demons."

They started West again, but had not gone far when a terrible storm arose, which blew the Master from his horse, and a tiger came rushing on him. Zhu Bajie took his nine pronged spear and said, "Come on, I will soon finish you." At a touch of his spear, the tiger, who was really a wind demon said, "We are a party sent ahead by the king of this mountain, to kill some mortals for dinner. What kind of Buddhist monk are you to carry deadly weapons like this?" Zhu Bajie replied, "You are greatly mistaken to think that we are ordinary mortals, we are come from China, and are going to the West in search of the Sacred Scriptures."

Meanwhile one of the demon chief's generals seized the Master himself, and carried him to the chief, who told him to be careful not to eat him, or harm him, as he had two terrible disciples. Xuanzang began weeping for fear. Sun Wukong and Zhu Bajie had not been there to protect the Master because they had been deceived by the demon who had taken the form of a tiger, and were busy chasing him down a mountain. But it turned out that the tiger was only a tiger's skin. The two disciples were in great distress, not knowing where their Master had been carried, but finally, they found him in the Cave of the Yellow Ridge, and cried out, "Deliver up our Master at once, or we shall destroy your nest!" At this the demon chief was frightened, and said to the tiger, "I sent you to catch some cattle to eat, why did you bring a Buddhist pilgrim?" The tiger ran away, but was killed by Zhu. Sun went to the cave to look for his Master.

Whilst the demon chief in the Cave of the Yellow Ridge was thinking of what to do, the Monkey outside killed a tiger door-keeper. At this the demon chief put on his clothes, took with him his trident and went out with a host of demon followers. At the sight of the Monkey, not four feet high, he laughed, and asked, "Who art thou to think that I cannot master thee easily?" The Monkey said, "Only strike me and I shall grow." He struck, and the Monkey at once was six feet, and then ten feet tall. They fought for a long time and neither was victor. Then the Monkey plucked a hair, chewed it, blew it out, and cried, "Change," and he was changed into ten identical monkeys, each holding a steel spear. At this the demon chief opened his mouth as wide as ten feet and blew out a typhoon, which made the little monkeys turn about in the air like paper mills. At this the Monkey recalled his magic monkeys and fought alone. The demon blew at him so hard that the Monkey could not open his eyelids and was blind. After this the Monkey went to a village to get eye medicine, and to lodge and rest for the night. His host said, "This is not ordinary wind, it is the epidemic wind of false religion."

> It can blow till the whole world is dark,
> It can blow till gods and demons are baffled.
> It is so terrible that rocks are split by it,
> And men will perish rather than give it up.

The Monkey got a plaster for his eyes, from his host, and the two disciples went to sleep. On waking they found no town at all, all had vanished. But there were some papers, hanging on the branches of the trees, on which was written:

> The dwellers in this village were not ordinary men,
> They defend the Truth with heavenly cures,
> They clear the sight with marvelous medicine.
> Strive to oppose falsehood, do not tarry near it!

The Monkey said to Zhu Bajie, "Stay here and look after the horse and baggage. I will go to the cave, and fight the demon again." This time he changed himself into a fly and flew inside and found the demons asleep. He flew behind to the inner room, and saw his Master there, praying for Sun and Zhu to come to his help. He lighted on the bare head of his Master and said, "I have found you, and we will rescue you." The hairy faced monkey heard the demon say, "Unless you have Guanyin herself on your side, we have nothing to fear."

The Monkey left Zhu Bajie to look after the horse and baggage, mounted the clouds, and appealed to Guanyin for help. She replied, "I have a pill for calming the wind, and a staff to conquer the demon whom I ordered to behave himself. But as he does not, I will go with you at once to the Cave of the Yellow Ridge. I will remain in the clouds, but you can descend to fight him again." Whilst they were fighting, Guanyin threw her staff, with eight prongs like dragon's claws, and the demon was wounded, and his true form as a yellow rat or weasel revealed. Guanyin said, "Do not kill him. He was once a rat in the basement of the Spiritual Mountain, and stole lamp oil so that the Celestial Palace became dark, and fearing punishment he fled. Let me take him to Lord Buddha for punishment." After this, Sun Wukong and Zhu Bajie went to the cave, rescued their Master, and started West again.

Having gone a short distance, they saw a great flood like the sea, but there were no boats in which to cross it. The Monkey in a minute jumped into the air, crossed and returned, saying it was too difficult.

> Quicksands 800 *li* wide,
> Weak water 3,000 *li* deep
> It cannot float a feather,
> And a floating reed would sink.

At this time a terrible demon appeared on the bank of the river, and Sun flew to protect his Master. The demon described himself:

> A great traveler from my youth,
> I providentially met a Taoist immortal
> Who taught me the way of the new birth.
> I extinguished all my passions,
> Had communion with heavenly beings.
> The Jade Emperor made me Chamberlain,
> Armed with sword and buckler
> I was leader of his bodyguard.
> But when the Queen of Heaven
> Ordered her peach banquet,
> By mischance some crystals broke,
> And I was sentenced to death.
> A bare footed Taoist begged to spare my life.
> I received eight hundred strokes

And was banished to these Quicksands,
Where to keep from starvation
I have eaten many a traveler.
Witness these skulls around my neck.
Today you afford me another meal.

At this Zhu Bajie started to beat him. Sun Wukong went to help, but the demon rushed back into the water, while the Master watched them from a little height. After two other unsuccessful fights, failing to get the demon to come out of the water and fight on dry land, they went and told the Master of their difficulty. The Monkey said to Zhu Bajie, "Stay here with the Master, while I go to see Guanyin again." He went and told his story that they had fought the demon three times without success. Guanyin asked, "Did you tell him that you were fetching the Sacred Scriptures? He is a disciple of mine, and if you had only told him so, you would have had no trouble. Hui Yan, take this red gourd, and go with Sun, and call for Seeker of Purity, and he will come and ferry you across."

On being called the demon emerged and apologized for the delay, because he did not know the pilgrim himself was there. He had already been accepted by Guanyin as a disciple, and he was called Sha Wujing, the Seeker of Purity. He was also called Sha the Monk. His head was shaved, a raft was built, and the whole party was ferried across in no time. Their feet washed by the water and the sand, they went their way westward.

沙和尚

Sha the Monk.

11
The Mandrake

THE MASTER SAID, "Let us rest at the next town for the night." The Monkey said, "Let us hurry on, every place is equally our home." Zhu Bajie said, "That is all very well for you to say, but I have a load to carry from day to day, do not forget that, and do not treat me as a common coolie. The horse is fat and strong and only carries the Master, why not put some of my load on the horse?" The Monkey said, "This horse was originally the third son of one of the dragon kings, and as he broke one of the laws of Heaven he would have been killed, but for Guanyin's mercy in sparing his life, on condition that he should carry the Master. Carry your load yourself!" On hearing this, Zhu Bajie started to wonder just what was going on.

When night came they arrived at a house occupied by a widow and her three daughters, and they asked for lodging. The mother welcomed them heartily, and told them how she became a widow and was now well to do. What troubled her was that there was no husband, or son, or son-in-law, to whom to leave her ten thousand acres of land. "Now that we are four women and you are four men, is it not providential that you have come here?" At this speech the Master pretended to be deaf and dumb. She went on to say there were 300 acres of dry land, 300 of watered land, 300 of orchard and forests, horses and cattle in droves, sheep and pigs without number, sixty or seventy farms, clothing enough to last for years, and grain and silver in abundance. "You had better stay here and have a comfortable home without care, rather than the troubles of travel to the West." The Master was silent. She again spoke, "I am forty-five years old, my eldest daughter is twenty, the second eighteen, and the third sixteen. None of them are betrothed. They are skilful with the needle and embroidery, and having no sons, I got a teacher for them, in order that they should study and sing." But the Master sat as if listening to frogs after rain, without saying a word. Zhu Bajie, however, was much attracted by their beauty and wealth, and said to his Master, "You should be civil and give some answer." The Master was annoyed and said, "We monks should not be moved by these things. What good is in them?" The widow smiled, and replied, "What a pity! What good is there in leaving your homes and becoming monks?"

> In the spring we make spring clothes.
> In the summer we change into light silk garments,
> In the autumn there comes harvest home,
> In the winter we have banquets and wine,
> Every season of the eight abounds with fresh dainties,
> Every night we rest in warm embrace.
> How much better than to travel in search of Amitabha!

The Master replied, "Yes, that is true, but our life has also its advantages."

> The vows a monk makes are uncommon.
> They give up their gracious homes,
> They do not speak of this world's good,
> They speak of another marriage,
> When work is finished, they remove to Heaven,
> That is their soul's eternal home.
> This is better than to enjoy one's self below,
> Which ends in mortifying rottenness
> Truly when one follows the right way, one must be careful,
> One must put away the desires of the flesh and be true.

The next morning dawned, and it was found that fairies had indeed tempted them, and that Zhu, the Keeper of the Eight Commandments, had succumbed. His repentance was in great sorrow and shame.

They next arrived at the mountain of Everlasting Life, the only spot in all the world where grew a root, which existed before creation, whose fruit ripened only once in 3,000 years. This root was in shape like a perfect little child, like a mandrake. By smelling it, one could live 360 years, and by eating it, one could live 47,000 years. On the mountain was the Taoist Temple of the Five Villages.

That very day the First Cause of All Things had called an assembly to hear him explain the story of creation.

The abbot of the Taoist temple took all his students of immortality with him to hear the First Cause of All Things, leaving two of the youngest at home. The age of one was 1300 and that of the other was 1200 years, and to them he said, "Soon there will arrive a Buddhist monk from the East in search of the Sacred Scriptures. He is the second great disciple of Buddha himself, and his name is Golden Cicada. When he comes, treat him well. He is an old friend of mine. Give him two of the magic mandrakes, which confer immortality." The two youths replied, "Confucius tells us not to be friendly with those of a different religion. We are servants of the First Cause of All Things." They were not pleased, but welcomed the pilgrims and led them to the temple. Above the door was a newly made beautiful tablet, on which was written two words only: "Heaven" and "Earth." The Master went in, burnt incense, and then said, "Your temple is beautiful, worthy of Heaven itself. But why do you not worship the Three Pure Ones and the Four Emperors of the North, South, East, and West?" They answered, "There is a suitable time and place for everything. In this place our abbot does what is suitable for him. Today he has been invited by the First Cause of All Things to come and listen to his teaching about the origin of things."

Then they gave him the two mandrakes as a rare gift, but which Xuanzang said was like a newborn baby, and indignantly refused to eat it. But the disciples knew of its rare value, so stole them for themselves. Fearing the consequences, all three decided not to confess, and returned into the hall. Xuanzang had refused the mandrakes but now they were missing, and enquiries were being made.

The Master called his disciples, and asked which of them had stolen the mandrakes, and said, "If you have done so, confess and apologize." But the two Taoist youths were rude, and made Xuanzang's disciples so angry that they went to the mandrake orchard and destroyed all the trees.

> When the Master reached the Mountain of Everlasting Life
> The Monkey stopped the growth of Fruits of Immortality.
> The leaves were fallen, the trees uprooted,
> The two Immortal youths were terror stricken.

五莊觀行者竊人參

Sun Steals the Mandrakes.

The two youths said, "We cannot fight them, for they are four and we are only two. Let us cheat them. First apologize to the Master, give them a good meal, and then lock them in that room, till our abbot returns."

This they did, but the Monkey burst open all the doors and they all went their way, leaving the youths fast asleep. The abbot of the temple returned, followed and arrested them, and took them back to his temple, where he tied them, each to a tree, to be flogged. But the Monkey transformed some willow trees into the likeness of the Master and his disciples, and in this way they escaped. They were caught again, and when the Monkey was beaten, he changed his legs into wrought iron. When about to be boiled in oil, he changed a stone lion into his form, to take his place.

> To be religious, one must have a keen edge to one's ear.
> One must ever keep close to one's conscience.
> Steel is hard, but steeled hearts are harder,
> The humble minded never is a fool.

The abbot said to the Monkey, "You have presumed too far this time. There is a day of reckoning. I will go with you to the West and get back my mandrake tree from Buddha himself." "Is that all? Why did you not tell me before? If you let my Master go, I will bring you a living tree." The bargain was made, and the Monkey went in search of the Old Physician, who could make the dead live. He first went to the Islands of the Immortals and found three persons playing chess, the angels of the Star of Long Life, the Star of Happiness, and the Star of Wealth. On seeing the Monkey, one said, "Great Sage, you have left Taoism and now follow Buddhism. How is it you come to see us again? Have you stolen the root of immortality, the mandrake? It far surpasses our laborious alchemical method." The Monkey said, "I destroyed the tree it grows on. Never mind. I can replace it. Give me a recipe for restoring it." They said, "We can heal wounds, but we cannot restore life." The Monkey then said. "Since you cannot, I will have to go to see the Jade Emperor himself."

Having arrived there, he told the Jade Emperor of his quest. The Jade Emperor replied, "We can cure living beings, but cannot cure trees." At this the Monkey left for Yongzhou and asked the same question, but none could tell him a remedy. He then directed his course to the Black Wind Demon, who was now doing good works as a disciple of Guanyin. He said, "I am grateful to you, Great Sage, for sparing my life." The Monkey was invited to see Guanyin, to whom he told his story. She said, "Do not be troubled, I have drops of water that will restore your trees to life." She at once returned with him, and although the trees were dead and uprooted, by application of the drops, they were fully renewed, leaves and fruit were produced and ten mandrakes were picked and shared by the assembled immortals. Even the Master ate one of the immortal fruit, and the Monkey and the abbot became sworn brothers.

Starting again, the Master felt he had new life in him. Soon they came to a mountain, and the Master told the Monkey to go and beg some food for him, as he was hungry. Sun said, "How foolish you are to ask me to beg on a mountain, where there are no living beings." However, mounting a cloud, he saw in the distance some peaches ripening, and made for them.

In the meantime a fairy came, saying that she had brought some food to give to the traveling monks. But it was a witch with some poison, and the Master would have taken it but for the Monkey, who returned with the peaches just in time. He suspected the witch and killed her, but he was blamed by the Master for his vengeance, and he would have been dismissed, but by begging hard he was permitted to continue, on condition he behaved better.

Then there appeared an old woman of eighty, whom the Monkey also attacked and killed. On they went, and met an old man, reciting his prayers on the roadside. Zhu Bajie said, "This old man must be a relative of the women just killed." So Sun struck him dead too. Zhu Bajie said to the Master, "This is terrible. The Monkey is the source of all our trouble; three persons killed in one day. Is this worthy of monks? You should repeat your incantation and let the cap of spikes pierce into his head." The Monkey said, "Zhu Bajie is a fool, do not listen to him! These are all demons, they cannot fool me. Master, look at this heap of bones. They are not of those just killed. You are fooled by their magic." But the Master had made up his mind to dismiss the Monkey, and give him a letter of dismissal. The Monkey thought of the many troubles and dangers from which he had saved his Master, and thought it hard that he should listen to the slanders of the foolish pig. He bade his fellow disciples take good care of the Master, and with tears in his eyes, left in the direction of his old cave in the Mountain Orchard.

The Monkey arrived at his old home, the Waterfall Cave. It was 500 years since he saw it last, and he was struck with the ruin everywhere. The seven brothers had burnt everything, and he was greatly distressed. Then a few monkeys appeared timidly, and when they knew who he was, they were delighted beyond measure, and gathered round him, telling of all the cruelties practiced on them, their dead being eaten, and the living having to make sport for their masters. "How is it that you, whom we heard had started with the Master, to fetch Sacred Scriptures from the West, are back again with us?" The Monkey King said, "I went with him and delivered him from a number of dangers, and destroyed many fiends and demons, who would have killed him. But he does not know how to employ men. He thinks me a cruel man and has dismissed me, never to engage me again."

Hearing of the Monkey King's return, the new rulers who were oppressing them came to attack him. The Monkey King gathered all the stones of the mountain into one heap, and sent the little monkeys to hide inside the cave. Then there was a sound of drums and over a thousand men and horses made a charge. The Monkey King with one big breath gathered together all the stones and then blew forth a terrible stone storm that annihilated all his enemies. He then laughed with great joy, and said, "My Master often said, 'Be good for a thousand days, and it is not enough; do evil for one day, and it is more than enough." Now I will order the restoration of the Mountain Park and Waterfall Cave, and will enjoy myself in peace."

As for the Master, he soon got into difficulties. Zhu Bajie led him into a dark forest. The Master told him to go and beg for some food. Zhu Bajie left him in the forest, and went in search of houses, where he could get food, but he could find none. Zhu Bajie became overpowered with sleep and, seeing some straw, rolled into it, and slept. Sha the Monk, finding that Zhu Bajie did not come back, went to look for him, and the Master, when neither returned, became alarmed, and went on alone. Seeing some light, he made for it, thinking he could get some food, but it was a demon's trap, and he was caught in it. The demon rejoiced greatly at the prospect of enjoying human flesh and thus becoming immortal. But the two disciples came, and discovering that their Master was inside, launched an attack on the demon.

The two disciples fought thirty times without being vanquished. The Master, who was bound inside, was praying for them. He was also weeping, fearing that he would be murdered, although he knew that his time had not yet come.

Then a woman of about thirty years old entered and, seeing the Master, asked him who he was. She told him she was the Princess from the Elephant Country, and had been carried away by this demon thirteen years before. If the Master would deliver a letter to her father on his way to the West, she would unbind him and let him go. This was agreed on, and through her help, the Master and his disciples were able to escape.

Having passed through a dark forest, they arrived at the court of the princess' father, where the Master delivered the letter begging for rescue from the demon husband. The king put this request before his military men, but being only mortal men they were afraid to attack demons, who came and went at will in the air. He asked if any of the pilgrims had fought successfully with demons. Zhu Bajie and Sha the Monk said that they had done so, and were willing to go back to deliver the princess. Zhu Bajie exhibited some of his magic tricks, such as stretching himself to eighty feet in height, and then went off in the air. Sha the Monk followed him in the air, to the great astonishment of all the court, and traveled through the Pine Forest to the demon's cave, and fought desperately some eighty or ninety bouts, but in vain. They were captured again, together with the horse, and all were bound in the cave.

The two disciples had gone back to fetch the princess, but they were no match for the demon. He would not allow the princess to go, but said he would go himself and pay his respects to his father-in-law. When he arrived there, he accused the Master of imposture. He said that it was the Master, in the form of a tiger, who had carried the princess away thirteen years before, and was now pretending to fetch Sacred Scriptures from the West. By his magic the demon changed the Master into a tiger, and frightened the king and all the ministers terribly. After that the demon drank wine and called for songs and dances in an outrageous manner. The Master's dragon horse could suffer this no longer, and said to Zhu Bajie, "If you wish to save your Master, you must send for help. You and the monk are no match for this demon." "Where can we get help?" "You must send to the Mountain Garden for the Monkey King." Zhu Bajie said, "I am afraid he will be angry with me and kill me, because I blamed him for killing those demons, who appeared as two women and an old man." "No, the Monkey King is a great and kind king. Tell him that the Master speaks of his ability and kindness often, and would like to see him."

Zhu Bajie therefore went to the Mountain Garden, where he interviewed the Monkey King. But the Monkey did not seem anxious to leave his beautiful place, and Zhu Bajie began to doubt his sincerity in serving the Master, and said so in the hearing of some of the Monkeys. These told the Monkey King of Zhu's Bajie's suspicions. At this the Monkey King was very indignant, and ordered them to fetch him back at once.

> It is righteousness
> Which religion arouses from the soul,
> All forces work together for good.
> Even the monkey heart, when it tastes immortality,
> Desires to go to Paradise.
> All religions meet in one Center.
> Sacred books are only general guides.
> Buddhism follows the origins of spirit.
> All leaders are harmonious brethren.
> Demons and fiends have to submit to nature,
> When they cut off selfish pleasure,
> They join in the grand harmony of life.

The little monkeys dragged Zhu Bajie back to the cave and the Great Sage began to curse him for his duplicity. Zhu Bajie denied it. But the Great Sage said, "You cannot deceive me! My left ear, turned upwards, hears every word in all the 33 heavens, and my right ear, turned downwards, hears everything down to the ten levels of hell." However, the Monkey King did go to see how his Master was. He transformed his Master from being a terrifying tiger into his usual form. The Master was most grateful to the Monkey King for coming to his rescue, and forgiving the wrong that had been done to him, and added that when he returned to China he would tell the emperor that he owed his safe traveling more to Sun than to any one else. The princess' father wished to give a handsome present to the travelers for their expenses, but the pilgrims would not take any. After this the king returned to his palace and his safe Elephant Kingdom, while the Master went on towards the Thunder Temple to worship Buddha.

12
The Lotus Cave

AFTER THIS SUN CAREFULLY WATCHED Zhu Bajie, who cheated in all he did. While professing to be on watch, he slept most of the time, but Sun discovered all. Arriving at Pingding Mountain, they were approached by a woodcutter, who warned them of their danger, saying, "In this mountain of 600 *li*, there is a Lotus Cave where there is a band of demons with two chiefs, lying in wait for the pilgrim from China to devour him and his party." Then the woodcutter disappeared. After this Zhu Bajie was ordered to be on the watch for the demons on the mountain. But on the way, seeing some hay, he lay down and slept in it. As a result, by his foolishness, he was carried away to the Lotus cave.

On seeing Zhu Bajie, the second chief said, "This one is no good, you must go out in search of the Master and the Monkey." At this time the Monkey, to keep his Master from fear, walked ahead of the horse swinging his club up and down to right and left several times. The Demon King was on the top of the mountain peak watching them and he said to himself, "I have heard much of this monkey and his magic, but I will show that he is no match for me; I will yet feast on his Master." Therefore he came down from the mountain, and transformed himself into a wounded lame man on the roadside, in order to appeal to the kindness of the Master. The Master, out of pity, persuaded the Monkey to carry him. Whilst on the Monkey's back the demon, by magic skill, threw Mount Meru on Sun's head, but the Monkey warded it off on his left shoulder, and walked on. Then the demon threw Mount Emei on his head, and this the Monkey warded off on his right shoulder, and walked on, to the great surprise of the demon. Lastly the demon, by another magic spell, made Mount Tai fall on his head. This at last staggered and stunned the Monkey. The demon then hurried after the Master and put his arm round him. At the sight of this, Sha the Monk drew forth his staff, but it was no match for the starry sword of the demon. He carried off Sha the Monk under one arm, and the Master under the other, and took them to the Lotus Cave, and called out, "Brother, I have now caught all the monks and brought them here." The chief replied, "It is no good unless that mighty monkey is caught."

It was then arranged that two young demons should take the yellow gourd of one, and the jade vase of the other, as the most precious things the two demons had, to bottle the Monkey in them. They were to take them upside down and call out the Monkey's name, and if he replied, he would be found inside them, and the demons were to seal them up, with the seal of the Ancient of Days.

When the Monkey found himself crushed under the three mountains, he was greatly distressed about his Master, and cried aloud, "Oh Master, you delivered me from under the mountain before, and trained me in religion, how is it that you have brought me to this pass, where I am under the mountains again? It is a thousand pities! If you must die, why should Sha the Monk, Zhu Bajie, and the Dragon Horse suffer needlessly?" Then his tears fell like rain.

The spirits of the mountains and the local gods wondered at this. The Guardians of the Five Regions asked, "Whose is this mountain, and who is crushed under it?" The local gods replied, "The mountain is ours, but who is under it we do not know." "If you do not know, we will tell you. It is the Great Sage, the Equal of Heaven, who rebelled there 500 years ago. He is now converted and is the disciple of the Chinese pilgrim. How dare you lend your mountain to the demon for this?" The local gods and the guardian angels then read some prayers and the mountains were removed, and the Monkey delivered. He sprang up, brandishing his spear at the spirits and local gods, and they at once apologized and kowtowed, saying that the demons insisted on their serving them daily. On hearing that the gods had to serve the demons, the Monkey was astonished and cried out in agony, "Oh High Heaven! Since you have created me, how is it that you have also created these demons?"

Whilst talking thus, Sun saw some light approaching and asked, "What is that?" The spirits who served the demons said, "This light comes from the demons' magic treasures which shine like lamps. We are afraid they are brought out to catch you." Then Sun said, "Now we shall have some sport. With whom does the demon chief associate?" They replied, "The man whom he loves most is a Tao-ist, who is daily engaged in alchemy." The Monkey said, "Return all of you, and I will catch them myself." He began by transforming himself into the very image of the Taoist.

Meeting the two small demons, Sun told them he was in search of a famous spirit among them, and asked them to show the way. In conversation he drew from them that they were going to catch the celebrated monkey, and that they had two magic treasures, a gourd and a vase, by which to catch and bottle him. They showed them to him, and added that the gourd, though small, could hold a thousand people. "That is nothing," replied Sun. "I have a gourd which can contain all the heavens." They were amazed at this, and bargained with him, that if he gave them his gourd, it was to be tried whether it could hold all the heavens and if so, they would give him their gourd and vase. The Monkey went to heaven and obtained permission, through Prince Nezha, to stop the light of the sun, moon, and stars for one hour. Then at noon the next day all was absolutely dark, and the little demons marveled greatly, and believed the Monkey when he told them that the reason of the darkness was that he had put the whole heavens in his gourd, and therefore there was no light. They therefore handed over the two magic treasures, the gourd and magic vase, to the Monkey, and he gave them in exchange his false gourd.

After this Sun mounted on the clouds and arrived at the South Gate of Heaven, where he thanked Prince Nezha for his valuable help. The Monkey then stood looking at the outwitted young de-mons. When the two young demons found that Sun had cheated them of their gourd to hold men, and had given them a false one to hold the heavens, sun, moon, and stars, they told all to the two chiefs, who said, "It is Sun who has outwitted you, by pretending that he was one of the Immortals. We had five magic treasures and now we have lost two, the gourd and the vase. There still remain three, the magic sword, the magic palm, and the magic rope. Go and invite our dear grandmother to dine on the human flesh we have caught for tonight's dinner." Sun himself went, impersonating one of the demons, and was invited inside. He told her that he wanted her to bring with her the magic rope, with which to catch Sun. She was delighted and started off in a chair carried by two fairies.

After traveling some four or five *li*, Sun attacked and killed them, and discovered they were in fact foxes. Sun carried away the magic rope, and thus had three of the magic treasures in his possession. Then he changed the dead to appear like the living, and returned to the Lotus Cave. Small demons came running, and saying that the old lady had been killed. Being frightened, the Demon King proposed to let the whole party go. His younger brother said, "No, let me fight Sun. If I win, then we shall eat them, if I fail, then let them go."

The demon called out to Sun, "Do not go away. I want to fight you again." After fighting some thirty bouts, Sun lost the rope, and the demon by the use of the magic rope lassoed him and carried him to his cave, and took back the magic gourd and vase, and the two chiefs rejoiced greatly. Sun now transformed himself into two false demons. One he placed, instead of himself, in the lasso bound to a pillar, and as the other, he reported to the second demon chief that Sun was struggling hard, and suggested that a stronger rope be used lest the other should break. Then by the change, Sun obtained possession of the magic rope again. After that, by a similar trick, he obtained the magic gourd and vase back.

> Originally the heart is in harmony with the Divine,
> But when caught in the various nets of the world,
> It finds it not easy to avoid mistakes.
> The attainment of immortality is not by following the many.
> It is one's lot to meet both good and evil.
> All the world has its appointed calamities
> Throughout countless ages,
> But there remains a divine light shining through the gloom.

The Great Sage and the demons wrangled much about the respective merits of their gourds, which, each assured the other, could imprison men, and make them do their own wish. Finally the Great Sage succeeded in putting one of the great demons in his gourd.

After that they had another fight concerning the sword and the palm fan, the magic treasures of the demons, and during the fight the fan was burnt to ashes.

> The fire was not ordinary fire,
> But that spark which nothing in nature can extinguish;
> It blazed, and all the world was red with its flames.

They continued fighting several times, and Sun gradually gained ground against great odds, and put the second demon in the magic vase, and sealed it with the seal of the Ancient of Days. Then the sword was delivered and the demons submitted to Sun. He returned to the cave for his Master, swept it clean of all evil spirits, and they marched off on their westward journey. Soon on the roadside they met a blind man crying, "Where are you going, Buddhist monk? I am the Ancient of Days! Give me back my magic treasures first! The gourd is my property, and I keep the Pill of Immortality in it. The jar is where I keep the Water of Life. The sword is that which I use to subdue demons. The fan is that which I use to stir up enthusiasm. The cord is that which I use to bind bundles. Those two demons used to look after my gold crucible, but they stole my magic treasures, and ran away to the world of human beings. Fortunately you have caught them, and deserve great reward." But Sun replied, "You should be severely punished for letting your servants do this evil in the world.'" The Ancient of Days said, "No, without these various trials, your Master and his disciples could never gain perfection of character!"

Then Sun understood and said, "Since you have come yourself for the magic treasures, I shall return them to you." After receiving them, the Ancient of Days and his two servants went away, one on his right and the other on his left, and returned to the Polar Star Mansion again.

13

The Baolin Temple

THEY HAD NOT TRAVELED FAR before the Master cried out, "There is a mountain of difficulties ahead of us, we must be careful." The Monkey said, "Master, do not be over anxious. So long as our hearts are upright, there cannot be any serious trouble." As the sun was setting, they saw a temple where they asked for lodging. But the abbot of the Baolin Temple was very rude, and said that if they went on some thirty *li*, they would find an inn and lodging. The Master asked why he did not treat them well. The abbot said, "We sometimes have to suffer for others' sins. Formerly some poor monks came and begged for lodgings. I took pity on them, gave them food and clothing, but they stayed on for several years, thinking more of their keep than of their religion."

When the Monkey heard of this refusal of lodging to his Master, he said to him, "You are far too gentle. Let me go and see this abbot." The novices ran in terror, to report that a man, with a hairy face and no cheeks, had come, and was very angry. The doors were shut against him. But the Monkey with his spear burst open the door, smashed the stone lions at the gate, as if they had been only of glass, and said, "Inside here, you have room for hundreds of monks, and yet you cannot give lodgings to these four!" When he found the abbot, he began beating him badly. The abbot cried for mercy, and Sun said, "Yes, I will show mercy on one condition. Bring out your five hundred priests, properly dressed, and give a proper welcome to my Master, or I shall beat you still more."

After this the abbot beat the great drum and rang the great bell, and the monks came running, and wondering what was the matter. When they were arranged in order, they fell on their knees, and welcomed the Master suitably. After supper, the Master dismissed all except Sun Wukong, Zhu Bajie and Sha the Monk. He took them out with him and said, "Look at that wonderful moonlight. It makes me long for the time when I can return to my dear old home."

The Monkey, on hearing this, said to the Master, "You enjoy the beautiful light and long for home. You do not think of the Great Purpose before the Sun and Moon were created, and how they are made to revolve from month to month without fail. This is a mystery. One thing is clear, what is not born is immortal."

The Master said, "My disciples, you are all tired, go to sleep while I read a chapter of my Sacred Scriptures." The Monkey said, "Are you not now traveling so far to get the Sacred Scriptures? How come you can read them now?" The Master said, "Oh, just sometimes I read over my old books, lest I forget them."

That night, the Master had a strange dream, in which the spirit of the King of Kashghar appeared to him and told his history. During a long drought he was deceived by a demon who slew him, and threw him into a well in the palace garden, where he had remained for three years, after which the demon had assumed his form and usurped his throne and deceived everyone. He begged the Master to allow his disciple Sun to rescue him. In proof of the truth of his story, be left behind a bar of white jade.

The Master told his dream to the Monkey, who thought there must be some truth in it, and departed to seek the palace. The Master then chanted:

> Religions vestments we need not heed,
> But the inward true Ideal is free from the dust of earth,
> The perfect character is seen through a thousand stitches.
> Pearls and jewels must harmonize with the Great First Spirit,
> Ministering angels respectfully serve,
> Devout monks will be sent to purify our lives.

For three years, the garden had been closed, and no one had been allowed to enter. The king's son was not permitted to see his mother, for the demon, having transformed himself into the same form as the king, was not suspected by the officials, who obeyed all his orders.

After a series of magic arts, Sun transformed himself into a two-inch babe, and hid himself with the piece of white jade in a small box, which was presented to the prince when he came to the Baolin Temple. After this the prince met the Master, who told all his dream. The prince recognised the piece of jade as really belonging to his father. He was told: "If you do not avenge your father's death, you have been born in vain!" But the prince remained still in some doubt. Sun therefore said, "Go straight back to the palace and see your mother in private, and hear what she will tell you."

Now after the Master had seen the soul of the king in a dream, the queen also had a similar dream. The prince learnt from her what had happened to his father. It was decided that Sun should attack the demon usurper. But first he wished to find the corpse of the murdered king. So he and Zhu Bajie went into the garden. Sun pointed to a palm tree, and ordered Zhu to dig underneath it. Beneath it was a heavy slab, which when removed disclosed a shining surface. Zhu Bajie cried, "Here is a mirror of light!" But it was a well whose waters reflected the moonlight. Sun then ordered Zhu Bajie to descend and recover a treasure he should find there. At the bottom he found an entrance into the crystal palace of one of the dragons of the deep. On asking for a treasure, Zhu was shown the body of a dead man in a yellow robe, with a crown on his head. This he was allowed to take up to Sun.

When the Monkey saw the corpse, he told Zhu to carry it to the temple, where the Master was resting. This he refused to do, but Sun gave him twenty blows with a heavy rod, and at last he carried the corpse to the temple. When the Master saw the corpse, with all the appearance of a live man, he wept to think of the usurper taking possession of the country. Zhu laughed at him, "Master, he does not belong to your family! Why should you be so distressed?" The Master replied, "The true Buddhist is always full of pity. Why are you so heartless?"

Zhu Bajie replied, "I am not heartless. Brother Sun said he can make the dead live. Do you think I would have troubled to carry the dead corpse here, if he had not said so?" The Master then called for Sun and told him to restore the dead to life. "It is better to save a man's life than to build a seven storied pagoda!" Sun replied, "Why do you believe that fool's talk? When a man dies, his soul returns only in the third week, the fifth week and the seventh week, but never after. This man has been dead for three years; how can you expect him to live again?" The Master assented.

But Zhu Bajie became angry and cried, "Do not be deceived by Sun. He is quite able to restore the dead to life if he should so choose. Recite the incantation to cause the spikes of his cap of spikes to pierce his head, and make him restore this man to life!" So the Master recited the incantation, and the Monkey's eyes became swollen and his head began to feel great pain.

The Great Sage suffered such terrible pain in his head that he begged the Master not to repeat the incantation any more, as he could not endure the pain. "I will make the dead live!" The Master said, "How can you do that?" Sun replied, "I will descend to hell, and beg that the king's spirit be allowed to return to his body." But Zhu Bajie said, "If you cannot give life to him without yourself descending to hell, where is your power? Master, do not let him deceive you. Go on, repeat the incantation." Sun, feeling the great pain again, said, "I can save him without going to hell." The Master said: And how can you do that?" "I will ascend to Heaven, to the Ancient of Days, and beg for the Pill of Immortality, that restores the soul nine times from death." He did so, and returned with the Pill, and the dead king was made alive again.

> In the West there is a secret by which to find the truth,
> Gold and straw and copper are tried by fire,
> The devout spirit is inspired with spiritual vision,
> The babe regrets it has no gift but a swollen body,
> But it grows like its father in the womb,
> And like the Ancient of Days in Heaven.
> The earthly must be lost before one gains the heavenly,
> Truly salvation comes from a higher realm.

The question then arose, how to restore the true king to his kingdom, and how to punish the demon. When he was just about to kill the demon, the *bodhisattva* Manjusri appeared and told the true history of both the king and the demon. In fact the king had done wrong, and the appearance of the demon in his place was a punishment permitted by Heaven. After this, Manjusri returned to his home in Mount Wutai. Having restored the dead king to his throne, the pilgrims took leave of the Court and went on their journey.

14
The Red Child Demon

BY THE AUTUMN THE TRAVELERS arrived at a great mountain. On the way, there appeared a red cloud that the Monkey thought must be a demon. It was indeed a demon child of seven, who, in order to entrap the Master, had himself bound and tied to a branch of a tree. The child cried again and again to the passers by to deliver him. Sun would not let the Master deliver the child, as he was certain it was only a trick to catch them all. Finally the Master could not endure the boy's cries for deliverance. He ordered his disciples to unloose the naked child, and the Monkey to carry him.

> When your virtue is great, your trials are great,
> When religion is not active, inactivity produces devilry.
> When the heart is upright, you walk in the right way.
> But if your mind is foolish, you make mistakes.

As they went on their way the demon caused a great whirlwind to arise. Whilst sheltering himself from the wind, the Master was carried away by the demon. Sun discovered that the demon was in fact an old friend of his, who, centuries before, had pledged himself to eternal friendship with Sun, so he comforted his comrades by saying that he was sure no harm would come to the Master.

> Men when wise reach a state,
> Where good and evil are effaced,
> Fame and failure ne'er disturb,
> Cloud and sunshine are alike,
> Eat and drink when needs arise,
> Well, their spirits calm remain,
> Ill, the demons trouble them.
> Wise men, vexed by life's turmoil,
> Find in temples rest and peace.

The travelers reached a mountain of dry pine forests, where they found the demon in his cave, looking forward with pleasure on feasting on the flesh of the monk. When Sun appeared, the demon refused to recognize their old friendship, and after an insulting altercation, they started fighting. The demon burnt everything, so that the smoke might blind Sun. Being thus blinded and beaten, he could not find his Master. In despair he said, "I must get the help of someone abler than myself." Zhu Bajie was sent to fetch Guanyin. The demon took a magic leather bag, in which to imprison Zhu Bajie and, transforming himself into the shape of Guanyin, invited Zhu Bajie to enter the cave. The fool went in, and directly he entered, he was seized and placed in the bag. Then the demon appeared in his true form, and said, "Now you see who I am. I am the naked child, and I mean to cook you for my dinner. A fine pig to protect his Master you are!" Then the small demons announced the arrival of Sun. The demon then called his six strong generals, with names such as Mist in the Clouds, Spreading Fire, Fleet as the Wind and so on, who came kneeling for orders. He ordered them to accompany him to fetch his father, the Ox-Head King, to dine on the pilgrim, and they disappeared. Meanwhile Sun opened the bag where Zhu Bajie had been imprisoned, and both went out of the cave after these six generals.

After the generals left, Sun thought, "Since the demon has played a trick on Zhu Bajie, I will play a trick on his generals." So he hurried on in front of them, and changed himself into the form of the Ox-Head King waiting for them. The generals were solemnly invited into his presence, and the demon child, the spokesman, said, "If anyone eats a slice of the pilgrim's flesh, his life will be prolonged indefinitely. Now he is caught and I invite you to feast on him." Sun, impersonating the father, said, "No, I cannot come, I am fasting today. Besides, the pilgrim is in charge of Sun. If harm comes to his Master, you will surely suffer, for he has seventy-two magic arts. He can make himself so big that your cave cannot contain him, and he can make himself as small as a fly, a mosquito, a bee, or a butterfly."

At this, the Monkey went south to Guanyin for help. She gave him a bottle, but he was surprised to find he could not move it. "I'm

観音慈善縛紅孩

Guanyin Saves the Red Child.

not surprised," said Guanyin, "for all the ocean forces are stored there." Guanyin took it up with ease, and said, "This dew water is different from dragon water and can put out the fire of passion. I will send a fairy with you on your boat. You need no sails. The fairy only needs to blow a little and the boat floats at will without any effort." Finally, the demon child, having been caught, repented and begged to be received as a disciple. Guanyin accepted him and blessed him, giving him the name of Sadhana the Page.

After Guanyin had said some prayers, Sadhana the Page commenced his duties by paying due respect to Guanyin. When Sha the Monk, who was still waiting at the Pine forest, saw Sun returning, he was very glad. They went in and unbound the Master, and told him of the conversion of the new disciple, on hearing which, the Master fell on his knees facing the south, and thanked Guanyin. They then marched westward for a month.

One day the Master cried suddenly, "What is that noise?" Sun said to the Master, "You are afraid, are you? Have you have forgotten the Heart Sutra, which says that we are to be indifferent to all the calls of the senses. The eye must not look at the beautiful, the ear must not be attracted by music, the nose must not seek sweet fragrance, the tongue must not long for fine flavor, the body must be indifferent to heat or cold, the mind must not have vain desires. These are the Six Thieves. If you cannot suppress these, how do you expect to attain enlightenment?" The Master thought awhile and then said, "Oh disciple, when shall we see Buddha face to face?"

Zhu Bajie said, "If we are to meet such demons as these, it will take us a thousand years to get to the West." But Sha the Monk said, "Both you and I are stupid. If we persevere and travel on, shoulder to shoulder, we shall reach there at last." Whilst thus talking, they saw before them a dark river in flood, which the horse could not cross. Seeing a small boat the Master said, "Let us engage this boat to cross over." Whilst crossing the river in it, they found that it was a boat sent by the Demon of the Black River to entrap them in midstream. Sun, needless to say, came to the rescue, and delivered the Master from their grasp. They were then ferried across and put on their way.

15
Buddhists and Taoists Compete

HAVING CROSSED THE BLACK RIVER, they traveled West against wind and snow. All of a sudden they heard a tremendous shout as of ten thousand voices. The Master was alarmed, and the disciples made wild guesses as to what it was. Sun laughed and said, "Let me go and see." He rose up on the clouds and saw a city, outside of which there were thousands of monks and carts full of bricks and all kinds of building materials. This was the city where Taoists were respected, and Buddhists were not wanted. The Monkey, who appeared among the people in the form of a Taoist, learnt that the country was called the Country of the Slow Carts, and for twenty years had been ruled by three Taoists who had succeeded in getting rain during drought. Their names were Tiger, Deer, and Sheep. They could call up wind or rain, and change stones into gold with ease. The Monkey said to the two leading Taoists, "I wonder if I shall have a spark of good luck and can see your king?" They said, "We will see to that after we have attended to other business." "What business could religious people like you have?" They said, "Formerly, in the time of drought, when our king ordered Buddhists to pray for rain they were not answered, then Taoists prayed and got rain. Since then all the Buddhist monks have been our slaves and coolies, bringing materials for building as you see. We must appoint them their work first and then will come to you." Sun said, "Do not go to any trouble, I am in search of an uncle of mine, who is a Buddhist monk from whom we have heard no word for years. He may be here among your slaves." They said, "You can look and see and let us know if you find him."

Meanwhile Sun went round to look for his relative. Hearing this many Buddhist monks surrounded him, hoping he would recognize one of them as his lost relative. Then after a time he smiled. They asked why he smiled. He said, "Why do you not improve and progress? You were not given life to be idle or stagnant." They said, "We cannot do anything. We are terribly oppressed." "What power have these Taoist priests?" "They can by magic call up wind or rain." "That is a small matter," said Sun. "What else can they do?" "They can manufacture the Pill of Immortality, and change stone into gold."

Sun said, "These are also small matters, common to many. How did these Taoists deceive your king?" "The king reads prayers with them night and day, expecting to attain permanent life without death. In this way the king believes in them." "Since things are in this state, why do you not all go away?" "Sir, you do not know that we cannot go away, for the king has authorized a picture of every one of us to be made, and these are hung up everywhere. The Country of Slow Carts is extensive with prefectures, counties, and market places, and a picture of the Buddhist monks is in each place, with a notice saying that any official who catches a runaway monk will be promoted three degrees, and that every non-official who catches a monk will get fifty taels. This is signed with the king's own hand. Thus you see we are helpless." Then said Sun, "You might as well die and end it all."

They replied, "A great many have died. We monks in this country at one time numbered over two thousand, but we perish in our sufferings. Six or seven hundred have already died, seven or eight hundred have committed suicide. There now remain only about five hundred of us and we cannot die. Ropes cannot strangle us, swords cannot cut us, we plunge into the river to drown ourselves, but float on top instead of sinking; we take poison, but it does not kill us." Sun said, "Then you are favored, you are all immortals." "Alas, we are only immortal in order to suffer. In the day we get only poor food. At night we have only this sand to sleep on. But at night there come spirits amongst us and tell us in our dreams not to kill ourselves, for there will come an *arhat* from the East to deliver us. With him there is a disciple, the Great Sage, the Equal of Heaven, most powerful and noble and tender hearted. He will put an end to these Taoists and ensure that we Buddhists are respected."

Inwardly Sun was glad to hear that his fame had gone abroad.

He then left the Buddhist monks and returned to the city gate. There he met the two chief Taoists. They asked him if he had found his relative. He replied, "Yes, they are all my relatives!" The two smiled and said, "How is it that you have so many relatives?" Sun said, "One hundred are my father's relatives, one hundred are my mother's relatives and the others are my adopted relatives. If you let all these monks depart with me, then I will enter the city with you, otherwise I will not enter." "You must be mad to talk in this way to us. These monks belong to us—they are gifts from the king. If you had only asked for one or two, we could have arranged it. What you ask for is altogether unreasonable." Sun said to them three times, "Do you really mean not to liberate them?" When they finally said they could not, Sun became very angry, took his magic spear from his ear and shook it, and their heads fell off at once.

When the Buddhist monks saw this at a distance, they ran and cried, "Murder! Murder! The Taoist priests are being killed!" They surrounded Sun, saying, "These priests are our masters. They go to the temple without visiting the king, and they return to their homes without taking leave of the king. The king is always spoken of as their chief priest. How is it that you come and make trouble here and kill his disciples? The Taoist chief priest will now say that we Buddhist monks have killed them. What shall we do? And if we go into the city with you, we are afraid you will have to pay for this with your life." Sun laughed and said, "Friends, do not trouble yourselves about this. I am Sun Wukong, the Great Sage, a disciple of the Holy Master from China, seeking Sacred Scriptures in the West, and I have come to save you." They all answered, "No, no, you cannot be Sun, for we know him." He replied, "You have not met him, how can you therefore know him?" They replied, "We have often seen him in our dreams. The Minister of Venus has described him to us and warned us not to make a mistake." "What did he say to you?" They replied, "He has a hard head, bright eyes, a round face, and a hairy face without cheeks, sharp teeth, pointed mouth, hot temper, and is uglier than the God of Thunder. He uses a steel club, made a disturbance in Heaven itself, but is now a penitent, and is coming with the Buddhist pilgrim for the express purpose of saving men from trouble and calamities." Hearing this, Sun was both angry and glad, and could not help saying, "Friends, it is true you know that I am not Sun himself. I am only his disciple come here to learn how to manage things. But is that not Sun Wukong himself coming?" He pointed with his hand. At this all looked in the direction in which he pointed.

During this interval, he changed from a Taoist and appeared in his true form. At this they all fell down and kowtowed, begging his pardon that their mortal eyes could not recognize him. "We implore you to enter the city, and compel the demons there to repent, and follow righteousness." Sun cried out, "Follow me," and they did, first to the sand, where they emptied two carts and smashed them into splinters, and then took the bricks and tiles and timber and threw them all into a heap calling upon all the monks to disperse. "Tomorrow," said Sun, "I am going to see the king and I will destroy these Taoists! They said, "Sir, we dare not go far, lest they attempt to seize you and there will be trouble." "Since you think so, I will give you a charm for your protection." So saying the Great Sage pulled out some hairs, and gave one to each to put on his ring finger, and to hold firmly. "If any one attempts to catch you, hold firmly to this, call out "Great Sage, the Equal of Heaven," and I will come and save you, though I should be ten thousand miles away." Some of them tried the charm and, sure enough, he stood before them like the God of Thunder. In his hand was an iron club so that an army of ten thousand men and horses could not get near him. After this about a hundred monks came up together and said, "There are a hundred Great Sages protecting us!" They kowtowed to Sun and said, "It is perfectly marvelous how your magic works!" So Sun went off to see the king to find out what was going on.

The king said, "Our country is suffering from drought, and although there are charges against you of murdering two Taoist priests, setting free five hundred slaves, and desecrating our temple, we will forgive you if you can bring rain. Can you do better than the Taoists? I will go to the top of the Five Phoenix Hall to watch you. First the Taoists will show their skill." The Taoist priest who was the Royal Wizard followed the king into the gallery while the Master and his disciples remained below. A messenger came running in to say that everything was ready for the altar. The Royal

Wizard said, "When you hear my first signal, the wind will come, at my second signal, the clouds will come, at my third signal, thunder and lightning will follow, at my fourth signal, rain will come, at my fifth signal, the clouds and rain will cease."

He mounted a platform about fifty feet high, all round which were banners with illustrations of the Twenty-eight Constellations. In the middle was a table, and on it was an incense burner and candles. Beside them was a golden tablet on which was written, "God of Thunder." Below these were five big jars full of clean water. Floating on the water were willow branches on which was an iron tablet whereon was written, "The Charm of the Master of the Thunder Hall." On the right and left were five boards on which were written the names of the Mistress of the Wind and the Master of Thunder. Beside each board there stood two Taoist priests each holding an iron banner. Behind them there were a great many Taoist fortunetellers and writers of charms.

A small Taoist presented the Great Wizard with a book of charms written on yellow paper and with a precious sword. The Wizard pronounced an incantation, took a charm and burnt it in a candle. Then he tapped the table as the first signal. Truly enough, at once it began to blow. Sun, at this, whispered to his companions, "Do not speak to me for some time, as I am going to attend to some private business." The Great Sage then plucked a hair and changed it into his own form to remain there by his Master, while he himself mounted the clouds and shouted out, "Mistress of the Wind, what are you doing? Instead of helping me, who is going to fetch the Sacred Scriptures from the West, you are helping a demon! Bid the wind to cease or I will give you twenty blows with my steel staff!'" The Mistress of the Wind at once bade the wind to cease.

The Wizard now struck the table as his second signal and the clouds gathered all over the heavens. At the sight of this, Sun shouted out, "Who is Master of the Clouds?" A young man came forward and bowed, and Sun threatened him with twenty blows if he did not disperse the clouds at once. Immediately after this, the sun shone forth brightly and there was not a cloud in the sky for ten thousand *li*.

At this, the Wizard cut loose his hair with the sword, recited an incantation and burnt another charm. Then he struck the table as his third signal. At this, from the south gate of heaven there appeared the Master of Thunder and the Mistress of Lightning before Sun and bowed to him. Sun reprimanded them, as he had done the others, for helping the demons so earnestly instead of helping him. They replied that the charms and dispatches had been burnt, and sent to the Jade Emperor by the Wizard, and the edict they had received was a genuine one ordering them to help in thunder, lightning, and rain. Sun said, "Since it is so, wait here and serve me now." There was no thunder and no lightning after this.

This made the Wizard still more anxious, and he burnt more incense and charms and recited more incantations and struck the table as his fourth signal. Instantly the dragons from the four oceans appeared.

Sun cried out above their heads, "Aoguang, where do you think you are going?" Aoguang and his companions came forward and bowed. Then Sun told them what he had told the other helpers before, and added, "You helped me before though not successfully. Today I hope you will help me with success." The Dragon King replied, "I gladly obey your orders." Sun said, "I beg of you to give me a helping hand. The Wizard's signal of the fourth performance is now finished. It is now my turn, and I expect you all to help me. I burn no incense and have no signal but my club. When I lift up my spear the first time, I want the wind to blow." The Mistress of the Wind said, "The wind shall blow."

"When I lift up my spear the second time, I want the clouds to gather." The Master of the Clouds said, "The clouds shall gather."

"When I lift up my spear the third time, I want thunder and lightning." The Master of Thunder and Mistress of Lightning said, "You shall have them in abundance."

"When I lift up my spear the fourth time, I want rain." The Dragon replied, "Your orders shall be obeyed."

"When I lift up my spear the fifth time, I want a clear sky without fail." Having arranged this, he restored the false Sun and took his place. He shouted out, "Master Wizard, your fourth signal for performance is now over and there has been neither wind, clouds, thunder, lightning, nor rain. Now it is my time to try."

The Wizard came down from his platform altar and went to the gallery by the king, and the Monkey followed him. The king asked the wizard how it was that none of his four attempts were success-ful. The wizard replied, "The rain king was not at home today." The Monkey angrily replied, "The dragon gods were all at home, but your Royal Wizard is not sufficiently skilful." The king then ordered the Buddhist monks to mount the platform. Sun invited the Master to go, but he said he could not command rain. The Monkey said, "You just pray, and I will do the rest."

The Master therefore mounted the platform and reverently prayed the Heart Sutra. Sun quickly took out his spear from his ear and raised the point of it to the sky. Immediately the sound of wind filled the place, not of ordinary wind, but of a great typhoon, and tiles were lifted off the roofs, and bricks rolled about, with gravel and stones.

Then he raised the point of his spear a second time, and mist and clouds darkened all like night.

Then he raised the point of his spear a third time, and then thunder and lightning broke forth as if the earth and mountains were split asunder, and so terrified the people that every family in the city burnt incense and paper money to their gods.

Then he raised the point of his spear the fourth time, and rain fell as if buckets were being emptied, and all the streets were run-ning with rivers, so that the king cried out, "Enough, enough!" The Monkey raised his spear point a fifth time, and immediately the wind, the thunder and lightning, and rain ceased, and the clouds cleared away to the great joy of all.

Then a second contest took place as to who could sit longest without moving when bugs and centipedes were crawling over their bodies. Then a third contest took place to discover what was in a closed chest, a peach kernel, or a Taoist priest. After failing in each of these, the Taoists proposed three feats, first, to cut one's head off and put it back on again, secondly, to cut out one's heart and put it back in again, thirdly, to be cast into boiling oil and not suffer. Sun accepted the challenge, but when the Taoist priests tried their arts, they perished.

> What is the use of playing with unknown materials?
> It is waste of labor, and small successes are of no value.

16
The Demon of the House

THE FALSE TEACHERS, the Tiger, the Deer, and the Sheep, were now exterminated. On leaving the city, Sun spoke to the king and people, "The three religions should be one. The Buddhists deserve respect, the Taoists deserve respect, and so also do the Confucianists, who train men's minds. If you protect these three religions the nation will be permanently prosperous."

The pilgrims then pursued their journey. Time flew and the autumn came. One evening the Master said, "Let us rest." They found themselves at the River of Heaven, 800 *li* wide. They saw a village, and sought lodgings there. They found a family named Chen, from whom they learnt that the monks, in a monastery close by, demanded the sacrifice of a boy and girl every year, along with offerings of pigs and goats, to avert a great calamity. In the house there were two old men, father and son, one over sixty, the other over fifty, but though they were very wealthy, they had but one son and one daughter of eight and seven years of age respectively, to perpetuate the family. Now the order had come from the Demon King of the river that these two children were to be given in sacrifice on the morrow. The old men were broken hearted at the cruelty and oppression of the Demon King and the monks. Sun proposed that he, possessing seventy-two magic arts, and Zhu Bajie possessing thirty-six arts, should transform themselves into the shape of this boy and girl, and offer themselves for sacrifice. They were carried to the temple and presented there.

After the people had made their offerings and dispersed to their homes the Demon King came to eat the sacrifice. Zhu Bajie and Sun then resumed their true forms and attacked him. After they had fought, Sun told him who they were, and demanded that he should restore to life all the children sacrificed to him in previous years. But the demon escaped into the River of Heaven, where he planned with his family how to revenge himself. A witch suggested that the demon should command a cold wind and snow to come, so that the river should be frozen, and that then, while the pilgrims were crossing, it would be easy to make the ice break. The demon was greatly pleased and commanded the snow to fall.

Meanwhile Zhu Bajie and Sun took all the offerings from the temple to the Chen family, and told their hosts and the Master what had taken place. Next morning, they awoke to find the land covered with deep snow. The hosts begged the pilgrims to wait till the weather was warmer, but the Master resolved to proceed. Zhu Bajie went on ahead to test the ice, and found it was quite solid. So they parted from their kind hosts, and the Master rode over the ice. Suddenly they heard a rumbling noise below and the white horse fell. Now the demon had been waiting for the sound of the horse's feet to make the ice give way. He seized on the Master and dragged him beneath, calling out, "Come, all of you! We will feast on his flesh so that we may become immortal!" But the witch, afraid of Sun's revenge, persuaded the demon to wait for two days, and they hid the Master in a stone coffer.

In the meantime, the disciples thought the Master was drowned. They went back to the Chen family with the sad news. The old men wept bitterly, but Sun said, "I am sure my Master is not drowned. This must be a trick on the part of the demon. Give us some food, and we will go in search of the Master." Then they all took their weapons and went into the river to find the demon.

Sun, Zhu Bajie, and Sha the Monk dived all three into the river and traveled about a hundred *li* until they found the Master imprisoned by the Demon King, who had been attacked at the temple. There ensued a fight, but the three of them alone could not conquer him.

Sun, in despair went in search of Guanyin. She gave him a bamboo basket, saying that he had only to show it to the old tortoise who was in charge of the river and he would liberate the Master and ferry them over the river. The old tortoise gladly did so, saying, "I have heard that the Buddha in Paradise is without Beginning or

End, and knows the Past and the Future. I have served him here for 1,300 years. I have lived long and my body has become light, and I can speak the language of man. I wish to get rid of this shell on my back. Please speak for me. That is all the reward I ask for this little service."

It was now winter, and the pilgrims were climbing a high mountain by a narrow pass, and the Master was afraid of wild beasts. The three disciples bade him not be afraid as they were all united, and were all good men seeking truth. Being cold and hungry they greatly rejoiced to see a fine building ahead of them, but Sun said, "It is another demon trap. I will make a ring round you. Inside that you will be safe. Do not wander outside it. I will go and look for food." By magic and skill Sun managed to get his begging bowl full of food, and returned to the Master. But the Master and his disciples had become tired of waiting inside the ring, and had gone to explore a fine building nearby. Zhu Bajie went in to look. Not a soul was to be seen, but when he entered one of the back rooms upstairs, he was terrified out of his wits, for there was a white human skeleton of immense size lying there. He was about to flee when he saw three wadded cloaks which he took to keep the pilgrims warm. The Master upbraided Zhu Bajie, and would have had him restore them at once. By this time, however, the Demon of the House descended on them, bound the Master and said, "We have heard that if we eat a bit of your flesh our white hairs shall become black again, and our lost teeth spring up afresh." So he gave orders to the small demons to bind the three. This they did, and thrust the pilgrims into a cave, and lay in wait for Sun. When he returned, there was a great fight. Sun by magic called forth a hundred thousand snakes which so frightened the small demons that they all ran to their cave. But they succeeded in robbing Sun of his magic club.

> When your virtue has grown one foot,
> The demon's tares have grown ten feet.
> What a pity the soul often has no steady purpose.
> But is led astray by circumstances.

The Great Sage, empty handed, having lost the battle, cried bitterly, and called out, "Master, I had hoped to bear testimony with you, and practice religion with you till I was saved by the same

Providence, and had the same magic power, little thinking that I should now be helpless without my weapons to do good." He then went up to heaven to ask for aid, but finally he was cast on his own resources, and managed to regain some of the stolen weapons.

At night Sun, by various magic arts, entered the demon's cave and tried to take possession of a magic coil belonging to him. But failing in this, he called forth a number of small monkeys, who took away most of the demon's weapons and set fire to the cave. Half of the small demons were burnt. But the Demon of the House, by means of his magic coil, put out the fire and Sun was not able to rescue the Master and his fellow pilgrims, who still remained bound. In the morning the Demon of the House again fought against Sun, and with the aid of his magic coil, recaptured all his stolen weapons, so that again they were helpless.

Sun then went to the Spiritual Mountain and sought the help of Buddha himself. Eighteen *arhats* were sent back with him to help him against the demon. When Sun once more attacked him, the *arhats* threw diamond dust into the air, which blinded and half buried the demon. But, throwing his magic coil, he was able to gather up all the diamond dust and carry it back to his cave.

The *arhats* then advised Sun to see the Ancient of Days, who knew more about this particular demon than any one else. So Sun went to the Palace of the Ancient of Days, where he found that the Demon of the House was none other than one of the deity's ox angels who had stolen the magic coil from the Palace and had gone down to earth as ox demons It was the same coil with which Sun himself had been subdued, when he had rebelled against Heaven.

The Ancient of Days mounted a cloud and reached the cave with Sun. He called upon the Demon of the House to come forth. When the demon saw who it was, he was terrified. The Ancient of Days recited an incantation, and the demon yielded up the magic coil to him. At a second incantation, all his strength left him and he appeared as a bull, and was led away by a ring in his nose. All the little demons were destroyed. The Master and the pilgrims were then liberated and set on their way.

Before long they heard a man cry out, "Holy monk, stop and take some food before you go." It was one of the *arhats* that had helped to subjugate the demon. He held in his hand a golden bowl of rice, saying, "Holy monk, this bowl of rice was collected by Sun when he left you within the magic circle. Because you would not wait for him, you fell into the demon's hands. Take it now and eat!" Thus was the bowl of food at last delivered to the Master. He was deeply grateful for his disciple's efforts. Sun replied, "All this trouble happened because you went outside the magic circle I drew round you, but you thought you would be safe in other folds. It is all owing to your foolishness, Zhu the Pig! Fortunately, Buddha and the Ancient of Days put an end to the trouble and saved us."

17
True Monkeys and False Monkeys

ON THEIR WAY THE PILGRIMS MET a band of robbers, and Sun killed two of them. At night they lodged in the house of the father of the robber chieftain. The father and mother treated the pilgrims kindly, and gave them food and lodging. At midnight the gang of robbers, led by the son, returned to the house and discussed how they should take their revenge on the pilgrims. The father, overhearing their talk, secretly advised the pilgrims to depart early, which they did. But Sun was angry with the wicked son and killed him. At this the Master was very angry. "Being a follower of my religion, how is it that you kill people? Yesterday you killed two, and today you have killed the son of our kind host. Being a blood thirsty man you must leave me, I cannot keep you any longer."

Alas, how true it is that when the heart is mad with passion the great treasure cannot be procured. When one's mind is not clear, it is difficult to succeed.

Sun, after being banished by the Master as unworthy to be his disciple, was in great distress. He was unwilling to return to his Waterfall Cave, for he would appear disgraced. He therefore decided not to return to his cave, but to go to Guanyin in the Southern Ocean. After mounting the clouds, he soon arrived and was admitted to her presence. He prostrated himself before her and shed bitter tears. Guanyin said, "What is the matter?" Sun replied, "Ever since you delivered me from the punishment of Heaven, and bade me go with the Buddhist pilgrim to fetch the Sacred Scriptures from the West, I have served him most faithfully and have risked my life many times in saving his. But now, just because I killed a few robbers who would, but for me, have killed him, he is most ungrateful, and sends me away in disgrace. Therefore I have come to you to do me justice. Guanyin said, "The robbers were human beings, and therefore you should not have killed them, even to save your Master. You should practice kindness as well as preach it." At this the Monkey confessed his sin, but added "I have rendered some service, and this should not be forgotten before sending me away in disgrace. I beg of you to pity me. I return to you the magic cap of spikes with which I am so often punished, and now let me return to my old home in the Waterfall Cave." Guanyin replied, "The magic cap was given me by Buddha himself." Then said the Monkey, "Let me go and return it to him." Guanyin said, "No, wait until I see your Master. He will soon be in danger again and will need your help."

Meanwhile, after Sun had been sent away, the Master on his horse traveled on his way a whole day without anything to eat, and he became weak from hunger. Zhu Bajie asked him to dismount and rest, while he would see if there were any habitations near, where he could beg food. The Master was also suffering from thirst, and Sha the Monk went away in search of some water, leaving the Master, the horse, and the baggage by the side of the road. Hunger and thirst seemed hard to bear, for the disciples were long gone away from their homes and their goal.

Suddenly there was a stir in the sky, and he saw what seemed like Sun appear with a cup of water for the Master. But seeing it was Sun who brought it, the Master would not touch it. He would rather die of hunger and thirst than touch anything given him by that bloodthirsty monkey. Sun Wukong said, "If you die, what will become of your great mission to fetch the Sacred Scriptures?" "What is that to you? Go away, go away, do not come and trouble me any more." Now this was in fact a demon impersonating Sun. He got very angry and struck the Master with his club, so that he fell fainting in the dust on the road. Then the false Sun went away, carrying the black felt bag, which contained the edicts and passports from the Emperor of China and the other rulers through whose regions they had passed.

During this interval Zhu Bajie had found a house, where an old woman had given him some food. This he carried back to the Master, after which he took him and Sha the Monk to the old woman's house, for a night's lodging. Sha was sent in search of the felt bag and documents and was told if he could not find them, to go on the clouds to Guanyin to ask her help.

> When the mind wanders from the body,
> The form is without life.
> When the passions are rebellious
> You must wait till they submit.

After three days and three nights, Sha arrived at the Waterfall Cave, where he found the false Sun seated on a rock, reading aloud the imperial edict spread out before him, in which it was written how the emperor had died and had descended into hell, but that the authorities there had allowed him to return to earth again, and he had made a vow to save the souls of the lost. Guanyin had also graciously said that the Sacred Scripture in the West could save the dead spirits from torment. "I have therefore commanded the monk Xuanzang to travel far to the West in search of these wonderful Scriptures so as to have them made known in the East. Let none of the rulers, through whose lands he must pass, hinder him in his holy mission."

This was dated the 13th year of Zhenguan and was stamped by the emperor's seal in nine places. The pilgrim was to be accompanied by his chief disciple, the Sun the Seeker of Emptiness, Zhu the Seeker of Strength, and Sha the Seeker of Purity. And so on and so on.

On hearing this Sha the Monk could not wait any longer, but cried out, "Brother Sun, the Master has lost his felt bag and the emperor's edict, and now I see you have them. Do not heed the Master's behavior towards you. Come back and let us continue our journey for the Sacred Scriptures. But if you are unwilling to return, I beg of you a thousand times to let me have the bag with the emperor's edict."

The false Sun laughed coldly and said, "Having read this edict, I will myself go to the West for the Sacred Scriptures and acquire merit and make a name for myself that shall never be forgotten." Sha the Monk replied, "That is impossible! It was never said that a monkey was to procure the Scriptures. If the Master does not go with you, Buddha will not give you the Scriptures." The impostor answered, "But I have provided myself with a duplicate Master."

So saying, he gave an order to one of the monkeys, who led out of the cave the white horse and the Master, followed by Zhu Bajie with the baggage, and Sha the Monk with his staff. When Sha saw the procession, he was filled with wrath and cried out, "How comes it that there is another Sha?" And he struck at the false Sha with his staff and killed him.

Then the false Sun brandished his magic club, and led out all the monkeys against Sha the Monk, but he escaped and fled to the Southern Ocean to seek help from Guanyin. There he found the true Sun with her. Thinking it was the impostor arrived there before him to tell a lying tale, he struck at him with the staff and cursed him. Guanyin told him to be calm and relate what had happened. Then after hearing his tale, she said, "Sun Wukong has been here for four days. It cannot be he that has created an impostor Master to fetch the Sacred Scriptures." Then Sha proposed that Sun should go with him to the Waterfall Cave and see the demon impostor for himself.

When Sun Wukong and Sha the Monk arrived at the Waterfall Cave, they found the impostor sitting on the stone terrace drinking wine. Then Sun's anger was kindled and he went forward and cursed the demon who was impersonating him, and taking possession of his home. They engaged in combat. Sha the Monk wished greatly to help, but was much perplexed: the two were so much alike that he feared he might aid the false one. So he went into the cave in search of the Master's bag with the imperial edict. But he could not find it.

When he came out, the two were still fighting. They both cried out to him to return to the Master, and tell him all that had taken place. Sha the Monk was still more perplexed, as their words were the same, and their appearance identical.

The two monkeys, still fighting, made their way to the Southern Ocean. Guanyin and her attendants came forth to see them. Both of them cried out to her, "This monkey has taken my shape, and we have been fighting all the way from the Waterfall Cave. I have come to beg you to help me." Guanyin and her fairies looked from one to the other, but could not detect any difference between them.

She bade them cease from fighting, and she again scrutinized them. Then she called for Mucha and the Red Child, who was now called Sadhana the Page, to come forth, and said to them, "I am going to pronounce a certain incantation and you must watch carefully and note which of them complains of pain in the head." So she recited the incantation to cause the spikes of Sun's cap to enter his head, but both of them cried out to her to cease, for the spikes were piercing the heads of both of them.

Finally they went up to Heaven so that the Jade Emperor should decide. The true Sun made his complaint that he was escorting the Buddhist pilgrim from China to fetch the Sacred Scriptures from the West, but that he was attacked on the way, and that the imperial edict had been stolen, and carried to his old home the Waterfall Cave, by the false Sun, who had appropriated everything there. The false Sun asserted exactly the same thing, and the Jade Emperor was not able to decide which was the true Monkey King.

Then all decided to go and see the Master, and let him decide which was which. On being confronted with them, the Master realized that the one who had robbed and beaten him must have been a demon. But the two were so exactly alike, and each asserted the same of the other, that even the Master could not decide between them.

Then they decided to go to hell and search the records there. But it was equally in vain, as no monkey name had been preserved there since the Monkey King had visited them and confused their records. Therefore none there could decide. However, before leaving, one of the Ministers of Hell said, "We know the names of all the demons, but must not disclose them in their presence, lest a riot should arise below. We dare not help the true one, for the magic powers of the false one are exactly equal to the true, and therefore the true is unable to arrest the false." The Doorman of Hell therefore said to them both, "Since you are identical in form and appearance, and have exactly the same magic powers, I advise you to go to Shakyamuni and let him decide for you." Thus the Gates of Hell were opened, and the two eagerly went to see Shakyamuni.

> A double-minded man gets into trouble,
> On land and sea he is in the midst of doubt,
> Trusting in his fine horse and three faithful servants,

Relying on magic spears and highest service.
In North and South without success,
In East and West troubles rise.
Seeking heaven you must sacrifice your own will,
Then there is new birth and growth into a saint.

The two Suns pressed and fought on, till they came to the Assembly of the Sages, where were the four great *bodhisattvas*, hundreds of *arhats* and innumerable other holy disciples, whom the Buddha had taught of the transcendental mysteries of Universal Law.

Lord Buddha said to the Assembly, "You are all of one mind. Now behold the double minded ones!" The two Suns quarreled fiercely, each claiming the same thing, and asked Lord Buddha to decide. He said, "There are but five classes of Immortals in the Universe: those of heaven, those of earth, those of gods, those of men, those of spirits.

There are but five classes of creatures: men, fish, hairy creatures, feathered creatures and worms.

These two Suns do not belong to any of these ten classes, but to the four classes of monkeys.

1. The first is the clever stone monkey, that knows magic, knows the times and seasons, and knows the treasures of earth and sky.

2. The second is a bare tailed horse monkey, that knows light and darkness and human affairs, is skilful in going in and out, and can avoid death and prolong life.

3. The third is the sliding long armed monkey, that holds the sun and moon in his hands, can compress a thousand mountains, knows what is lucky and unlucky, and plays with heaven and earth, as if they were mere balls.

4. The fourth is the six-eared monkey, that hears at great distances, understands the principles of things, knows the past and future, and all things are perfectly clear to him.

Lord Buddha said, "It is this six-eared monkey who is the false one." At this the false monkey was greatly alarmed, transformed himself into a bee, and tried to fly away, but Buddha put a pot over it, which prevented its escape. The true Sun could not contain himself any longer, and struck it dead with his club, and so ended this species of monkey, and none have appeared since.

Meanwhile Zhu Bajie had gone to the Mountain Cave and found the false Master and the false disciples. He killed them and discovered they were only monkeys transformed. He then brought back the felt bag and stolen documents. Thus once more the four true pilgrims started on their westward journey.

> Discord on the way disturbs all things.
> Demons take advantage and unite in mischief.
> When one's soul is at rest, religion is well founded,
> The senses are clear, and life is assured.

18
The Flaming Mountain

HAVING THROWN OFF THEIR SUSPICIONS, the Master and Sun marched on together, but they began to feel the heat greatly, although it was autumn. They were in the Land of Sahar, where everything was red—red walls, red tiles, red varnish on doors and furniture. Sixty *li* from this was a place called Flaming Mountain, which lay on their way westwards.

An old man there said it was only possible to cross the Flaming Mountain if they had a magic Iron Fan which at the first shake could quench fire, at the second shake could produce strong wind, and at the third shake produce rain. This magic fan was kept by a wizard called the Iron Fan Wizard in a cave at Kingfisher Green Cloud Mountain, 1,500 *li* away. On hearing this, Sun mounted a cloud and was there in a moment. After arriving there, he found there was no Iron Fan Wizard, but an Iron Fan Princess, a typical *raksha* or female demon.

She was the mother of the red Demon Child with whom Sun had fought earlier, and who had since become a disciple of Guanyin. On hearing that Sun the Monkey King had called, she was very angry, and wanted to have her revenge for the outwitting of her husband, the Ox-Head Demon, and for the taking away of her son. He said, "If you lend me the Iron Fan I will bring your son to see you." She did not believe him and struck him with a sword. He then fought her long, and she, feeling her strength failing, took out the Magic Fan and gave it a shake. With the wind it raised, Sun was blown away 84,000 *li* and whirled about like a leaf in a whirlwind. But he soon returned with increased magic powers provided by a helpful *bodhisattva*. But the *raksha* deceived him, and gave him another fan, which increased the flames instead of lessening them. So Sun and his party had to retreat more than twenty *li,* or they would have been burnt by the flames of the mountain.

Then the local mountain gods appeared, bringing them refreshments, and urging them to get the Magic Fan before they could proceed. Sun pointed to his fan and said, "Is this not the Magic Fan?" They smiled and said, "No, this is a false one which the princess has given you."

The local gods said, "Originally there was no Flaming Mountain here, but when you upset the furnace in Heaven 500 years ago, the fire fell here, and has been burning ever since, and we have had to look after it as a punishment for not having taken more care in Heaven. The Ox-Head Demon married the *raksha* only to desert her some two years ago for the only daughter of a fox king. They live at Jilei Mountain, some 3,000 *li* from here. If you can get the true Magic Fan through his help, you will be able to end the fire, take your Master to the West, save the lives of many beings around here, and enable us to return to Heaven once more."

Having heard this, Sun mounted on a cloud and arrived at Jilei Mountain. There he met the fox princess, the present wife of the Ox-Head Demon, whom he upbraided and pursued back to her cave. The Ox-Head Demon came out and became very angry with Sun for having terrified her. Sun asked him to return to his previous wife, the *raksha*, and beg the Magic Fan of her. This the Ox-Head Demon refused to do. Then they fought three times together, and Sun was victorious. With the consent of the Ox-Head Demon, Sun assumed his shape and visited the *raksha*. He was very nice to her. She, thinking he really was the Ox-Head Demon, gladly received him back, and finally gave him the Magic Fan to keep. Having obtained this, he hurriedly left, and set out to see his Master.

On the way back, the Ox-Head Demon followed after Sun and saw him, joyfully carrying the Magic Fan on his shoulder. Now Sun had forgotten to ask how to make it small, and like an apricot leaf, as it was at first. The Ox-Head Demon, wishing to revenge himself on Sun, changed himself into the likeness of Zhu Bajie. He went up to Sun and said, "I am glad to see you come back, brother Sun, have you succeeded?" "Yes," replied Sun, and he described his fights, and how he had deceived the Ox-Head Demon's former wife into giving him the magic fan. The Ox-Head Demon, now impersonating Zhu Bajie, said, "You must be very tired after all your efforts, let me carry the Magic Fan for you." As soon as he got it into his hands, he appeared in his true form, cursed Sun with all the evil names he could think of, and they fought with all their might. The Ox-Head Demon wished to use the Magic Fan to blow Sun away 84,000 *li,* but did not know that the Great Sage had swallowed the wind-resisting pill, and was therefore surprised to find him immovable. He then put the Magic Fan in his mouth and fought with his two swords. He was a match for Sun in all his magic arts, but Sun, being helped by Zhu Bajie and the local gods whom the Master had sent, proved himself stronger. The demon changed himself many times into a number of birds, but for each of these Sun was able to change himself into a swifter and stronger one. Then the demon changed himself into many beasts, such as tigers, leopards, bears, elephants, and an ox 10,000 feet long, then laughed and said to Sun, "What can you do to me now?" Sun took his steel club and cried out "Grow!" and suddenly he grew to be 100,000 feet high, with eyes like the sun and moon. They fought till the heavens and the earth shook with their onslaughts.

> When one's virtue is one foot high, the Demon's arts are ten
> thousand feet high in order to overcome virtue.
> If the flames of passions are to be put out, we must get the
> Magic Fan to cool our desires.
> When the will is not supreme, one must seek the help of the
> Supreme,
> The passions and the supreme will must live in harmony.
> Then all classes of society will be at peace.
> Demons are turned, the unclean are purified, and all go together
> towards Heaven.

As this Ox-Head Demon was so terrible, both Buddha in Paradise and the Jade Emperor in his Celestial Palace sent down whole legions of celebrated warriors to help Sun and the others. The demon tried to escape by the North, by the South, by the East, and by the West, but in all these efforts he was baffled. Being defeated,

孫行者調三芭蕉扇

Sun Puts Out Fire by the Magic Fan.

both he and his wife promised to give up their wicked ways and follow the Buddhist principles of kindness.

The Magic Fan was given to Sun, who tested its magic. After the first shake, the flames of the mountain died out. After the second shake a cool gentle breeze arose. After the third, gentle rain fell everywhere, and the pilgrims proceeded on their journey in comfort.

19

The Demon of the Thunder Temple

THE MASTER AND HIS DISCIPLES TRAVELED on till they came to a city. On entering the city, they saw a number of monks, clad in rags and locked with handcuffs. On enquiry they were told that the city had formerly been the capital of a great country in the West. Four nations had paid tribute to it yearly: Yue in the South, Gaochang in the North, Xiliang in the East, and Benbo in the West. These tributes were precious stones, beautiful women, and fine horses. The country was at peace, and the surrounding nations had honored it as chief amongst them. Then the Master said, "Your king and his ministers, civil and military, must all have been fine men." The monks replied, "On the contrary, all were bad. Our monastery, the Temple of the Golden Light, with its thirteen storied pagoda, which was once most beautiful, is now falling rapidly into ruins. Three years ago there fell a shower of blood, which made the whole temple stink, and nobody comes near it now. Its glory has departed."

The Master determined he would cleanse the pagoda himself that very night. Sun helped him, but the Master at the tenth story got tired. Sun said, "Go to rest, I will clean the upper stories myself." When he reached the top story he found two demons feasting there. He at once attacked and arrested them.

Next morning the Master asked to see the king to present his credentials. Then it was disclosed that the ruin of the monastery, of the monks, and of the capital was owing to the work of these demons. When examined by the Master, they had confessed that three years before a Dragon King of ten thousand powers, ruling about four hundred *li* to the South East of this country, in a mountain called the Wild Rock, had a lovely daughter, whom he gave in marriage to a Nine-Headed Demon of unparalleled magic power. These two, father and son-in-law, had caused the shower of blood to fall, and then had stolen the gold off the cupola of the pagoda, and the reliquary now illuminated the Dragon Palace, so that the night had become like day. The daughter had also stolen the magic mushrooms from the Queen of Heaven. The two demons were not the chiefs of the Wild Rock, but were simply minor officials sent to the pagoda to look after things.

The king asked that Sun should lead an army to put down these robbers. Sun Wukong and Zhu Bajie, however, said they needed no army, but wished the two prisoners to act as their guides to the Wild Rock. Sun Wukong and Zhu Bajie went to the Dragon Palace and fought hard. They obtained the assistance of seven brothers coming back from a hunt, to whom they told their story.

Finally the Dragon King and his nine-headed son-in-law were killed, and the reliquary belonging to the top of the pagoda, and the magic mushrooms of the Queen of Heaven, were restored. The Temple name was changed from that of the Temple of Golden Light to the Temple of the Conquered Dragon. The King gave a banquet to the pilgrims, and wished to present them with silver for their journey, but they would not receive any, and the party departed.

The travelers now entered a forest of thorns, through which it would have been impossible to pass but for the labors of Zhu Bajie in clearing a path. On the top of the pass they saw what appeared to be a temple, where the Master wished to rest for the night. But Sun said, "I fear that in this place, good fortune is small and the danger great." At this moment the Master saw, as in a dream, some old men appear, who said, "You had better stay here for the night, for there are 800 *li* of wilderness before you." A gust of wind seemed to separate the Master from his disciples. He fancied that the three old men at the temple told him that they had heard of his coming, and that they invited him to stay and match some verses of poetry with them. They were in reality idle spirits in league with fairies, trying to seduce him. The Master, when asked about his religion, answered and said, "Our religion is quiet, our law is to save. It cannot be done without understanding. To understand one must first be pure in heart and without anxiety, and be rid of evil habits. It is not easy to be born as a man, or in the Middle Kingdom, and find the true religion. It is a great blessing to obtain all these three privileges, which few enjoy, by which one can avoid the mistakes of the senses and tradition. Wisdom is to know how to get rid of the necessity of rebirth, how to die without debt to anyone in the universe, to become beyond all form and no form, both human and divine, to seek truth and the origin of things, and link cause with effect, to understand the real miracle of enlightenment, the Enlightened One, to see through the net of illusion which surrounds us, and to attain enlightenment. For this, we must examine our understanding, and examine our comprehending, and get sure hold of that vital flame, which will illuminate the world, and reveal the spiritual world through all, in all its mystery and preserve it firmly. Who knows the passage from death to life? I strive to study the great depth of my religion. It is only those who have a will to follow it and who are called who can master it." After these words the spirits vanished and he regained his disciples. Soon there remained but a few trees instead of the structure the Master thought was a temple. It was no more than an illusion.

The four traveled on over a hill and saw a temple, on which was written "The Sound of Thunder Temple." The Master thought it must surely be the home of a famous *bodhisattva*. "Guanyin lives in the Southern Ocean, Samantabhadra lives in Mount Emei in Sichuan, Manjusri lives in Shansi, but I do not know what famous *bodhisattva* lives here. Let us go in." But Sun said, "I fear it is not safe to go in." But the Master insisted on going in. Sun said, "If you get into trouble, don't blame me."

They went in. There was the image of the Buddha, surrounded by 500 *arhats*, as well as the usual Four Temple Guardians and innumerable other images.

These figures filled the Master, Zhu Bajie, and Sha the Monk with awe, and they knelt and worshipped at every step; but Sun paid no respect to any of them. Then a loud voice cried out, "How is it that Sun, the chief disciple, does not worship Buddha?" At this Sun plucked up his steel club, and cried, "How dare you, false one, pretend to be the Buddha?" Suddenly Sun found himself imprisoned inside a metal sphere, where neither head nor hands were visible, while the Master was carried to one of the rooms behind. Sun became alarmed lest his Master should suffer harm. He applied his magic arts to enlarge himself, but the metal sphere grew equally large. Then he tried to become as small as a mustard seed, in the hope of getting out through a small hole, but the metal sphere became equally small also. Then, by magic, he called the spirits from the four quarters to come to his help. But none could move, nor turn over the sphere. They then hurried up to heaven for help, and the Forces of the Twenty-eight Constellations were ordered to go and help. When they came, they bored, after infinite labor, a tiny hole through which Sun came out. Then with his steel club he smashed the sphere into atoms. This awoke the Demon of the Thunder Temple, and he called all his followers to fight Sun and the Forces of the Constellations. They surrounded the Demon of the Thunder Temple, but he seemed in no way alarmed. He took out a magic bag in which he caught Sun and all his allies and carried them away as prisoners. Then he bound them all one by one with ropes, to keep them secure for his banquet. About midnight Sun made himself so small that he slipped out of his ropes. After that he went round and, loosening each of his fellow prisoners, he led them out. Unfortunately the demon again succeeded in putting the Master, Zhu Bajie, and Sha the Monk, together with the heavenly forces, into the bag. Sun wept at this, for he was loath to go again to Heaven to ask the Jade Emperor for aid yet again. Then he remembered that there was a military spirit of the Northern region, called The True Conqueror, and of him he decided to ask for help.

Now The True Conqueror was the ruler of the Pure Land Country, and had an all-powerful queen who, after swallowing a beam of light, had given birth to a son.

> Brave when he was young,
> Wise when he was grown,
> The throne he did not covet,
> Only virtue was his quest.
> Against his parents' wish,
> Palace joys he left,

> To study the Mysteries,
> In lonely hill retreats.
> When his work was finished,
> He ascended up in light,
> Received the name of Conqueror,
> The Equal One with Heaven.
> All demon forms and spirits
> That caused man's sin and woe
> Were put under his control.

Two generals, of the Tortoise and Serpent Stars, and five dragons were sent to help Sun against the Demon of the Thunder Temple. But after several fights they were captured. Sun was greatly disheartened, but the local gods told him not to lose courage, but to ask the *bodhisattva* of the Southern Continent for aid. He was a chief of exceeding mighty power, who had formerly subdued the Queen of the Ocean. After hearing Sun's tale, he sent his son and four of his generals to help him against the demon. But after fighting a long time, the demon captured them all in his magic bag, and, binding them, threw them into a vault. Then Sun went to the top of a hill near and wept in despair. In the midst of his grief, he saw a bright cloud approach from the Southwest and heard a voice calling him. This was no other than Lord Buddha himself.

Lord Buddha told Sun not to lose heart, but to attack the demon once more. This time, however, he was to retreat before the demon and lead him to a little temple at the foot of the hill, where there was a garden of melons. Sun was then to transform himself into a fine ripe melon, and Buddha would give him to the demon to eat. Once inside his enemy, Sun could have his revenge.

This plan greatly pleased Sun, and all was done as had been proposed. So Buddha, in the form of a gardener, gave the demon a large ripe melon to quench his thirst. As soon as Sun slipped down his throat, he caused such agony to the demon that he rolled on the ground, and the tears ran down his cheeks. Then Buddha made himself known to the demon, who was greatly terrified, and begged forgiveness. Lord Buddha then bade Sun come forth, and taking the demon's treasures from him he shut him up in the magic bag.

Then they returned to the Sound of Thunder Temple. The little demons could see that that their chief had been vanquished, and fled away in terror. But Sun pursued and killed them all. The Master and pilgrims were then discovered, and the heavenly allies were all liberated from the vault, and thanked Sun and the others for their assistance. Before the pilgrims resumed their journey they set fire to the temple which had been used to deceive worshippers. And that was the end of that.

20
Sun Becomes a Doctor

The Good get the help of ten thousand Providences.
Their fame spreads to the four continents,
Their wisdom shines on the life to come.
They are blown about to the ends of heaven.
All things serve them and they enjoy themselves forever,
They no longer believe in the dreams of earth.
They have cleansed themselves from all the dust of time.

THE PILGRIMS TRAVELED ON. Having arrived in the Land of Vermillion, the pilgrims presented the king with the imperial edict from the Emperor of China, in which he described his experiences in hell, how after three days he had been allowed to return to earth, and how, in order to commemorate the event, he had sent the Master in search of the Scriptures, which could save those who were suffering in hell.

Now the king of the Land of Vermillion was himself very ill, and had not been able to give audience for some time, therefore he was much interested in this story of the Emperor of China. He issued a proclamation that very day authorizing any able doctors to come and prescribe for him, adding that the one who could cure him would be rewarded with a share in his kingdom. At the sight of this proclamation, Sun decided to have some fun out of it. He offered to cure the king. But when he appeared, the sight of his face, and the manner of his speech, so terrified the king that he fell into a swoon, and the attendants were afraid to let him see the king again. But Sun said that it was not at all necessary for him to see the king again. "If you tie a silk thread to his wrist, I can at the other end find out his disease and prescribe for him." So a string attached to the king's palm, and the disease diagnosed by Sun the doctor at a distance.

The king admitted that his illness was a grief for the loss of his wife, whom an evil spirit had carried away. Sun at once mounted the clouds to find and attack the evil spirit.

> To pacify a nation, first attend to the king's illness.
> To obtain true religion, one must put away the love of evil.

Sun, accompanied by the king, went forth in search of the evil spirit who had imprisoned the king's wife. They found he possessed three great bells, the first of which, on being shaken, could produce smoke, the second of which could produce fire, and the third such a thick sand storm that the sun could not be seen. Now at first there appeared great smoke and fire. The Monkey, not knowing what it meant, changed himself into a fire cricket that the fire might do him no harm. He further took a cup of wine, which the demon was offering him, and threw its contents into the air. Soon there came a messenger who related that, when the fire was burning fiercely, a shower of rain, which had the smell of wine, fell and had extinguished the fire.

The demon then said, "Excuse me, Holy Pilgrim, asking you a question. Your face looks like a monkey. How is it that you know all these wonderful arts, and can travel enormous distances in no time?"

The Monkey answered and said, "Although my face has been like that of a monkey from my childhood, I have studied the way of life and death, and have everywhere sought a competent teacher to give me the right teaching. I have retired to the mountains and studied night and day, and relied on Heaven for eternal principles, and on earth for my practical experience. I have combined the two elements to produce a new one, I have mixed positive and negative properties as different as fire and water, and in time have discovered Nature's secret that all depends on trials under different conditions. Experiments with different elements are easy, and a little addition of one or of the other produces all Nature's combinations, according to the definite proportions of the various forces. When the positive and negative follow their respective laws, and the three forces of mind, matter, and life unite to form the Golden Pill of Immortality, then we can understand the laws which permeate all things.

> By trying to be wise, one becomes foolish,
> By playing with a vice, it becomes a bad habit.

So Sun transformed himself into one of the ladies in waiting on the queen, in order to gain possession of the three bells. To get the demon to show the bells, which were concealed under his clothes, Sun caused lice, fleas, and bugs to worry him, till he was compelled to take off his garments. The Monkey then took the genuine bells himself, and substituted false ones for the demon.

Sun then appeared outside the gates and called upon the demon to come out and fight him. He shook the three bells together. At once there appeared dense smoke, fierce flames, and blinding sand, such as were never seen before. The demon meantime, used his false bells, but could do nothing.

Infuriated at being tricked, the evil spirit wished to avenge himself on the queen for being in league with Sun. But a Taoist wizard came to her aid, and produced pins and needles all over her body, so that the demon could not approach near enough to injure her.

Finally Guanyin appeared, riding on a peacock, and called on Sun not to attack the evil demon any further. She also ordered Sun to give her the three bells, as they had been stolen from her a long time ago.

濯垢泉八

戒忘形

Zhu Bajie at the Bathing Pool.

21
The Spider Women

HAVING TRAVELED FAR ACROSS MANY MOUNTAINS, and passed both spring and autumn on the way, the pilgrims came to a village. The Master said, "You, my disciples, are always very good to me, taking round the begging bowl and finding food for me. Today I will take the begging bowl myself." Sun said, "That will never do! You should let us, your disciples, do this for you." But the Master insisted on going himself.

When he reached the village, there was not a man to be seen, but only four lovely women. He did not think it was right for him to speak to women. On the other hand, if he did not procure a supper, his disciples would laugh at him. After deliberating for a long time, he went forward and begged food of them. They received him heartily and invited him into their cave home. Having learnt who he was, they ordered some food for him, but it was all human flesh boiled or fried.

At the sight, the Master said he was a vegetarian. If he ate any of this meat he would never reach Paradise. He begged to be excused and rose to go. But the women would not let him go. They surrounded and bound him, thinking he would be a fine banquet for them the next day.

Then seven of the women went out to bathe in a pool. Meanwhile Sun, in search of his Master, found them bathing and would have killed them, only he thought it was not right to kill women. So he changed himself into an eagle and carried away their clothes to his nest. This so frightened the women, that they crouched in the pool, and none dared come out.

But Zhu Bajie, coming also in search of his Master, found the women bathing. He changed himself into a fish which the women tried to catch, chasing him hither and thither through the pool.

Then Zhu Bajie came out of the pool and appeared in his true form, and threatened the women for having bound his Master. In their fright the women fled out of the pool into a pavilion, round which they spun spiders' threads so thickly that Zhu Bajie became entangled and fell. Then they escaped to their cave and put on some clothes.

When Zhu Bajie was able to disentangle himself from the webs, he saw Sun Wukong and Sha the Monk approach. When they heard what had happened, they feared the women might do some mischief to the Master, so they made for the cave to rescue him. But on the way, they were beset by the seven dwarf sons of the seven women, who transformed themselves into a swarm of dragonflies, bees, and other insects. Then Sun pulled out some hairs and, changing them into seven different swarms of flying insects, destroyed the hostile swarm, and the ground was covered a foot deep with the dead bodies. Then the pilgrims reached the cave, and found it deserted by the women. They unbound the Master, making him promise never to beg for food again. He mounted on his horse and they proceeded on their journey.

The four pilgrims had only traveled a little way when they saw a great and fine building. It was a Taoist temple. Sha the Monk said, "Let us go in here, for Buddhism and Taoism teach the same things. They only differ in their vestments." The Taoist abbot received them civilly and ordered five cups of tea. Now he was in league with the seven women, and when the servant went in for tea, the sisters put poison in each cup. Sun, however, had suspected treason, and did not take his tea. Finding the rest poisoned, he then went and attacked the sisters, who transformed themselves into huge spiders. They could spin ropes out of their bellies and bind any enemy. He attacked and killed them.

At this the Taoist abbot showed himself in his true form, a demon with a thousand eyes. He gave fierce battle to Sun, and finally succeeded in putting him under an extinguisher. This was a new art which Sun could not understand. However, after trying to break out at the top and sides in vain, he thought he would bore downwards, and finding that the extinguisher was not deep in the earth, he escaped from below. But he feared that his Master and fellow disciples would die of the poison. In this dire distress there came the *bodhisattva* Vilamba to his rescue. By her magic he broke the extinguisher, gave his Master and fellow disciples pills to counteract the poison, and so rescued them.

> Desires and passions have the same beginning.
> With passions and desires, how can there be peace?
> The scholars, with all their differences,
> Have but one aim: to end desire and passion.
> To set the mind upon a single purpose.
> When fully cleansed from the stains of earth,
> One is perfected for Heaven.
> To continue in virtue is never wrong.
> When good work is full and accomplished,
> One then attains to sainthood.

The pilgrims, having escaped out of the net of desire, traveled westwards, and the autumn commenced.

Being warned not to travel in a certain direction, as it was full of demons, the Master was anxious to find a safer way, but there was none. Sun was sent forward to make inquiries about the way, the names of the local demons, and where they lived. He transformed himself into one of the soldiers of the chief demon, put on their uniform, and carried a bell and a wooden clapper, like theirs. From his companions he learnt that they lived in the Lion and Camel Cave, with ten thousand small demons in attendance. The three chiefs, having learnt that the Chinese pilgrim was approaching, under the escort of the terrible Sun, had decided to unite in watching and attacking them. Being in a sentinel's uniform, Sun boldly approached the cave. He was asked if he had seen the terrible Sun. He replied, "Yes, he is more than a hundred feet tall. In his hand he bears an iron club as stout as your leg, and he has already killed ten thousand of our soldiers." At this, the rest were struck with terror and fled. Sun was very pleased at this, and went inside the cave to see the three chiefs.

The chief demon realized that the speaker must be Sun himself, who was impersonating one of their soldiers. Sun was arrested forthwith, stripped, and placed in a jar, where in a short time he would be reduced to a pool of blood. He first felt cold, then hot, as if he were burning in flames. Then he remembered that Guanyin had given him three hairs which could save him in extremity. He tested their powers and escaped out of the jar. Then Sun called on the chief demon to come out of the cave and tight him. The demon said, "Let us two fight alone without any assistance." The demon asked, "Who are you who dares to fight with me, and whom no weapon seems to hurt?" Sun replied,

> "When young I went into the crucible of the Ancient of Days,
> Four dipper stars watched the work,
> The Twenty-eight Constellations assisted.
> They manufactured a thousand indestructible weapons.
> Such as never existed before.
> To complete my armor, the cap of spikes was added."

They fought a terrible battle, and the demon was allowed to strike three times before Sun began to strike. At one stroke Sun was cut in two like a melon. But he laughed, saying, "I am now two complete Suns, and if cut into ten thousand pieces I shall be ten thousand Suns!" The demon said, "To multiply yourself is easy, but you cannot unite yourself again." At this Sun turned a somersault and was united into one as before. Then the demon chief opened his gigantic mouth and swallowed him alive. Now Sun gave him great pains, so that the demon took emetics to cast him out. But Sun said he was too comfortable to come out; he meant to pass the winter there as it was warm; he would set up a kitchen, and cook the demon's vitals on a tripod of bones, from time to time, as he required food. Soon he produced such terrible agony inside, that the demon was thrown into convulsions on the ground.

The demon chief at last begged Sun to come forth as he acknowledged his defeat. But the two younger chiefs privately urged him to close his jaws as Sun came out so as to make an end of him. But Sun overheard the suggestion, and would not come out without making careful arrangements in case of any mishap.

After Sun had conquered the chief demon, the two younger ones came forth and challenged him. But he sent Zhu Bajie to fight with them instead. After seven or eight bouts he was defeated and fled. The demons pursued him and took him, by the snout, back to their cave. The Master, seeing this, urged Sun to rescue him. So, transforming himself into an insect, Sun alighted on Zhu Bajie's ear and entered the cave. The two demons brought their captive in triumph to the elder chief. But he said they had been foolish to capture Zhu Bajie, since he was of no use at all. On hearing this, Zhu Bajie cried out, "Since I am no good, why then, let me go, and you can capture my fellow pilgrims instead!" The demons, however, threw him bound into a tank, where he floundered, half swimming, half sinking, and blowing through his snout in a ridiculous fashion.

Sun thought this an excellent opportunity to revenge himself on Zhu Bajie for having made the Master repeat the incantation against him so often, causing the spikes to enter his head. He resolved to give Zhu Bajie a good fright. So he impersonated a messenger from Hell and told Zhu Bajie that his last hour was approaching. Zhu begged that his death might be postponed, and gave Sun some money he had been secretly hoarding. Then Sun made himself known, and roared laughing at Zhu Bajie, who cursed him roundly, still wallowing in the water. After this, Sun rescued him from the tank, unbound him, and led him to a small side door. They rushed out together and finished off the demons.

Then the demon chiefs met together and agreed to carry the Master across four hundred li of the mountain. They treated him with great honor, and he was carried by eight bearers. But the younger chiefs resolved to have their revenge on the pilgrims on the other half of the mountain, where they alone ruled. All this time, Sun would not trust the young demons, so kept a careful watch. When they reached the first city of the district ruled by the younger demon chiefs, his suspicions were further aroused.

Sure enough, the demons showed their true nature, and took the Master, Zhu Bajie, and Sha the Monk captive, and brought them back to the city, and all four were bound in the order they were to be eaten, and were made ready to be cooked.

Seeing this, Sun changed himself into a false Sun, and, leaving the false one bound, escaped outside. The demons retired to sleep, expecting to feast on the Master next morning, in the hope that all who ate of his flesh would become immortal.

The cooks were ordered to attend to their fire and roast. But Sun sent the cooks sleeping insects, that made them all fall asleep, and forget the fires. Then he went round and unbound his Master and his fellow pilgrims, but found all the gates locked. The three disciples could easily pass through the locked doors, but their Master, being a mortal, could not get out, so Sha the Monk and Zhu Bajie remained behind with him. Meantime, finding that Sun had outwitted them and escaped, the demon chief said, "In the garden there is an arbor where there is a cupboard, let us hide the Master there. And circulate the rumor that we have eaten him alive." This news was told to Zhu Bajie and Sha the Monk.

When Sun heard of his Master's death, he wept bitterly, and seemed to lose his faith altogether, and thought within himself, "It is all very well for Buddha to live an idle life in Paradise, while troubling my Master to seek for Scriptures. If he really means to save men, why does he not send the Scriptures himself to the East? Why does he expect us from the East to go through all these interminable dangers, and thus end our life without accomplishing his purposes? This will never do, I will go and see Buddha myself, and tell him all this. If he gives me the Scriptures to take back with me to the East, then some good will have been done, and the original purpose will be accomplished. If he does not give them to me, I shall ask him to take back the cap of spikes, which he gave me to wear, and let me return to the cave in my old mountain home."

So he went to see Lord Buddha in his Paradise, and after prostrating himself before him, said, "Since my conversion, I have escorted the Master to fetch the Sacred Scriptures, and have suffered unutterable hardships. Now I have arrived at the Lion and Camel Cave, where there are three terrible demons, who have taken my Master captive and eaten him alive, and his disciples Zhu Bajie and Sha the Monk are also taken and bound. Being driven to despair, I have come to beg for a great favor. Take back the cap of spikes and let me return to my old mountain cave. You know that since I became human, well almost, and was converted to Buddhism, I have never failed in my duty. But this time these demons are more than a match for me." Buddha said, "Do not be alarmed, I know these particular demons quite well." Sun shouted back, "You must be in league with them!" Buddha said, "Just listen, will you? The first and second demons are really a peacock and a roc. They are servants of Manjusri of Mount Wutai in Shansi, and Samantadhadra, of Mount Emei in Sichuan. In the beginning, when all things were produced, among the beasts the *jilin* was chief, among birds the phoenix was chief. The phoenix gave birth to the peacock and the roc. When they appeared, they were great eaters of men. Once, aeons ago, I was swallowed by a peacock, but I bored a hole through his back, and rode him to the top of Snow Mountain. It's name is Buddha's Mother. The great roc is born of the same mother as the peacock. So that is how we are related. But now I must go with you to subdue these demons."

Then Lord Buddha summoned Manjusri and Samantabhandra to help in recalling their servants, and they all went to the Demon Cave. Sun attacked the demons again, but when he was apparently defeated, Manjusri and Samantabhadra cried out to their former servants, "Why do you two demons still refuse to follow the right way?" At this the demons appeared in the forms of a blue lion and a white elephant, and Manjusri and Samantabhadra fitted them with lotus saddles and rode off into the distance. The Master was found unhurt in the arbor.

> The true Scriptures, must be got from a true man.
> The assumed teaching of demons are all false.

22

The Golden-Nosed White Rat

AFTER TRAVELING FOR SEVERAL MONTHS the pilgrims arrived at a city where little boys were laid out in cradles at each house door. The Master was curious to know the meaning of the custom. He learnt that a Taoist priest had deceived the king, and persuaded him that he could obtain immortality by taking a certain medicine, which was manufactured from the livers of little boys. These boys were to be presented and killed on the morrow, to cure the king.

Sun called on his friendly spirits to carry away each of the cradles and children in the night, and hide them for a day or two.

On the next day all the officials, civil and military, presented themselves at the temple, and announced that by some magic all the children had been spirited away, so that the king could not procure the much-coveted medicine. The king was much displeased at this, but the proud Taoist said, "You need not be troubled, for Heaven has sent you what is much better than the livers of little boys. There is a pilgrim here who has been a Buddhist all his days. Let him be killed and his heart used instead."

At this the pilgrims were in the greatest danger again. But Sun said, "I can save my Master." He said to his Master, "Let us exchange places. You take my form, and I yours." When the king's orders came for the arrest of the Master, the pilgrims were ready.

By the king's orders, soldiers came and took away the Master to the temple, where his heart was to be cut out to cure the king.

"I have many hearts" said the substitute Master. "Which one does the king require?" The Taoist wizard replied, "Your black heart." With this Sun cut himself open before the astonished gathering, and his insides tumbled out in heaps before them. The Taoist

wizard said, "This Buddhist monk is full of all kinds of black arts."
Sun picked out various hearts dripping with blood, but none of
them were black, and he asked, "Is it this white heart, this yellow
heart, this heart, ambitious for riches or fame, or this jealous heart,
filled with desire to be first and foremost, or this heart full of desire
to be honorable, or to be careful? These I can give you, but there
is not a single black heart or desire in the whole lot." At this the
king was bewildered and said, "Stop, we do not want any more of
this." But the substitute Master said, "How blind you have been,
Oh king! It is this Taoist priest who has the black heart. Let me
show it to you!" In a moment Sun changed into his own form, and
made for the Taoist priest, who recognised him as the Great Sage,
who had thrown Heaven itself into turmoil 500 years before.

The priest then fled with the queen, but Sun followed them,
and by the aid of the local gods found their hiding place. The old
Minister of the Star of Longevity assisted in capturing them, and
bringing them back to the city. There they changed into their true
forms, one a white deer, and the other a fox.

The whole city was thus delivered, and the parents of the boys
would not let the pilgrims leave, till they had shown their great
gratitude.

The saved boys naturally became Buddhist disciples.

After having traveled some twenty *li*, they entered a dark pine
forest where they found a young woman bound to a tree with the
lower half of her body buried in the earth. She begged them to save
her. Sun warned the Master that it was a deception. But the woman
pleaded that to save a life was better than to travel far to fetch
Scriptures, or to spend money in building pagodas. The Master
therefore ordered his disciples to unbind and help her. Sun said, "If
you do save her, do not blame me if you get into trouble." She was
rescued and traveled with them much against Sun's will.

When night came they arrived at a great temple. The first and
second courts were fallen into ruin, and were left as quarters for
robbers at night. But the inner court was occupied by lamas who
had beautiful rooms and lived in luxury. Still, they were astonished
that the pilgrims had a woman with them.

Having arrived at the temple the Master fell ill. He called for paper and ink and in a fit of despair wrote a dispatch to be delivered to the emperor in Chang'an. Sun said, "There are many things I cannot do, but though Chang'an is very far, I can deliver that in no time. Let me hear what you have written." The Master read, "When by your command I left the East to go to the West, I did not realize the dangers, nor expect to be taken ill, when only halfway, so that I fear I cannot proceed farther. Though I have entered the Buddhist religion as a disciple, I still find Heaven's gate is very far away. If I do not live to obtain the Scriptures, all the trouble will have been in vain. I beg your Majesty not to insist on my traveling any farther for the Scriptures."

When Sun heard this, he smiled and said, "Tell me frankly whether you want to live or die. I have some ability. I can see the Judge of Hell if you like, and make such a confusion in hell as I did in Heaven. You, Master, were the second of the Buddha's great prophets, and you were called Golden Cicada, and showed much promise. But now you have lost heart, and even want to abandon your mission. No wonder you suffer all these difficulties. You will be quite well in a day or two." The Master called for water, and Sun went out to ask for it. When he went out, he found all the monks in a terrible plight. Some demons had broken into the temple, and carried away six of their number to be eaten.

The Master was greatly alarmed at this, wondering who the demon could be. Sun knew very well that it was the woman who had misled the young monks, and he determined to attack her that evening. He did so, and she assumed her natural form, and fought desperately till she was obliged to yield. But in yielding, she caused a great wind to arise and the Master was carried away by it.

The disciples at this were greatly alarmed, and searched for him all through the pine forest. Finally they learnt that he was not there, but a thousand *li* away.

Eventually the pilgrims learnt their Master was in the deepest cave of a dangerous hollow mountain. They overheard the talk of two witches drawing water at a well, in preparation for the wedding of their mistress with the Master, whom she had carried away to her cave.

Sun advised his Master to agree to take the witch into the garden that night. Sun transformed himself into a peach, which the Master presented to his bride. As soon as she had swallowed the peach, Sun caused her terrible pain, and threatened to kill her outright, unless she promised to carry his Master on her back, out through the long labyrinth entrance of the cave, and set him free.

The Master was carried out, and Sun was then spat forth as a date. Then he and the witch had a terrible fight with each other.

> One was naturally a heaven sent heart and body,
> The other was a human spirit in the witch.
> The one sought a partner of Heaven's appointment,
> The other sought against nature to produce a holy mix.
> When two extremes like fire and water meet, then harm is done,
> When two laws of nature cannot unite, let them be apart.

Having rescued the Master, Sun and his two comrades began discussing what to do next, and the Master sat down bewildered. Seeing that she could not fight Sun successfully, once more the witch caused a great wind to rise, and whirled the Master away again into the cave, together with his horse and baggage. She was determined he should marry her. At this time Sun was in great perplexity about his Master, for the cave was 300 *li* in extent and not easy to search. But during his search he smelt incense. Going in its direction he found a tablet on which was written, "To the honor of my father, Li, Guardian King of Heaven." There stood an incense burner before it.

At this, Sun carried out the tablet and burner to the mouth of the cave, and said with great glee, "We have found her secret now. She is none other than the daughter of Li the Guardian King of Heaven, and a sister of Prince Nezha. So it is she who has come to earth, and carried away our Master." Sun's comrades asked him, "But have you found our Master?" Sun replied, "No, but I have thought of a good plan that will save him." "What is that?" "I am going to charge the Guardian King of Heaven with treason. That will soon bring him. Bring me paper and ink at once." Then he wrote a charge against Li the Guardian King of Heaven, who has been so careless about his family as to let one of the ladies of his family go down to earth, and live in a deep cave as a witch. Zhu Bajie and

Sha the Monk said, "That is true, and Heaven should know about it. Go at once!"

Sun mounted the clouds and in a short time reached the South Gate of Heaven. The four great generals paid him their respects and asked, "Why does the Great Sage come here now?" Sun replied, "I have come to make complaint against someone." The generals were astonished and said, "We wonder whose skin will get it now." They were obliged to lead him to the Palace of the Jade Emperor. Sun Wukong then put down the tablet and the incense burner, made his obeisance to the Jade Emperor, and then handed over to him his complaint. The Jade Emperor read it through, and ordered that the Minister of Venus should go, together with the plaintiff, to the Palace of Li, the Guardian King, and let him explain the matter. Sun and the minister mounted the clouds for that court.

They soon arrived there and the pages announced them, saying, "His Honor the Minister of Venus has come." The Guardian King came out to meet him. Seeing that the minister carried an edict, he ordered the burning of incense. On turning round he saw Sun following. The Guardian King quickly asked, "What kind of edict do you bring?" The minister replied, "It is Sun, the Great Sage, who makes a charge against you." The Guardian King, hearing of a charge against himself, became very angry and asked, "With what does he charge me?" The Minister of Venus replied, "He charges you for keeping a witch to injure people, and allowing incense to be burnt to other gods. Please look at the charge yourself." The Guardian King, full of anger, had incense burnt, worshipped towards the Throne of the Jade Emperor and then opened the edict. It was as the minister had said. Full of anger, he struck the incense table, and said, "This monkey has made a mistake in charging me. The minister said, "Do not be angry, look at the evidence of the tablet and the incense burner which say that she is your own daughter." The Guardian King said, "I have only three sons and one daughter. My eldest son serves in the Office for the Defense of the Faith. My second son, Mucha, is in the Southern Ocean, studying with Guanyin. My third son is Nezha, who is with me, in constant attendance at court. I have one daughter named Baoying, who is just seven years of age. Being too young to understand human relations, how can she do the work of a witch? If you do not believe, I will have her carried out for you to see. This monkey is really outrageous in his charges. Remember too that I am of the celestial world, and am given power to execute any one, without memorializing for permission first. Even if I were one of the common people on the earth, I should not be falsely accused, for the law says a false charge should be punished threefold. Let my men bind this monkey!" Instantly the great generals in waiting came forward and bound Sun. The minister cried, "Guardian King Li, take care you do not get into trouble. We bring you a celestial edict. How can you order your officers to bind one who bears this edict?"

The Guardian King said, "Tell me, Minister, how I should deal with a false charge like this. Please sit down. Let me get the sword with which I execute demons, and have this monkey beheaded, and then we can go together and report to the Jade Emperor." When the minister saw the sword, he was really alarmed about Sun, but Sun, not in the least afraid, smiled and said quietly, "Do not be alarmed about me, I am accustomed to losing at first, but in the end I always win." Before he had finished his sentence, the Guardian King raised his sword and was going to strike Sun. But before the stroke fell, Prince Nezha came forward and seizing the sword cried, "Father, do not be angry!" At this the father, instead of being more angry that his son should resist him, was alarmed. There was a reason for it.

Prince Nezha had once gone to bathe in the sea, and got into trouble by going into the Dragon's Crystal Palace, and seizing a dragon there, in order to make a bow string out of his muscles. When the Guardian King heard of it, he was afraid of future troubles, and wished to kill his son. The son became very angry, took a sword and cut off his flesh and gave it to his mother, and cut off his bones and returned them to his father. His soul departed and went to Paradise. Lord Buddha had just dismissed his pupils, to whom he had been preaching, when he heard a cry, "Murder, help, help!" Buddha knew it was Nezha. He gave him a new body, and read over him the magic words which give life to the dead, and Nezha was given a new life to rule over 96 demons, and with wonderful magic powers. He wished to kill his father for attempting to kill him. In these dire straits the Guardian King was obliged to beg for his own life. The Buddha gave him charge of a golden pagoda. That is why the Guardian King was also called Li the Pagoda Bearer. From then on Nezha came to regard Lord Buddha as his father, so as to end the strife between father and son.

Guardian King Li said to Nezha, "Son, you have something to say." This was the reason why the father showed no anger. Nezha went on his knees, kowtowed, and said, "Father, there is a daughter in the earthly world, whom you have forgotten, and she is a witch. Three hundred years ago she stole some fragrant candles from the Spiritual Hall. Lord Buddha sent you and me to arrest her, and by rights she should have been put to death then. But we spared her life, and she in gratitude worships you as her father, and honors me as brother, and that is the explanation of tablet and incense burner in her cave." The king was astonished and said, "I had completely forgotten her. What is her name?" Nezha replied, "She has three names. Originally she was called Golden-nosed White Rat. On account of her fondness for fragrant incense she was called Half-of-a-Guanyin. Now she is called the Brave-Lady-of-the-Earth."

After hearing this, the Guardian King ordered Sun to be unbound. But Sun would not hear of it. "Carry me bound to the Jade Emperor, or if you will not carry me, I will roll myself into his presence." At this the Guardian King became much alarmed. The Minister of Venus strove to make peace and said to Sun, "Oh monkey, you are too willful, you should remember past kindness." "And what kindness have you shown me?" The Minister of Venus replied "I recommended you to be made the Great Sage, the Equal of Heaven, but you did not behave yourself." Sun said, "I committed no crime, I only made a disturbance in Heaven. Still, for your sake, I will let the Guardian King come himself and unbind me."

Then, instead of disgracing the Guardian King, Sun agreed to the minister's suggestion that, if a celestial army were sent to put down the witch, he would say nothing about his bonds, or the sword drawn to kill him.

Then the soldiers arrived and captured the witch, while Sun hurried away with his Master on their journey.

23
Sun Shaves a Village

THE SUMMER HAD NOW ARRIVED. On the road they met an old lady and a little boy. The old lady said, "You are clearly monks, so do not go forward, for this country before you is called the country that exterminates religion. They have vowed to kill ten thousand monks. They have already killed that number with the exception of four noted ones whose arrival they soon expect, and then their number will be full."

This old lady was Guanyin and the little boy was Sudhana the Page, who had come to give them warning. At this, Sun changed himself into a candle moth and flew into the city to examine for himself. He entered an inn and heard the innkeeper warning his guests to look after their own clothes and belongings when they went to sleep. In order to travel safely through the city, Sun decided that they all should put on turbans and clothing, like the rest of the people, or they would be killed. Knowing from the innkeeper's warning that thieving was common, Sun stole some clothing and turbans for his Master and comrades. Then he returned, and fetched them to the inn at dusk, representing himself as a horse dealer.

Sun, fearing that in their sleep their turbans would fall off, and their shaven heads be revealed, arranged for them all to sleep in a cupboard, which they asked the innkeeper to lock.

During the night, robbers came and carried the cupboard away, thinking it was full of silver to buy horses. When the watchman saw many men carrying this, he became suspicious, and the soldiers were called out. At this, the robbers ran away, leaving the cupboard in the open. The Master was very angry with Sun for getting him into this danger. He feared that at daylight they would be discovered and all executed. But Sun said, "Do not be alarmed I will save you yet!" He changed himself into an ant and escaped outside the cupboard. Then be plucked out some hairs and changed them into a thousand monkeys like himself. To each he gave a razor and some sleeping insects. They were to place the insects on the king and all the officials and their wives, and when they were asleep, the monkeys were to shave their heads.

On the morrow there was a terrible commotion in the whole city, as all the leaders and their families found themselves shaved like Buddhists.

When the ministers came to court next morning, all weeping and begging the king to save their lives, the king confessed that the same thing had been done in his palace, and no more shaved heads were to be executed. All bowed before the Master in repentance for having vowed to massacre monks. The pilgrims then went on their way.

They had not gone far when the Master, seeing smoke coming out of a mountain in front, was alarmed. In front of this mountain was a demon with some scores of smaller demons on his right and left. One of these advised the chief to be careful in attacking the Master. "His chief disciple, Sun, has terrible powers, which I witnessed at the Lion and Camel cave, before escaping here. If you have decided to attack the Master and eat his flesh, so as to live for ever, I advise you to choose the best hundred among a thousand of your warriors, and of these select the best ten, and of these again choose the best three. With their help you may attack the pilgrims, divide their forces, and when none of the disciples are near, you can snatch the Master away."

In this way the Master was caught and bound. There was a woodcutter bound in the same place waiting to be cooked. He told the Master he had a mother, 83 years of age, dependent on him, and if he died no one would look after her. The Master said, "That is small trouble compared with mine. If I am killed, the Emperor of China's vow, to save all the sufferers in Hell, will not be accomplished. Still, some may say that filial piety to the parent is as important as loyalty to the sovereign."

When the Monkey returned from chasing the demons, the Master had disappeared. Having searched the district for a distance of about twenty *li,* the disciples came upon a cave inscribed with the words, "The Cave of the Cold Mountain Mist." This was the home of the demon, and here the Master was kept. But the little demons resolved to deceive the pilgrims. They brought out a head, saying that they had all taken part in eating the Master, and that only his head remained. Zhu Bajie began to weep, but Sun believed it was a false head, and taking it, struck it against a rock. Then they found it was made of the root of a willow.

The little demons withdrew into the cave once more, and brought out a real man's head, dripping with blood. This time all three disciples believed it was their Master's. They wept bitterly and reverently buried it. Leaving Sha the Monk to take care of the grave and the baggage, Sun Wukong and Zhu Bajie determined to take revenge on the demons for their Master's death. The demon led out all his forces against them, but Sun, plucking out some of his hairs, changed them into monkeys like himself, each armed with a terrible spear. They killed numbers of demons, so that the chief fled to his cave.

Sun then left Zhu Bajie at the grave with Sha the Monk, and, changing himself into a winged ant, crept through the door of the cave. He found the Master and the woodcutter bound in a little courtyard at the back. Returning to the cave, he caused number of sleeping insects to crawl over all the demons, so that they fell fast asleep. Then he liberated his Master and the woodcutter, and led them to Sha the Monk and Zhu Bajie. When they realized it was the Master and not his ghost, they were overcome with joy. The woodcutter then showed Zhu Bajie where to find dry fuel to burn the cave, and when it was set alight, Zhu fanned the flames with his long ears. The little demons were all burnt, and the chief demon, when he awoke, was struck dead by Zhu Bajie on the spot.

The woodcutter told the pilgrims that they had only a thousand *li* more to travel, and that they are nearing the borders of India. The Master and disciples set forth on their journey with great joy.

The party now arrived at Fengshan city under the rule of India. In the city they found the Prefect had put out a proclamation offering a thousand *taels* to any one who could bring down rain, for there had been a drought for three years, and two-thirds of the people had died of starvation. Grain cost a hundred *taels* a bushel; girls of ten years of age were sold for three pints of grain; boys of five years of age were given away as slaves, to any one who would have them for nothing. All clothes and furniture were being pawned in order to raise money to keep body and soul together. There was no security for life in the land, and desperate men carried people away, and ate them to keep themselves from starvation. This was the reason why the great reward was offered.

Sun told the Prefect that he could call down rain. He summoned the Rain Dragon, who said to him, "Obtain an Edict from Heaven to sanction rain and I will give you as much as you desire." At this, Sun flew away to Heaven. Meanwhile the Prefect ordered each family to reverence the Tablet of the Rain Dragon, and burn incense to him, to put out water jars and willow branches at their doors, and to worship Heaven.

When Sun presented his request in Heaven, he was told by the Jade Emperor that the city did not deserve rain, as their Prefect had committed a great sin. On the 25th day of the 12th moon, which was the day when the Jade Emperor went forth to inspect Heaven and Earth, he had found an altar prepared for worship in Fengshan city, but, owing to a quarrel between the Prefect and his wife, the altar had been upset and the offerings prepared for the gods had been thrown to the dogs. This was an offence beyond pardon, so the prefecture was punished with drought. This was to last till a mountain of rice 1,000 feet high had been all eaten up by a chicken the size of a man's fist, and till a mountain of flour 200 feet high had been licked up by a little pet dog, and a metal lock 13 inches long, which had a bolt of the thickness of one's finger, had been burnt through by an ordinary lamp. But one of the great spirits told Sun, "Do not be discouraged at this, for if the Prefect truly repents, all this will come to pass."

Sun returned from heaven, and told the Prefect that repentance was necessary before Heaven would grant pardon. Then the Prefect and people vowed to repent, to repair to the temples, recite prayers, and worship Buddha with the monks. Sun carried this promise to Heaven to show the Jade Emperor. Whilst he was presenting this, the spirit, whose duty it was to report the quantities of incense burnt, announced that the rice and flour mountains had both fallen and disappeared, and that the metal lock had been broken. After this, rain fell to the great joy of all. The people offered money to the pilgrims for what they had done, but they would not receive any. The officials and people escorted them thirty *li* on their journey, and parted with them in tears.

The Master, much pleased with the events at Fengshan, rode on his way, and arrived at a religious gathering at Yuhua, a most flourishing place, where rice was sold at four *candarins* per ten bushels, and oil for ten cash per catty. By this time they had traveled eighteen thousand *li* from China, and had been fourteen years on the road.

> The True Illustrious Religion is not human,
> The Great Way, whose origin is in all space,
> Whose influence pervades the Universe,
> Has balm to heal all suffering.

The ruling sovereign of this place at first regarded the pilgrims as ordinary mortal travelers, but soon found they were immortals. The pilgrims showed their miraculous powers in wielding their magic weapons, one weighing 13,000 catties, and the others weighing 5,048 catties each. When his three sons saw the magic power of the pilgrims, they begged to be taught how to wield such weapons. The disciples promised to instruct them. But the young princes found they had not sufficient strength to wield the pilgrims' heavy weapons. Sun told them they must learn to acquire more power. He ordered the three young princes to go to a quiet room, where he drew the seven stars of the Great Bear on the floor, and made the princes kneel on them. He told them to close their eyes, concentrate their thoughts on some scriptural truth, and let the breath of Heaven enter their bodies, so that it might dwell in their heart. After this, they would receive renewed power, being born again, their very bones transformed. The princes then spent the whole night and day absorbed in a trance of new life. When they awoke and rose on their feet, they found themselves endowed with new strength.

Three lighter magic weapons were made for the princes, to be always carried with them. But one evening a Yellow Lion Demon from a mountain seventy *li* off, saw some strange lights shining in the sky, and discovered that they came from the weapons of the pilgrims. Knowing them to be precious, he stole them and thereby increased his power greatly.

Sun changed himself into the shape of a butterfly, and flew to the demon's cave. There he heard a demon tell the others of the capture of the magic weapons, and they decided to hold a banquet to celebrate the event. On hearing this, Sun returned and told the others of the demon's plans. Then the three disciples, transforming themselves into the shapes of the demons sent to buy animals for the feast, gained entrance to the cave, where they found their weapons displayed. Changing back into their true forms, they seized their arms, and gave battle to the demons. The chief of them, the Yellow Lion Demon, escaped, but the others were slain and the cave was set on fire. The disciples, bearing their weapons, returned in triumph to the city, and related to the ruler and the Master what had taken place.

Meanwhile the Yellow Lion Demon fled to a certain Nine-headed Demon, whom he had invited to attend the feast, and begged his aid against the pilgrims. It seemed to the pilgrims, more than once, a hopeless task to conquer him and the Lion Demon. But Sun in this extremity appealed to the chief of the Taoist gods, as this Nine-headed Demon was under his jurisdiction, and in this way they were finally saved. The guardian of the demon in Heaven confessed that he had once become drunk, during which time the demon escaped down to earth, and it was then that he almost ended the life of the Master.

After they had traveled five or six days from Yuhua, the pilgrims arrived at a flourishing city called Jinping, a dependency of India, and stayed at the Temple of the Merciful Cloud Temple. This was on the 13th of the 1st moon. They were pressed to stay over the Lantern Festival on the 15th. The pilgrims had lost their reckoning of days and months and were glad to start afresh. The lanterns were very brilliant with silk gauze and horn, and were to burn for three nights only. Only the best quality of oil was provided and the expense was enormous, amounting to 48,000 *taels*. Buddha was to appear the last night, and on his appearance all the lamps would go out before the brightness of Buddha himself, and all the people would disappear in honor of his presence. But the Master, having come all the way from China to see Buddha, determined he would stay and see Buddha there and then. Sun looked on, and declared it was all a false deception. At this moment, a great wind arose and carried away all the oil, and the Master was whirled away to the Blue Dragon mountain, where demons had lived in a cave for 1,000 years.

When the pilgrims discovered where their Master was hidden, they attacked the demons, demanding the Master's liberty, and fought a hundred and fifty pitched battles, but were not successful. They returned to the temple, and related their failure to the monks. After consultation, they decided to go again and attack the demons in the night, lest it should be too late if they waited till the morning.

The disciples hastened to save their Master. Sun changed himself into a fly and having got in, found his Master, and unbound him whilst all the demons were asleep. But on their way out, owing to some accident, all were aroused and the Master was retaken, and again bound. Zhu Bajie and Sha the Monk were also taken and bound.

In this extremity, Sun decided to go to Heaven and seek celestial soldiers to help him. First he went back to the temple, and told the monks what had befallen him and that he was going to Heaven to ask for help. At this they were astonished, and asked. "How can you go to Heaven?" He replied, "There is no difficulty about that, for Heaven is my old home." With this he whistled, and was transported to the West Gate of Heaven at once. There he met his old friend the Minister of Venus, and one of the Guardian Kings, and the Four Great Messengers, and having told his story, saw the Jade Emperor, who promised to aid him with celestial soldiers. These were legions under the star generals, who were ordered to help.

They accompanied Sun, and subdued the demons, who changed into rhinoceros form. Finally, the officials and gentry were told that they would never be imposed on again by these demons, nor forced to contribute towards buying this expensive oil, which, owing to the credulity of the people, was only used by the demons themselves. The officials and gentry were most grateful for the deliverance, and built a temple to commemorate the victory of the star generals over the demons, and erected a memorial temple to the four pilgrims.

24

The False Princess

ON THE PILGRIMS WENT, till they came to the Golden Temple where Shakyamuni had once preached. There they were hospitably received by the abbot, who said grace before eating. Attached to the temple was an orphanage. There they met a monk 105 years old, who told them, privately, that the king's daughter was in the orphanage. She declared she had been carried off and placed in this temple by the demons, whilst a witch had been substituted as the royal princess in the palace. He begged them to find out the truth of this, as every night the true princess begged him to help her. The pilgrims promised to do what they could.

On entering the city in search of the king's palace, to get his passport signed, the Master and Sun found a strange ceremony taking place. The king's only daughter had fixed on that very day and hour to throw a colored silk ball on the head of her chosen husband. She threw it at the Master, and carried him to the palace, amid the congratulations of all the people. But the Master said he was on an important mission, and must consult his three disciples, as to what was to be done. He was warned that if he did not accept the princess' choice he would he killed. This threw the Master into a great fear and he waited anxiously for the appearance of his disciples, for whom he had sent.

The three disciples were invited to the royal palace. On entering the royal presence, the three stood upright, and none of them knelt. The king asked them their names, and business. At this, the three moved nearer the king to speak, but the guard sternly rebuked them for their rudeness in approaching so near. Sun smiled, and cried out with a loud voice, "Those who insult others insult themselves. Since my Master is to be your son-in-law, how is it that he is standing and not sitting in your presence? I have never heard of such manners before." At this the king changed his countenance, but submitted to the rebuke.

Then the chief disciple spoke:

"My name is Sun Wukong, and my ancestors lived in the country of Aolai, in the Flower and Fruit Mountain. My father was Heaven and my mother was Earth; a peach stone split and I was born. I sought for a famous man to be my teacher, and studied the best religion. Then I studied the magic of the immortals, and sought happiness at the Cave of the Blessed. I went to sea and conquered the dragons, went to the mountains and captured the demons, erased my name from among mortals in Hell, and was registered with the immortals. Officials acknowledged me as the Great Sage, the Equal of Heaven. I met the spirits of heaven daily, and we sang together in the most sacred places. But, because I spoilt the peach banquet, and greatly disturbed the Heavenly Court, I was arrested and subdued by Buddha, and imprisoned under Nature's mountain. When hungry, I had only iron rust to eat, and when thirsty I was given only copper syrup to drink. For 500 years I never tasted tea or food. Happily, when my Master came from the East to go to the West, Guanyin taught me how to avert the punishment of Heaven by repentance, and rescued me from my terrible distress. I was named the Seeker of Secrets, and I am also known as Sun Wukong, Aware of Emptiness.

The king was greatly astonished, then came down from his throne and congratulated the Master, rejoicing in the great providence which had brought them together.

The second disciple then spoke:

"My name is Zhu Bajie. In a former life, I was a man fond of pleasure and idleness, and I was stupid all my life. But I met a Taoist immortal and after a few words from him, my mind was aroused, and I was awakened and decided to follow him. After studying for sixteen years, I acquired about nine arts, and was able to mount on the clouds, and enter the Celestial Palace. There I was fortunate enough, by the grace of the Jade Emperor, to be appointed the General of the Celestial Fairies, and had control of the River Legions.

All in all I was most happy in Heaven. But because I became drunk during a peach banquet, and played with the fairies, I lost my official position, and was condemned to be reborn on earth. By mistake I entered the womb of a sow instead of a woman, and that is how I have the snout and ears of a pig. I lived a life of ease, full of all kinds of mischief. Then I met Guanyin who showed me the way to virtue, by following the teachings of Buddha, and by escorting the Master from China, who is on his way to fetch the Sacred Scriptures from the West. My Buddhist name is Seeker of Strength, also known as Zhu Bajie, the Keeper of the Eight Commandments."

The king was much astonished on hearing this, and then asked the third disciple why he followed Buddha.

He replied:

"My name is Sha the Monk. I was originally a mortal man. But, because I desired to avoid the transmigration of souls, I searched high and low, far and wide, for a way of deliverance. I was reckoned among the saints, and learnt spiritual arts for some 3,000 years. I understood the four great forces of nature, and at last succeeded in entering the celestial world. I accidentally broke the glass dishes at the peach banquet and was banished to the Quicksands River, where I did great damage. Happily Guanyin gave me a chance to redeem myself by accompanying the Master to the West, and in this way bring forth good fruit. I understand religion much better now. My name is Sha the Monk, also known as the Seeker of Purity." When the king heard this, he was very glad, because his own daughter had chosen to marry a living Buddha, and also very much alarmed, because all three disciples were strange spirits. Then an official came to announce to the king that the propitious day for the marriage was the twelfth of that month, and so it was fixed for that day.

As it was only the eighth, the king provided daily feasts for the prospective son-in-law, and the disciples. But the Master became very much annoyed with Sun, and said, "You always bring me into trouble. If you had not taken me to see the throwing of the silk ball, this present difficulty would never have occurred. What am I to do?"

Now the bride also began to fear what Sun might do to her. So, on the night before the wedding, she begged her father to let the disciples leave before daylight, and proceed to fetch the Sacred

Scriptures by themselves, while the Master remained with the king. She said she feared to see the frightful faces of his disciples. And so it was arranged that they should go before daylight.

The Master was greatly alarmed at this. But Sun, plucking a hair, made a false Sun and let that one proceed with the other two disciples, whilst he himself remained to watch over his Master. At night he flew, as a bee, to his Master's side, "Do not be alarmed, I am with you!"

When the princess appeared the next day for her marriage, Sun at once recognised her as a witch, and attacked her in the midst of the court. She in turn appeared in her true form, threw away all her royal garments and jewels, and took up a club, and fought with Sun in the air. She fled away, and he followed her, till she disappeared in a cave. But he found her in one of the caves and fought her again, and was pressing her hard, when the Minister of the Yin Star appeared, and begged Sun to spare her life for his sake. He then related the story of the true princess. She had been a rabbit fairy in one of the Heavenly Mansions twenty years before, and had boxed the ears of one of her companions. After this, to save herself from revenge, she decided to go down to earth, and entered the womb of a queen. The insulted fairy had never forgotten her treatment, and a year before had carried her enemy off in the wind, and taken her place in the palace.

When the king discovered that the false princess was a witch, he wished to know where his true daughter was. Sun told him that she was at the orphanage. The king and queen went and fetched her and the temple was rebuilt at royal expense. To reward the old abbot for his care of the princess, the king commanded that the successive abbots of that temple should be specially honored.

Sun said to the king, "I have another matter to inform your majesty. This mountain is called Centipede Mountain, and they say that many people suffer annually from these pests. The greatest enemies of these centipedes are cocks." The king ordered a thousand cocks to be sent to the mountain to devour all the centipedes.

> Form, form, form, yet there is no form,
> Vain, vain, vain, yet there is no vanity
> Loud wrangling and silent thought are alike in vain.

Why trouble to speak in your dreams?
In usefulness there is uselessness,
In no merit there is merit,
Like change of color in ripening fruit.
Do not ask how this can be.

It was now the beginning of summer, as the pilgrims proceeded on their journey. They arrived at Dongtai, and were most hospitably entertained by a good family, who had vowed, twenty-four years before, to aid ten thousand monks. The chief was now 64 years old and had already helped 9996. By helping the four who had just come, he would now be able to complete his vow. His wife and two sons were also most kind and attentive, and would not let the pilgrims leave in a hurry. They said, "Why not stay a year with us?" Twenty-four monks were invited to hold a three days' service, and dine with them. The day before they left, a large number of neighbors were also invited, and they were treated most royally during the whole fortnight of their stay. On leaving, they were offered money for their expenses, but this the Master refused. They had scarcely started before a great rain fell and they had poor shelter in an old ruin through the whole night.

Seeing the lavish reception given to the pilgrims that night, some robbers decided that the host must be the wealthiest in the city. They therefore took advantage of the dark night and rain, burnt his house, robbed him of his treasure, and killed him.

Next day the injured family of the rich man falsely charged the pilgrims of robbing and killing, and a band of five hundred and fifty soldiers was sent after them for their money. Meanwhile the robbers had got their booty outside the city and divided it. But, seeing the pilgrims coming on they said, "These were well treated, and must have money on them; let us rob them also!'" Sun used his magic skill and, delivering his company, got the robbers' booty, which he decided to return to his former kind host. The pilgrims were then set at liberty, and went on their way.

The earth is broad; good and evil are acting both at once.
Heaven is high, and does not always shelter the good.
Far away and safe is the Way of Heaven,
And leads to the Spiritual Mountain in the Blessed Land.

25

The Mortal Body Cast Aside

AFTER SOLVING THE MYSTERY of the robbery, the pilgrims went on their way, and found the country most beautiful, like the land of the gods; every family followed virtue, and students studied religion in the woods. In about a week, they saw, in front of them, a building several stories high, even a hundred feet, the top of which reached the stars. At this the Master said to the Monkey, "This is a fine country." "Truly it is," answered Sun. "But when traveling through other countries, you wished to dismount, and worship each poor representation of Buddha; now that you are in the real country with true Buddhas, how is it you do not dismount and worship?" At this the Master felt rebuked and jumped off his horse. Soon after they reached the gate of the high building, where a fine student leaned on the gate, and called out to some one, "Is this not the holy pilgrim from the East in search of the Sacred Scriptures?" The Master quickly raised his head, and saw an Immortal of surpassing loveliness. He was robed in fine garments, and had a dust brush in his hand, straw sandals on his feet, and a Taoist charm on his arm. He had been a Taoist priest, who had cultivated long life by living in beautiful surroundings, in order to enjoy eternal life, free from earthly sorrow. The Master did not know that he was an Immortal sent from the Golden Thunder Hall to welcome him. But the Monkey knew, and called out, "Master, this is the Great Immortal of the Taoist temple at the foot of the Spiritual Mountain come to welcome us." It was only then that the Master understood, and went forward to bow to him. The Great Immortal smiled and said, "You, holy monk, have only arrived this year. I was misled by Guanyin, who informed me ten years

ago, that she had received Buddha's command to go to the East
and find a man, who should come to India and fetch the Sacred
Scriptures. I therefore expected you would have arrived in two or
three years. I have been waiting for you every year, but have never
received any news till now." The Master put his palms together
and said, "Many thanks for all your kind thoughts." Then the four
pilgrims, their horse and baggage, were taken into the mansion,
and each of the disciples was introduced to the Great Immortal.
Tea and refreshments were ordered for them, and a young monk
was ordered to prepare a fragrant bath for the pilgrims, before
they ascended the Spiritual Mountain.

> When your work is done, then cleanse yourself,
> Train your spirit in harmony with nature,
> Then you may disregard all troubles.
> By seeking the three refuges, and the eight commandments, you
>   begin a new life.
> When the demons are conquered, then you reach the land of
>   Buddha.
> When struggles cease, you can join the happy few,
> All impurity is washed away
> And you attain the original perfection and incorruptibility.

When the pilgrims had finished their bath, it was evening, and
they rested in the Taoist mansion. Next morning the Master changed
his clothes, put on his beautiful cassock, and his miter, and took in
his hand the silver staff. He then entered the hall, and there made
obeisance to the Great Immortal, who said, "Let me show you the
way." Sun said, "I know the way. We must not trouble you." The
Great Immortal replied, "You might know the way through the
air, but you have never trodden this way on foot. Your Master has
not yet traveled by the clouds, and therefore you should follow
the road." Sun said, "What you say is true, kindly show us the
way. My Master desires with all his heart to see Buddha. Have no
doubt about that." The Great Immortal smiled, took the hand of
the Master and led him on, burning sandalwood incense. "By this
way one does not go outside the mansion gate, but through the
central hall and out at the back gate."

The Great Immortal pointed to the Spiritual Mountain, and said, "Your Reverence, half way up the sky you see beautiful light of all colors shining forth in a thousand rays. That is the top of the Spiritual Mountain, where Buddha dwells." At this sight the Master was going to worship. But Sun laughed and said, "Master, you have not yet arrived at the place of worship. The place to dismount and worship is still some distance off. If you begin to kowtow now, you will have too many obeisances to make." The Great Immortal then said, "Holy monk and you three disciples, the Great Sage, the Celestial Fairy Chieftain, and the Celestial Chief of Pages have now arrived at the Blessed Land and can see the Spiritual Mountain. I shall now return." The Master bade him farewell.

The Great Sage led the other pilgrims, and they ascended gradually. Not more than two miles distant, they saw a stream of living water rolling down with high waves. It was about three miles wide, with no sign of roads anywhere leading to it. The Master was surprised and said to Sun Wukong, "The Great Immortal must have shown us the wrong way by mistake. This water is so wide and strong, and I see no ferry boats, how can we get across it?" Sun smiled and said, "No, the Great Immortal made no mistake. Do you not see there is a great bridge? We must cross the river by that bridge." When the Master and his disciples came near it, there was a tablet on the bridge with these words "Cloud Ferry."

> It was a single tree across the river.
> From afar it was like a beam across the sky,
> Near by, it seemed a rotten broken tree trunk.
> It was narrow and slippery and dizzy to cross,
> By this the gods trod over the brilliant clouds.

The Master was frightened and said, "This bridge is not for mortals to cross over. We must look for some other way." Sun smiled, and said, "It is the right way." Zhu Bajie said, "If it is the way, who dares to cross it? The river is broad and the waves are high, and there is only this single tree, both narrow and slippery, spanning it. Who will attempt to cross it?" Sun said, "If you all wait here, I will show you how to cross it." At this he ran and jumped on the bridge, crossed it jauntily, and in a minute was over it. Then he called on the others to follow. The Master shook his head, Zhu Bajie and Sha the Monk bit their nails, and said, "It is far too difficult!" At this Sun Wukong ran back over the bridge and, taking hold of Zhu Bajie's hand, dragged him towards it, saying "Stupid fool, follow me!" But Zhu Bajie rolled on the ground and said, "Forgive me, it is far too dangerous. Let me just mount on the wind and cross over that way." Sun urged him, "This is not the place for you to mount the wind. To become a Buddha you must cross by this bridge." Zhu Bajie said, "Brother, if I cannot become a Buddha without this, I will have to renounce my hopes. It is really impossible to pass over it."

While these two were wrangling at the bridge end, they saw a man floating down in a boat crying out, "Take the ferry boat, take the ferry boat." The Master was overjoyed at this, and called out to his disciples, "Do not wrangle any more, there is a ferryman coming." When he came near, they saw he had only a raft. Sun was not dismayed at the raft, but called to the boatman to come closer. In a twinkling the raft was alongside the shore. At the sight, the Master was frightened and said, "How can such a broken raft take us over?" The boatman said:

> My boat since chaos famous is,
> Unchanged it is from first to last,
> Spite wind and waves, still firm it is,
> Ever safe, without beginning or end.
> Passions never infect it, they submit to The One,
> Through countless troubles it moves firmly on,
> Though a weak raft, yet it can cross an ocean
> It has safely ferried innumerable souls.

The Great Sage united his palms, thanked him and said, "I am deeply grateful to you for your thoughtfulness in coming to meet my Master. Master, get into the boat! Although it has a leaky bottom, it is steady, and no wind or waves can upset it." The Master was still afraid and doubtful. Sun Wukong pushed him, and the Master lost his footing, and fell into the water. But the boatman at once rescued him, and stood him on the boat. The Master wrung his clothes, blaming Sun. Then Sun helped Sha the Monk to get on, while Zhu Bajie led the horse, and carried the baggage also, onto the raft.

The boatman then gently guided the raft across. They saw a dead body floating. At sight of this, the Master was greatly frightened. But Sun smiled and said, "Master do not be alarmed! That corpse is none other than your own." Zhu Bajie said, "It is you, it is you!" Sha the Monk clapped his hands, and also said, "It is you, it is you!" The boatman also remarked, "It was yours, I congratulate you." The three pilgrims congratulated him, and they quietly crossed over the Cloud Ferry in safety. The Master's shape was changed, and he jumped ashore on the other side with a very light body.

> When casting off the flesh and bones of the mortal body,
> The permanent soul is loath to depart,
> Now that the work is finished and it is become divine.
> All the past impurities of passions are washed away.
> To reach the other shore of eternity is called the greatest and
>   widest wisdom.

When the four pilgrims looked round, the raft had disappeared. Sun Wukong told them that the boatman was Lord Buddha himself, welcoming them to Paradise. It was now that the Master understood. Then he quickly turned round and thanked his disciples. Sun replied, "Let neither of us thank each other, for we all helped one another. Thanks to our Master, we were saved by following Buddhism. Happily we have succeeded in bearing good fruit, and we were able to defend our Master and persevered, till he was able to cast off the mortal body. Master, look at this wonderful land of beauty, of forest, of flowers and birds! How vastly superior to the old world!" The pilgrims could not cease rejoicing. With light and strong bodies they marched up the Spiritual Mountain, and soon saw the Central Hall of the Great Buddha.

> Its roof touched the clouds,
> Its foundation was on Spiritual Mountain,
> It stood amidst high peaks and wondrous rocks,
> O'erhanging precipices and deep valleys,
> Adorned with grasses and flowers,
> With winding paths and fragrant air.
> The roofs dovetailed with golden tiles,
> The walls built up of colored agate,
> With carved pillars without number.

The many mansions bloomed with flowers.
And high palaces were innumerable.
The roof of the palace of Lord Buddha
Shone forth with rainbow light.
In front of the Sacred Hall burning flames came forth.
The Buddha shrine was visible.
Rarest flowers gave forth their perfumes
Beyond compare of the best on earth.
There was eternal day among the clouds,
The lightest dust did not reach there,
Such was the Purest Land,
No trouble came near the Sacred Hall.

The pilgrims climbed leisurely to the top of the mountain, and there they saw green forests of pine and other trees, where were gathered the saints. The Master bowed to them. The groups of saints, men and women disciples, were embarrassed, put the palms of their hands together and said, "Holy monk, do not bow to us until you have seen Shakyamuni. After that we can talk." Sun smiled and said, "It is too soon for this. Let us go and worship Lord Buddha first."

The Master gladly hurried up after Sun till they reached the door of the Temple. There were two doorkeepers who met them, and said, "Holy monk, welcome! You have arrived at last!" The Master bowed, and said, "Yes, your disciple, Xuanzang from China, has arrived" He was about to enter, but the doorkeepers said, "Holy monk, please wait until we have announced you, and then you can go in." One of them went round a corner, and announced him to the four great temple gods at the inner door, and at the second gate they announced him to those at the third door. Inside the third door there was a religious function in progress. So they hurried on to the Sacred Hall, and announced the Master to the most Honorable Shakyamuni, saying, "The Chinese monk who has come to get the Sacred Scriptures has arrived." The Buddha was much pleased and assembled:

The Eight Bodhisattvas,
The Four Messengers,
The Five Hundred *arhats*,
The Eleven Shining Ones
The Eighteen Guardians.

These were arranged in two rows and then the Buddha invited the Chinese monk to come in. Xuanzang entered, followed in order by Sun Wukong and Zhu Bajie. Sha the Monk followed, leading the horse, and carrying the load of baggage. They had traveled 10,000 *li,* and crossed a thousand rivers, in the hope of seeing the Buddha at last. This day was going to be the day of their lives.

When the four were in front of the Grand Central Hall, they fell on their faces and worshipped Lord Buddha, and then they worshipped the two on his right and left, each three times. After kneeling before Lord Buddha for a long time the Master presented their credentials and passports to him.

After looking them through, Lord Buddha returned them to the Chinese monk. The Master made a profound bow and said, "Your disciple, Xuanzang, appointed by the Chinese Emperor of the Tang dynasty, has come from afar to your Spiritual Mountain to humbly beg for Sacred Scriptures to save all men. I hope Lord Buddha will be gracious, so that I may soon return to my country with the holy books." Lord Buddha opened his lips and, with great kindness of heart, spoke to the Master:

"You in the East belong to the Southern Continent. The heaven is high, and the earth is deep, products are extensive and men numerous. But most of them are covetous and cruel, licentious and wild, insulting and deceitful. They do not respect the Buddhist religion and do not seek goodness, they do not reverence the sun, moon and stars, and do not value agriculture. They are neither loyal nor filial, neither just nor kind. Their hearts are full of deceit, using big bushels with which to buy, and small weights with which to sell. They delight in cruel, destructive deeds, and gather for themselves a harvest of trouble in hell, where they suffer many poundings and grindings of affliction before they are changed into animals. Then they will suffer much from horny creatures in payment of their sins. Their flesh will feed men. They are lost forever into the lowest hell without hope of deliverance, on account of their wickedness.

Although they have had Confucius in their continent, who established the teaching of benevolence, righteousness, propriety, and knowledge, and have had a succession of rulers, who have imposed the punishments of banishment, of strangulation, and of beheading, they are still foolish.

Now I have three kinds of sacred books by which men can be delivered from their troubles and by which an end can be put to their sins. The three kinds of sacred books are the *dharma*, which deals with the laws of Heaven, the *sastras*, which deal with the laws of earth, and the third are the *sutras,* which deal with they ways to save lost souls. In all, they number 35 works and 15,144 books, and are all sacred in that they show men how to be upright and good.

All the knowledge of the four great continents, of the heavens, and the earth, of the races of men, of birds, and beasts, of flowers, of forestry and manufactures are complete in them. Since you have come a long distance, I must give you a complete set to carry back. But your people are ignorant and gross, calumniating the true scriptures and not understanding the deep meaning of our teachings. Call my two chief disciples, Ananda and Kasyapa. Let them lead these four travelers, first to the dining hall to dine, and then to the Library, and from each of the 35 works select a few to take back with them to circulate in the East."

Ananda and Kasyapa led them below, where they saw strange precious things in thousands. Gifts were provided for each of the pilgrims, and a vegetable banquet spread before them. All was of the very best, the choicest food, the most delicate tea, the finest fruit of all kinds, different from anything on earth among men. The Master and disciples raised the dishes to their heads in thanks for Buddha's grace and then enjoyed them.

> Truly, their reigns golden light as bright as day,
> All kinds of nameless sweet incense,
> The eye meets a thousand trees in the beautiful palace,
> And the sweetest music charms the ear beyond all earthly strains,
> There the saints never grow old,
> Once partaking of celestial food, they live forever.
> All the sorrows of life are past,
> And now eternal glory and joy are attained.

It was great bliss to Zhu Bajie and Sha the Monk to be at Buddha's palace, and enjoy to their hearts' content the banquet of immortals, who had cast off their mortal coils of bones and flesh and blood. Ananda and Kasyapa honored their guests with their presence. When their meal was over, the pilgrims were led to the Sacred Library, where books were stored in cupboards and boxes all with red labels of their names.

After the four had seen the list of books, Ananda and Kasyapa said, if they were going to pay for the volumes, they would be given them at once. The Master replied that he had not been prepared to pay, as he understood the Scriptures were to be presented to them. The two smiled and said, "If we give away our Scriptures for nothing, we shall die of starvation."

When Sun Wukong heard this, he paid, "Then we shall go back and tell Buddha about this!" At this the two said, "Take it easy! Just take whatever you want!" Thus the Master and disciples took several loads of books, which Zhu Bajie, Sha the Monk, and the horse carted away, after which they went to thank Lord Buddha. On the way they passed the Light Giving Buddha. He had overheard the conversation about the price of the books, and knew that they had been given "wordless scriptures." He thought within himself, "Serves them right! Still, since the people in the East are unintelligent they will not understand the subtlety of the wordless scriptures, and as the Master has traveled far, he should have the written scriptures."

He ordered the pilgrims to be followed, and when their loads were opened, the pilgrims were indignant to find that they had no written scriptures, but only white paper. They decided to return and inform Buddha that they had been cheated, because they had not offered to pay for the books. The Master offered Ananda and Kasyapa the golden bowl, which the Chinese emperor and given him, in payment for the written scriptures. Kasyapa then went in and brought out the written scriptures to the Master, who ordered his disciples to examine each volume carefully and see that they were not white paper this time. The Three Treasures dealing with Heaven, Earth, and Lost Souls numbered 5,048 works. These were loaded on the horse. The Master took the staff in his hand, put on his miter and cassock, and went, with great joy, to thank Lord Buddha.

> The Sacred Scripture is joyful reading,
> It is a rare gift of Lord Buddha,

It is full of priceless pearls,
One word cannot be bought for ten thousand coins.
Who can read the Wordless Scripture of Ananda?
The Written Scriptures must not be lightly used,
The common people should not desecrate them
Believers will then understand this Boundless Law.

Then Buddha ascended and sat on the Lotus Throne, and ordered the two great tamers of dragons and tigers to beat the cloud
drums, and invite the 3,000 Buddhas, the Four Temple Guardians,
The Shining Ones, the *Bodhisattvas*, the 500 *arhats*, and all other
denizens of all quarters of the Blessed Land of the Spiritual Mountain, together with all honored ones and all the holy monks. They
were seated all in their respective places. Then heavenly music commenced simultaneously. When all the Buddhas had arrived, they
bowed before Lord Buddha. Buddha asked Ananda and Kasyapa
how many scriptures they had given him. They said 5,048 books
had been selected and given to the holy monk from China. Each
of the four pilgrims then folded his palms together and bowed
towards Lord Buddha.

Buddha spoke to the Master and said, "These Scriptures are
priceless in value. Although they are Buddhist canons, they really
contain the essence of the three religions of China, Confucianism,
Buddhism, and Taoism. When you take them to your Southern
Continent for the instruction of all, be careful not to desecrate
them. Do not read them till you have bathed and fasted from flesh.
Reverence them as great treasures, for in them you find the mystery
of how to become divine, and you will receive wonderful light for
the understanding of all things." The Master bowed in thanksgiving, and received them all.

When the Master had gone, Lord Buddha was about to dismiss
the assembled court, when suddenly Guanyin entered, united her
palms and said, "Some years ago I received your commands to go
to the East and look for a man to fetch the Sacred Scriptures. Today
that work is accomplished. It has taken 14 years, which is 5,040
days, which is eight days less than the number of books in the three
collections of Sacred Scriptures you have given them. I beg that you
authorize me to have the additional Scriptures sent to the East in

eight days." Buddha was greatly pleased at this, gave her an edict authorizing this, and ordered the Eight Messengers to have the holy monk return to China with the Scriptures within eight days, so that the days might tally with the number of the books in the collection. On no account should there be any delay. The Messengers then at once caught up the Master and said, "Scripture Seekers, follow us." Then, feeling their bodies light and strong, they could feel themselves flying on clouds.

26
The Mission Fulfilled

WHILST THE MESSENGERS WERE escorting the Master on his return journey, the Guardians of the Five Regions went to Guanyin and said, "We were formerly commanded by you to provide protection to the holy monk. Now that his work is accomplished, we beg to be released from our duty." She said, "Certainly, but tell me how the pilgrims behaved on the journey." They said, "They were most sincere and devoted. But the poor Master suffered countless troubles all the way. We have written a complete list of them. They number eighty in all."

Guanyin looked at the list of trials and said, "It is not complete. The perfect number is nine by nine. To be perfect there should be eighty one trials." She ordered the messengers that they must let the monk suffer one trial more.

After receiving this order from Guanyin they slackened down on the wings of the wind, and gradually descended to the ground, where they left the pilgrims.

> To attain perfection in religion is not easy.
> A firm will is needed to penetrate the Divine Mysteries.
> One must often fight and overcome demons,
> Before one can reach the end.
> One must toil and encounter many sorrows,
> And not make superficial study of books.
> If one errs by a hair's breadth, one cannot attain to truth.

It was a strange sensation for the pilgrims to be on the ground again. They had come down near some water. The Master asked, "Can any one tell me where we are?" Sun said, "Master, this is the mouth of the River of Heaven." It was also a lonely place, without houses or boats, and they were on the Western side. How could they get across? Two of them suggested that since the Master had left his mortal body behind, they could cross the river by magic. But Sun said, "No, it cannot be done." He knew that there was one trial more to undergo, and it was for this that they had stopped on the way. Then they heard a cry, "Chinese monk, come this way." They went, and found that it was the old tortoise, who had ferried them over as they were traveling towards the West. The tortoise said he had been waiting for their return for a long time, and was glad to see them. Sun said, "Formerly we had to trouble you. Now we meet again." At this the four pilgrims rejoiced to see the tortoise. He took them and the horse all on his back, and swam across to the other side.

> The one way of salvation is full of mystery.
> All evil spirits distinguish between Divine and Human.
> They know when the Perfect Man appears
> And the stages by which perfection is attained.
> They know the three ways of the Buddhist Faith
> They know the nine ways of perfection,
> There is no need to resort to magic.

As they neared the Eastern shore and it was getting dark, the tortoise said, "Master, when you went to the West I asked you to enquire of Buddha for me how I might return to my former state, and when I might get a human body. Did you remember to ask?" But the Master had been so absorbed in his own affairs, that he had completely forgotten the tortoise and his request and so he had nothing to say. The tortoise, finding that he had been forgotten, turned a somersault and threw all and everything into the river. Happily the mortal body of the Master had been exchanged for an immortal one, and therefore he was safe in the water. Zhu Bajie and Sha the Monk were also at home in the water, but the books were all soaked.

Suddenly a great sandstorm arose, the sky grew dark and there was thunder and lightning. The Master was so alarmed that he put weights on the books lest they should be blown away. Sun brandished his club, for he knew that the storm had been caused by an evil spirit who wanted to rob the Master of the books. They fought the whole night till dawn. Then the Master in his wet clothes and in great fear said to Sun, "What can be the meaning of this trial?" Sun blurted out, "Master, you know it is my duty to protect you. To get these Scriptures is to rob human nature of its forces by which men can be made to last as long as heaven and earth, and be as bright as the sun and moon, living in eternal youth, with an incorruptible body. On this account all the evil spirits are jealous, and wish to rob men of these scriptures. First, they made the books wet, and now, they have succeeded in bringing your spiritual body down to earth again, it was necessary that your perfect powers should be brought to test for your protection."

When the sun rose, the books and other effects were spread out to dry. Soon the local people found the pilgrims and, full of gratitude for what had been done for them on the way West, insisted on their going to the village to see their new temple. There they found images of the four set up, and the whole village most prosperous. Sun said they should worship Buddha, not his disciples. The pilgrims were prevailed on to rest for the night.

Before daylight, however, the Master called his comrades up and said, "We must not yield to more invitations to stay. Let us start at once." When they got outside, they heard the eight messengers in the sky calling out, " travelers, follow us!" They felt the air full of sweet fragrance, and mounting the wind, flew on their way.

At the second drive of the wind, the messengers brought the four travelers in one day within sight of Chang'an. There they saw the Library built by the emperor for the reception of the scriptures. This had been erected three years after the master had started for the West. Every anniversary after that, the emperor had visited the building. On the very day that the messengers arrived with the travelers, the emperor was there. The messengers would not descend to earth, but let the four travelers down, with their loads of scriptures, telling them that they would wait there till they returned to say the books had been delivered, adding, "But be quick, for we are to be back in eight days, and more than five are already spent."

When they neared the library, the emperor and officials saw them arriving, and came down from the upper story to meet them.

The emperor said, "Imperial Younger Brother, Holy Monk, you have returned!" The Master fell on his knees and kowtowed. The emperor raised him up, and asked, "Who are these with you?" Xuanzang said they were his disciples, and introduced each, saying what they had been, and how they had been converted by Guanyin to Buddhism, and how they had volunteered to escort him on the whole journey.

The news of the Master's return soon spread through the city, and crowds ran to see him. He entered the palace with the emperor and thanked him for his great interest, and the loads of scripture were brought in by his disciples. The emperor asked the number of the scriptures, how they had fared by the way, how they had reached the Spiritual Mountain and seen Lord Buddha. The Master told how he had been given wordless scriptures the first time, and how, after he had presented the emperor's golden bowl, he had then been given the written scriptures, which comprised selections from thirty five works, numbering 5,048 books from the three collections. The emperor was greatly pleased and ordered refreshments for the pilgrims. Seeing the three strange disciples below, the emperor asked if they were foreigners. Then the Master gave the history of each.

"My chief disciple is Sun the Monkey. His religious name is the Seeker of Truth, and he is also called Sun Wukong, Aware of Emptiness. He is from the Southern Continent, the country of Aolai, the Orchard Mountain and the Waterfall Cave. Five hundred years ago, he made a great disturbance in Heaven and on that account was imprisoned under a mountain. After listening to the exhortations of Guanyin, who pitied him, he was willing to repent. When I reached that place I delivered him out of his prison and I found him a most valuable escort.

"My second disciple is named Zhu the Pig. His religious name is the Seeker of Strength and he is also known as Zhu Bajie, the Keeper of the Eight Commandments. He is a native of Fuling mountain, and lived in the Cloud Inn Cave. On account of his robberies at Gao village, he was punished. But Guanyin had mercy on him and exhorted him to repent. On account of his strength, he was ordered to carry our baggage all the way. He could also work well in water.

"My third disciple is named Sha the Monk. His religious name is Seeker of Purity. He lived at Quicksands River and was a robber. He too was converted by Guanyin to Buddhism.

"The horse is not the horse which Your Majesty gave me."

The emperor said, "It is very much like it." The Master replied, "When I arrived at Snake Mountain, in one of the torrents there your horse was swallowed by this horse, who was then in the shape of a dragon. My chief disciple found out the history of this horse. It was a foal of the Dragon King of the Western Sea. Owing to its lawlessness it had been punished, but was afterwards forgiven and was also converted by Guanyin. It was taken to carry me on the journey, and in a moment it was changed into the semblance of the other horse. It was very useful in crossing mountains and rivers, and in riding great distances. On our return it carried our load of scriptures."

On hearing this, the emperor was full of wonder and gratitude. Then he asked about the distance they had traveled. The Master replied, "We have traveled about 108,000 *li*, but we did not keep a careful record. But I know that we spent 14 years on the way, met many robbers and evil spirits. We had our passports examined in many lands." He then called his chief disciple to bring the passport to show to the emperor the many seals stamped on it.

At this time dinner was announced, and the Master and his disciples dined with the emperor. After that the officials, both civil and military, came, and the emperor seated himself in their midst. The pilgrims were invited to join, and singing and dancing and instrumental music crowned the day with rejoicing.

> It was a royal banquet worthy of the ancient kings.
> To have received the Scriptures was a joy to overflowing.
> They were to transmit to future generations the best of the past
> The Light of Buddha to illuminate the kingdom.

Next morning the emperor came and said he had no means of thanking the Master properly for his great services, but he presented him with a *Preface to the Sacred Scriptures* which he had especially written for the occasion:

"We have heard how the invisible forces of *yin* and *yang*, that brood over and produce all life, are represented by the visible sun and moon. The four seasons, though themselves unseen, by the action of heat and cold, produce all growth. By looking to heaven above or earth beneath, even the most ignorant know this influence of *yin* and *yang*. But the wisest cannot explain them fully. By what we see, it is easy to know that there are these forces. They cannot be fully understood because they are invisible. But their influence is known by what is visible. Even the ignorant have no doubt about them. Their form is invisible, and their workings beyond the knowledge of the learned. How much more difficult, therefore, is it to understand the religion of Buddha, which deals entirely with the unseen, the dark and the quiet, but which exercises profound influence over all beings throughout the universe. It is unsurpassed in high majesty, and in the smallest details it is divine. Its greatness penetrates all space; there is no space so small that it does not permeate. It is not born; it does not die. It remains throughout all time, and never ages. Whether visible or invisible, it brings all blessings even now. Wonderful doctrine, most mysterious! Those who study it find it unlimited; its influences reaching everywhere in silence. They try to grasp it, but they cannot find the fountainhead. How much less can the ordinary man with his small ability and knowledge find out its full secret.

On examining the origin of this great religion, we find it arose in the West. During the Han dynasty we heard of it as of a dream, which flowed with its mercy to the East. At first by Buddha's example and teaching, before the doctrine was fully understood, the people believed he appeared on earth to do good, and honored him. But after he returned to paradise, and generations passed, they forgot the true character of the founder, but made beautiful images, fine paintings, and devised the thirty-two marks or forms of the Buddha. Thus his main doctrines spread far and wide to save men from the three roads of transmigration, hell, demons, and animals, and left traditions everywhere to lead men along the ten paths of Buddhism. But true religion is not easy to spread without varying views arising. Plausible views are easily followed, and thus arose both true and false interpretations. Therefore the doctrine of the seen and unseen is expounded in various ways, according to the customs of the world; some asserting one view and others denying it.

So the schools of Primitive Buddhism and Higher Buddhism flourish according to time and circumstance.

Then the holy monk Xuanzang appeared. From his youth he was resolute and intelligent, and understood the vanity of the world. When grown he comprehended the spiritual, the laws governing life and death, and underlying providence, and making for contentment, as clearly as the wind in the forest, or the moon mirrored in the water, and more beautiful than the dews of heaven. Therefore he knew everything, even before it took visible form, and was above being influenced by the senses, and in all the past he had no equal. He cultivated his heart, the whole time, and mourned over the mutilation of the true doctrine. Studying the doctrine, he deplored that even the best books had many mistakes. He thought of revising them all, for wide publication, by striking out the errors, and preserving only the true, for the benefit of students. He thought of visiting the Pure Land, for the purpose of improving his knowledge of religion. Leaning on his staff he went alone; he risked danger, and traveled far. In the morning drifting snow would bury the paths. In the evening clouds of sand would blow so that the sky was invisible. Ten thousand *li* of mountains and rivers he crossed. Through mist and fog, through heat and cold, through frost and rain, he pressed on. Because his zeal was great, he considered his trials light, being determined to succeed. He spent fourteen years in traveling from country to country, in order to find the truth. Through two great forests and across eight rivers he learned various truths. In fine parks and on high mountain peaks he saw strange sights. He learned the sublime thoughts of Buddha, and their purposes, from the best teachers studying the mysteries of religion and its very essence. Thus he learned by heart the six teachings of the three schools, and a hundred collections of scriptures, and like waves their truth bubbled from his lips. He received the most important works of Higher Buddhism, thirty-five works in all, consisting of five thousand and forty eight books for the purpose of translation and distribution in China. He brought the merciful clouds of the West to fall in fine rain in the East. Thus the imperfect doctrines of religion have been corrected. By the power of religion, sinful men can subdue evil and be saved, just as water can put out fire. Traveling through the sea of life, it affords the voyager calm water instead of tumultuous waves, whereby he can reach the other shore in peace. Thus we know that if we do sin, we must have punishment; if we do good, we shall be raised to heaven. Good and evil are reached by man himself. The cinnamon grows on the mountain ridge, nourished by clouds and dew, and impurities cannot reach it; it brings forth flowers, not because the nature of the cinnamon is good, but because its growing place is pure. Again, the lotus grows in clear water, and dust cannot fall on its leaves; this is not because the nature of the lotus is pure, but because impurity cannot reach its home. Thus, if even the vegetable kingdom knows the importance of good environment, how can men attain perfection except by abiding in virtue?

I hope these scriptures will abide for ever as the sun and moon, and that the great blessings found therein will spread over the earth and heavens."

Many officials congratulated the emperor on his Preface. The emperor said he would now like to have some of the new scriptures explained. The Master replied, "Let there be a suitable fine place prepared, from which I may expound the scriptures, and as the scriptures should be preserved carefully, copies should be made for wide distribution." The emperor at once commanded the scholars of the Hanlin Academy, the best calligraphers, to make copies. Meanwhile a stage was erected from which the Master was to read. The disciples were also asked to go on the platform, and the reading was about to commence when the eight messengers appeared in the air and called out, "Reader of the Scriptures, return with us at once to the West." Then in a moment the Master, his disciples, and even the horse, rose in the air and were spirited away. The emperor and his officials were greatly terrified at this, and worshipped towards the sky.

> The holy monks exerted their energies to procure the scriptures.
> They had spent fourteen years on their travels,
> They had suffered many trials on the way,
> Many hardships, crossing mountains and rivers,
> Their good work was now accomplished,
> Through a thousand efforts.
> The wonderful scriptures of the greatest wisdom
> To their country had been brought
> And to this day are studied in the land.

The emperor, as he had vowed, established a Society for the Salvation of All Souls, and eminent monks were appointed to read and study the holy scriptures.

The messengers led the Master, his three disciples and the horse, in all five individuals, back to the Spiritual Mountain, and the whole journey, both coming and going, was accomplished in eight days exactly. When they arrived, Lord Buddha called a great meeting of all the gods and sages, who were listening to his teaching. The eight messengers announced the return of the pilgrims, having accomplished their mission of delivering the holy scriptures to China, and they brought them forward to receive the honors that Buddha wished to confer on them. Buddha thanked each one for his long and faithful service, saying, "Holy monk, in a former life you were my disciple, second in rank, called Golden Cicada. But at that time you had no respect for my teaching, and you were condemned to be reborn in China. Fortunately you have now come to believe in our religion and fetched the true scriptures for the salvation of souls."

Then Buddha conferred special honors on the pilgrims:

> The Master was canonized as the Buddha of Sweet Incense
> Sun Wukong was canonized as the Buddha Victorious in War
> Zhu Bajie was canonized as a Guardian of the Pure Altar.
> Sha the Monk was canonized as the Golden Arhat.
> The horse was canonized as Commander of the Dragons of Heaven.

> The members of the body of the True Ideal on earth
> Were in harmony with him.
> Both matter and spirit were once more quiet.
> No evil spirits were to trouble any more,
> The fruit of the Spirit was seen
> In following the Greatest Wisdom.
> Thus perfection was attained and hell escaped.
> The Scriptures filled the world with light,
> The five pilgrims were elevated to the highest state.

During this ceremony of canonization all the Buddhas and *bodhisattvas*, the holy monks, *arhats*, all saints from all mountains and caves, all local gods and spirits, and all who had attained to immortality from the beginning of time, attended and sat in their respective seats in the midst of glory indescribable.

The faithful messengers gathered on gorgeous clouds.
In the blissful atmosphere of Paradise,
Where great dragons and fierce tigers lie together in peace,
Where sun and moons come and go,
Where great dragons play together,
Where birds of paradise flit happily about,
And black monkeys and rare white deer are found.
There beautiful flowers of all seasons,
Ripe fruit of all kinds abound,
Tall pines and lovely bamboos,
Flowers of all colors,
Immortal peaches all ripe.

Then they all folded their hands, worshipped, and chanted the following litany:

Homage to the Buddhas of the Past, Present, and Future.
Homage to Sakyamuni Buddha.
Homage to Vairocana Buddha.
Homage to Maitreya Buddha.
Homage to Amitabha Buddha.
Homage to the Nagaraja Buddha.
Homage to the Buddha of Goodness.
Homage to the Buddha of Precious Moonlight.
Homage to the Buddha Free of Stupidity.
Homage to the Buddha of Meritorious Talent.
Homage to the Buddha of the Torch of Wisdom.
Homage to the Buddha of Great Virtues.
Homage to the Buddha of Great Compassion.
Homage to the Wise and Good Leader Buddha.
Homage to the Buddha of Golden Splendor.
Homage to the Buddha of Brilliant Talent.
Homage to the Buddha of the Banner of Wisdom.
Homage to the Buddha of the Lamp of the World.
Homage to the Buddha of the Golden Sea.
Homage to the Buddha of Universal Light.
Homage to the Bodhisattva Guanyin.
Homage to the Bodhisattva Mahasthama.
Homage to the Bodhisattva Manjusri
Homage to the Bodhisattva Samantabhadra.
Homage to the Bodhisattvas of the Ocean of Purity.
Homage to the Bodhisattvas of the Lotus Pool Assembly.
Homage to the Bodhisattvas of the Blissful Western Heaven.

Homage to the Three Thousand Protector *Bodhisattvas*.
Homage to the Five Hundred *Arhats*.
Homage to the Golden *Bodhisattva* of the Eight Treasures.
Homage to the Heavenly Dragon of the Eight Classes of Being.
Homage to all the Buddhas of the Past, Present, and Future, in
    all Ten Regions, all the *Bodhisattvas* and *Mahasattvas*.

Maha prajnaparamita.